Saved by the SEAL

Also by Diana Gardin

The Battle Scars Series

Last True Hero

The Nelson Island Series

Falling Deep
Ever Always (novella)
Wanting Forever

Saved by the SEAL

Battle Scars, Book 2

DIANA GARDIN

FOREVER
YOURS

Copyright © 2016 by Diana Gardin
Excerpt from *Last True Hero* copyright © 2015 by Diana Gardin

Cover design by Elizabeth Turner
Cover copyright © 2016 by Hachette Book Group, Inc.

Forever Yours
Hachette Book Group
1290 Avenue of the Americas
New York, NY 10104
forever-romance.com
twitter.com/foreverromance

First published as an ebook and as a print on demand: March 2016

Forever Yours is an imprint of Grand Central Publishing.
The Forever Yours name and logo are trademarks of Hachette Book Group, Inc.

The publisher is not responsible for websites (or their content) that are not owned by the publisher.

The Hachette Speakers Bureau provides a wide range of authors for speaking events. To find out more, go to www.hachettespeakersbureau.com or call (866) 376-6591

ISBNs: 978-1-4555-9473-3 (ebook), 978-1-4555-9474-0 (POD)

To all the veterans who risked their lives for our freedom, and the women and men who love them. Thank you so much for your service.

Acknowledgments

Thank you to my Lord and Savior first and foremost. I am so blessed to be able to do this wonderful thing called a writing career, and it's through You that I can.

To my superman, Tyson. True love isn't a fairy tale. It's a battle every day, and I'm blessed to be fighting through it with someone as strong and steady as you. Thank you for picking up my slack around the house and with the kiddos when I'm a crazy woman on a deadline. I will always love you.

To my busy bees, Carrington and Raleigh. Thank you for being patient with Mommy when I am just letting you run around like maniacs while I type away on this computer. You're always in my thoughts and I do it all for you.

To my mama, Inez. Thank you so much for passing on your love of books. It meant everything. You are and have always been my inspiration.

To my crew, the Fab Five: Crystal, Emilee, Beth, Christy, and Maria. Without you hot mamas and our girls' nights, our girls' trips, and our group texts, I would go stark raving mad. I'm infinitely blessed to have you in my life, and I hope Dare keeps your hubbies happy for a while! Love and kisses, Kitty.

To my BFF of the South, Natalee, you are truly one of my favorite people on this planet. Thank you so much for being the first one in line to buy each and every book, and for your unwavering love and support. With each new hero I write, I can't wait to see what you'll think of him. I heart you.

To Stacey Donaghy. What a lucky day it was when you agreed to be my agent. I'm still not sure how it happened, but I'm so thankful it did! Your hard work and positive words, especially about this book, are incomparable. I would not want to navigate this publishing world without you, because what I've learned with you by my side can't be traded. Every time I write something new, I can't wait until you read it, because you're my biggest cheerleader. Thank you!

To my editor, Dana. Thank you for falling in love with Dare and Berkeley! Your input is awesome, and I can already tell this will be a wonderful relationship.

To my Forever publicist, Fareeda. Thanks for helping to get the word out about my books. You are an excellent guide through this process, and your quick responses feed my type A complexes. Thank you!

To the rest of the team at Forever Romance, including the wonderful Caroline Acebo, who edited this book, thank you for all the hard work you do in order to make authors look good. You are all so spectacular to work with!

To my special correspondent who helped me get the SEAL aspects of this book right:. Thank you for letting me grill you for your SEAL intellect. Your help with this story was terrific! You helped me bring Grisham to life in a realistic (I hope) way.

I never could have gotten him right without you! Also, a big thank you to your wife, one of my oldest and dearest friends, for lending you out!

To Tracy Comerford. You are a one-woman wrecking team. You were one of the earliest reviewers to love my books, and I'm lucky enough now to be able to call you so many things: friend, reviewer, publicist, and even my trusty PA from time to time. Your time is so valuable, and the fact that you spend some of it on me and getting the word out there about my books blows my mind. You're über talented and knowledge-able about the book world. Can't wait to see where BMBB goes from here!

To my critique partner for SBTS: Marie Meyer. We share so many things: a writing group, a publisher, and a genre. I admire you and the beauty that is your writing so very much! Thank you for your advice and the encouragement you gave me on this book. Love you, girl!

To my warm and fuzzy writing group, the NAC. Kate, Ara, Marie, Sribindu, Meredith, Jamie, Jessica, Sophia, Marnee, Missy, Laura, and Amanda. I found you guys when I was already well into this biz, and now I don't know what I ever did without you. I wouldn't trade any of you, and I can't wait for the day when we can all have dinner together. Remember, I would cut a bitch for any one of you.

To my mentor, Rachel van Dyken. I'm very certain you have no idea how much your effortless kindness and encouragement mean to me, but my admiration and love for you runs deep! Thank you for every returned message, sweet word, and wonderful blurb you've done. You're a complete rock star in the romance world, and I hope to make it as big as you one day!

To the bloggers and readers who find this book: THANK YOU. Thank you so much for reading, purchasing, reviewing, and spreading the word about the Battle Scars series. Without you, what would I be? You make this possible, and I want to hear from each and every one of you soon!

1

Grisham

The cool, blue Atlantic sprays my face as I sit in the sand. My eyes are fixated on the breaking waves. My good buddies—my brothers—are taking advantage of the larger-than-normal swells while they cut in and out of the waves on their boards. I lay back on my elbows and watch...the same way I've been watching for the past month and a half—the time it took for me to muster up the balls and the strength to get back to the beach.

I glance at the board lying beside me. If I can do it, today will be my first time back in the ocean. It's *supposed* to be my first day back. I just haven't been able to get off my ass and into the water just yet.

It's early; the sun just broke over the horizon about half an hour ago, and the morning is flawless. I take a deep breath and close my eyes, letting the morning's rays touch my face.

I'm utterly relaxed on the beach, but I'm also at home when I'm working, when I'm strategizing, planning, or embarking on a mission with my team. Working in the mission field is about as far from the dream my father laid out for me as possible, and this is one of the reasons I love it so damn much. He pulled all the strings he could so that, as an officer graduating from the Naval Academy a couple of years ago, I'd be placed behind a desk and rise quickly through the ranks without ever touching a battlefield.

He didn't anticipate that I had my own plans for my life, my own goals and ambitions. I wasn't going to be just a douche in a uniform telling other guys what to do, never having lived it myself. If I was going to order other men around, it was going to be while I was risking my life right there beside them.

And my father, Admiral Michael Abbot, would just have to deal with it.

Lawson Snyder disturbs the sand beside me as he dives into place and sprawls out. He places his hands behind his head and closes his eyes. His wet suit is hanging out down around his waist, and his tattoo-covered torso is on display.

"Dude." I slap him on the chest. "That was awesome out there. You've been practicing."

He chuckles. "Thanks, man. That's high praise coming from a beachcomber like you. Us corn-fed Nebraskan boys don't grow up riding the waves. Took me a while to learn."

True. But now that Lawson has found surfing, he'll never quit. There's something about getting lost in the sea and letting the waves guide you back to shore that's addictive.

We sit, the quiet stretching around us, while Lawson catches his breath, and before long our other surfing buddy and team member, Ben McBride, joins us. We don't call him Ben, though.

"Get your ass up, Abbot!" yells Ben as he runs out of the waves. "You said today was the day!"

I watch him approach. "Did I say that? I meant today was the day I'm keeping my ass planted in the sand. Tomorrow's the day I get back on the board."

"Bullshit!" Ben runs at me, feinting like he's going to land right on top of me. I dodge left, laughing as he ends up on his face.

"Still too fast for your ass." I gloat. Grinning at Lawson, we high-five.

"Too slow, Cowboy." Lawson sounds ashamed of Ben as he shakes his head. "Even missing a limb, Abbot's got you beat every single time."

"That's why he's team leader. That, and the fact that he's an officer and I'm not. I don't give a shit. Can we go grab some waffles now if you ain't surfing today?"

I nod, dusting off my hands. "I'll be there in a minute."

They grab their boards and take off toward the steps that lead to the parking lot. I have my own car; I'll meet them at the Waffle King in a few minutes. They'll probably be scarfing down their piles of food by then. I just need another minute with the ocean.

Just months ago, I was still stuck in a place with no ocean. I was in that faraway desert for four months before I was flown to a naval hospital in Germany, only two weeks shy of my assigned homecoming. I let my mind temporarily drift back to that last fateful day in Syria. The things I remember with vivid recall are the smells.

The smell of gasoline. The smell of burning rubber and plastic. The smell of hot, dry air as the darkness exploded with orange light. The smell of blood. Your own blood smells really fucking distinct. It's a scent you can never erase from your memory.

Yeah, the smells are still with me every single day.

I'm torn from my thoughts when I hear the scream. It was short and staccato, possibly cut off by the waves.

I sit up straight, my eyes scanning the ocean for the source of the scream. Without even realizing it's happening, adrenaline surges through my body in a way I haven't felt in months. My muscles tighten, alert. My senses kick into overdrive as my eyes continue to search the blue-green sea and my ears strain for foreign sounds.

This is a private spot on the beach, usually occupied only by surfers. At seven-fifteen on a Wednesday morning, it's nearly deserted. I scan the sand and notice there's a beach bag and towel about twenty feet to my left and behind me. I'm not sure when that person got into the water, maybe when my eyes were closed. Maybe when I was thinking about the desert.

When I turn my eyes back toward the ocean, I see it. There's an orange and pink surfboard drifting in the waves, minus its rider. I'm up from the sand in seconds, raising a hand to my eyes to scan the water for the missing surfer. I don't need to search the small stretch of beach behind me to see there's no lifeguard stand here. There's a sign on the old, twisty steps leading down to the shore that this is a private stretch and there's no lifeguard on duty.

I step forward, and the foamy sea rolls over my foot. I stare down at it. It's been so long since I've felt it; I'm having a weird reaction. Blood pumps in my ears, and a thin sheen of sweat breaks out all over my skin that has nothing to do with the sun and the heat.

Then, out past the breaking point, a small figure surfaces, floating on top of the rising and falling swells. I watch for movement and don't see any.

I don't think. I react.

Taking two running steps, I rush into the waves and dive headfirst into the ocean. I use my arms to pull my body through the rolling waves, kicking out hard behind me. I'm a skilled swimmer; it's kind of mandatory in my job description, but I've been a good swimmer for my entire life. Even though this is my first time in the ocean since the accident, it doesn't take long at all for me to reach the girl floating facedown in the water. Her raven-colored hair floats around her. My eyes scan her, noting her surfboard still floating feet away, attached to her slender ankle. Without a second look, I flip her on her back, pulling her under one of my arms. Then I use the other to cut through the saltwater once more, this time with the beach set in my sights.

I'm winded when I reach the sand, but I stumble up onto the beach carrying the still girl in my arms. Her head lolls against my chest, her limbs hanging limply from my hold. She's a rag doll, and fear courses through my blood, heating it until it feels like it's bubbling in my veins. I fall to my knees, laying her gently on the sand. My hands are steady as I unstrap the surfboard from her foot, but my heart crashes against my ribs.

Then, still running on autopilot, I brush her hair back so that I can assess her.

As soon as her face is clear of her long, dark mane, I suck in a breath as recognition slams into me like a jacked-up truck.

"Holy shit," I murmur. "Greta? Come on, girl, you gotta wake up for me."

She doesn't move.

Breathe for her.

Her gorgeous face is turning blue. I use my fingers to tilt her chin back, and then I lean in and breathe into her mouth twice.

Chest compressions.

My hands are centered on her chest, and I'm riveted to her face as I press down again and again, counting aloud each time I pump. After thirty compressions, I return to her mouth, pinching her nose closed and breathing in twice.

Again.

I repeat the process, pushing all fear out of my head. "Come on, Greta! Berkeley will kill me if I let you die. Wake up, dammit!"

Suddenly, she splutters, takes a huge, gasping breath, and ocean water pours out of her mouth. Lightning fast, I turn her on her side, and she retches, coughing again and again. When she's finished, I help her sit up on the sand, and I brush her hair out of her face as her crystal blue eyes finally focus on me.

"There you are." I breathe. "Hey, beautiful. You're okay. You're okay."

I repeat the phrase again and again, rubbing her back with one hand while she gains her bearings. She blinks rapidly a few times, and then croaks out in a hoarse voice.

"Grisham? Grisham Abbot?"

I smile, grateful to hear my name falling from her mouth right now. "It's me. Been a while, huh?"

She nods, coughing again. She raises a hand to her head and winces. That's when I see the blood, nearly hidden in her hair at the top of her forehead.

"Damn. That's a nasty cut. That probably happened when you fell off your board. Let me take you to the hospital, okay?"

She shakes her head. "I hate hospitals. I was just there with my little sister a few days ago. I'll go to urgent care."

I shake my head. "Not by yourself. I'll take you."

She looks reluctant, but nods her head. "Okay."

I stand, holding out my hand to her. "Do you think you can stand and walk? If not, I'll carry you."

She allows me to help her up. She's a little unsteady on her feet, but she seems like she'll be able to make it up the steps and to my four-door Jeep Wrangler.

"Wait!" she cries, turning toward the ocean. "My board!"

"Shhh, I got it," I reply, pointing to where it's lying on the beach. "We towed it in on your ankle."

She nods in relief.

"Let me get you to the car, and then I'll come back for our boards. Okay?"

Her eyes stray down to my leg, following the metal trail to my prosthetic foot. I've almost forgotten about it. It usually doesn't take people this long, but I'm going to give Greta credit because she was unconscious for part of the time we've been together today.

"Oh, Grisham," she whispers. Her eyes fill with tears.

"Hush," I admonish her. "I'm used to it by now. Hey, I'm good as new, Greta. I got out there to pull you in, didn't I?"

She nods and rewards me with a small smile. My heart stutters, remembering what it was like when I really saw that smile for the first time.

I met Greta well over two years ago when she and my best friend, Berkeley, became roommates. But Berkeley wasn't just my best friend; I'd also been secretly in love with her since we were kids. When Berkeley moved in with her, I didn't pay Greta much attention. But after Berkeley got together with her boyfriend, Dare, my heart took a beating. There was one morning when I was at their apartment, giving Dare the business, when Greta walked into the room wearing really tiny pajama shorts complete with a thin tank top.

The image is still burned into my mind.

I couldn't help but follow the trail of her long legs, past her little shorts, pausing at the small patch of skin exposed on her stomach. Then, when I made eye contact and saw those baby blues, clear as the fucking sky above and filled with desire, I almost lost my mind.

I left, because my head wasn't in a place to deal with feelings for another girl.

But right now, connecting with her again like this...something inside of me is pulling me toward her like a magnet. I can get lost in eyes as big and as blue as hers.

I think I might even want to.

"I'm sorry, Grisham," she says sincerely as she blinks.

I'm distracted as she pulls her soft, plump bottom lip into her mouth and bites down. I'm mesmerized as the nipped skin turns pale.

"What?"

"I said I'm sorry? About the explosion that caused you to lose part of your leg. I heard about it..." She trails off, her eyes closing briefly as if she's in pain.

I reach out and grab her chin, causing her eyes to fly open and lock with mine once more. A stirring in my suit grabs my attention, but I push my physical reaction to this girl out of my head so I can finish this conversation. Her eyes stay locked on mine, instead of straying back down to my foot.

This surprises the shit out of me, because usually I can't keep anyone's attention for more than a few seconds before they're looking at it again.

"I can do everything I did before," I tell her, my voice soft. "Except lead my boys out into the damn desert again, that is. My career focus has shifted a bit, that's all. But I'm okay, Greta. Thanks for worrying about me."

She nods, giving me a real smile for the first time.

Good Lord.

I'm floored. Two rows of perfect white teeth and plump, full lips form a smile that's just a little bit crooked. She's like seeing the sun again after months in the dark. Holy shit. I'm screwed. I'm not ready for this right now. I'm in no better state of mind than I was a year ago. In some ways, I'm worse. So I'm going to chalk whatever I'm feeling right now up to residual attraction from two years ago and from the high I get from saving someone's life.

"Let's get you to the car." I take her elbow and steer her toward the steps.

It's slow going, but we make it to the little parking lot. Her forehead wrinkles in confusion as we approach my Jeep.

"Where's your little sports car? The Audi?"

"Kind of hard to haul my board and my bikes around on that thing. I like to do shit outside…a lot. My Jeep is better for that type of stuff."

And my father bought me that Audi. After I graduated from school, I decided there was no way I was going to let him keep paying my way.

But I kept that thought to myself.

She raises her hands to the top of her wet suit, but I notice them trembling as she attempts to pull it down. Then I'm touching her shoulders without thinking.

"Let me help you," I say as I graze her soft, soft skin.

The simple touch does something wild to my insides, turning me from strong and steady to something gelatinous and wobbly. Her eyes fly to meet mine, and I'm left wondering if she felt it, too. Slowly, together, we slide the suit down her body, still slick from the ocean water I just pulled her from. The pink and black material peels away, and my gaze fixes on her pale skin like I've spotted a shiny new coin. She wiggles a little, shimmying out of the wet suit to reveal a tiny black bikini underneath. The sight sends a jolt of awareness straight to my cock. Coupled with miles and fucking miles of milky skin, she's an incredible sight. I let my gaze sweep up and down her frame just once before finding her face again. Her cheeks are pink, probably because she noticed my through once-over.

She nibbles her lip again, and I bite down hard on a groan.

"My towel is in my bag, down there." She points toward the beach.

"I'll get it when I get your board. Anything else, ma'am?"

I exaggerate my southern accent on the last line, making her giggle.

"Nope, I think that's it, *sir*." She picks up my game, exaggerating hers, and I feel warmth spread through my body starting in the very center of me.

"Funny girl."

After I help her into the Jeep—ignoring her protests about her being wet—and turn down the radio as the Marshall Tucker Band blares from the speakers. I turn and jog back down to the beach. I grab my surfboard and hers under one arm and load her bag onto the other.

Even though I'm only taking her to the doctor, and it's been months since I've seen her, I can't stop the feeling of giddy anticipation overwhelming me at the thought of seeing her sitting there in my car.

After Berkeley, I changed a lot about my life. I stopped answering to my asshole father. I gave my mother a very specific ultimatum. I changed my job trajectory in the navy, entering the SEALs training program against my father's wishes. I sold the Audi and bought a Jeep. I also bought a small house in Lone Sands close to the beach I'd always loved so much instead of living on base.

The one thing I hadn't changed was my relationship status. I was definitely in the *single* category. My parents and I had basically planned my life around their goal for me to marry

Berkeley one day. And like an idiot I'd bought into it; because she and I were so close there wasn't anyone else I could imagine spending my life with. Any girl I dated before then was just a distraction.

And now any girl I dated was the same thing. A distraction. A way to pass the time. I chose girls who knew the score, girls who typically dated guys in the navy because they weren't going to be around for long. Nothing serious, no strings attached.

But as I climb into my Jeep and glance over at Greta sitting there with a genuine, sweet-and-sexy smile on her face and with a body that could cause men to jump off bridges, something inside me stirs and stretches. Something that had been dormant for a long time. Something that tells me Greta Owen isn't going to be like other girls. I'm not going to be able to love her body one night and then walk away the next day.

Without even saying a word, she demands to be more than that.

I look down at my left leg. I'm not even a whole man anymore. I'd been through some shit in the last year that had changed me fundamentally, both inside and out. There's no way I can be everything to someone else.

I know it in my gut.

I'm going to drive Greta to the doctor and make sure she's okay.

And then I'm going to walk away.

Because at this point in my life, that's the best possible thing I can do for a woman like this.

Just walk away.

2

Greta

Grab the turkey bacon. Shred the cheddar. Place the chicken in the baking dish. Season it.

My brain has been taking a vacation all day. First, falling off my board (something I never do) and ending up unconscious in the ocean. And now I haven't been able to think of much else other than the way Grisham's intense forest-green eyes practically swallowed me whole when I woke. And the way one of his strong hands remained on me at all times, making sure I was okay. I wonder idly if the skin underneath those hands felt as hot to him as it did to me. And I also can't forget about the way his thick, dirty-blond hair fell into his eyes as he leaned over me.

So basically, my usually smart brain has turned into a big ol' dumb-dumb. And although I know the last thing I should be thinking about right now is Grisham Abbot, my dummy brain just won't let me stop.

So that's probably the reason I slice my finger open while

I'm chopping up the red onions to go on the smothered chicken I'm preparing for dinner.

"Ouch, dammit!" I hiss in pain as the blood immediately begins to seep from the wound. And then, because I'm one of those people who can't stand the sight of my own blood, I promptly become too woozy to stand and end up on my butt on the kitchen floor. My head is spinning in a complicated, wild dance.

The front door opens with a bang. Somewhere in the back of my fuzzy head I know it's Mea, because Mea always enters a room with a flourish.

"Greta! Ohmigod, are you okay?"

Mea crouches down beside me and takes my hand in hers. As soon as she notices the blood, she acts like a flash. Grabbing a towel from the cabinet behind, her she wraps it around my hand, applying an almost painful amount of pressure.

"There," she says. "All covered up. Come on back to the land of the living."

I take deep breaths. In through my mouth, out through my nose. For some reason, it helps me best when I take breaths in the opposite pattern normally used.

"Better?"

Mea's voice is full of sympathy as she scrutinizes my face. I nod, and her eyes narrow in on the butterfly bandage covering up the fresh stitches in my forehead.

I sigh, standing up on wobbly legs. "I'm fine. Just...the blood. You know."

"I know."

Mea goes to fetch a Band-Aid for my finger. I continue

holding the towel on my hand until she returns. My finger is now throbbing sharp beats of pain, but I'll live. There's no way I'm going back to urgent care for more stitches today. They'll assume someone is beating me up on a regular basis. And it's too difficult to tell them that I've just suddenly come down with a case of the klutzes.

When Mea returns, she sweeps gazelle-like into our apartment kitchen like a fierce little ballerina and begins wrapping the bandage around my finger while I avert my eyes.

"There," she announces. "All done."

I shoot her a grateful smile as I watch her chuck the Band-Aid wrapper in the trash and leave the kitchen. I get back to fixing our dinner. I throw the raw chicken breasts on the indoor grill and hum with satisfaction as they begin to sizzle. The rest of the ingredients are neatly lined up in little bowls on the counter.

Cooking is one area of my life where I have complete and utter control. I can cook the pants off of any meal, anytime. There are many areas in my life where control is out of my grasp, but usually when I'm cooking and when I'm surfing I'm 100 percent on my game.

Except for today, of course.

Today, I'm off my game in all areas.

"So how's your sister?" Mea kicks off her shoes and flops onto the couch. Of course she looks like a little winged bird as she does it, where I'd probably look like a stork on skates.

"She was released this morning. It wasn't anything she hasn't been through before. With her cystic fibrosis, you know she's no stranger to the inside of a hospital room."

Mea nods, sympathy pooling in her deep brown eyes. "Bless her sweet little heart. I hate to see her sick."

"Me, too. Mom takes good care of her, though. It just sucks that she doesn't have two involved parents. A sick sixteen-year-old girl would really appreciate having her dad by her side sometimes."

Mea folds her hands in her lap. I know she feels torn in two directions when I speak ill of my father. It's not like I don't love my dad. He's always been good to me, in his own way. And my mom will never have to worry about my sister's medical bills, because Jacob Owen has done more than well for himself. As Gemma would put it, he's loaded. But at the end of the day, a kid just wants her dad to show her love by *being there*. And that's where my dad gets it wrong every single time.

"Do we need to let Gemma spend the night here tonight so your mom can take care of Gabi?"

Shaking my head, I turn back to the grill. "No, Gabi's just going to take it easy tonight. I'm sure Gemma won't want to do anything besides get on Snapchat and talk to her friends, anyway."

Mea giggles. "Oh, to be fifteen again."

My insides melt when I think of my little sisters. They're the reason I moved back to Lone Sands after college. If it weren't for them, I probably wouldn't have moved away from the bigger city. But my mom needs help with my two teenage sisters a lot. Being there for them is as natural as breathing for me. It's second nature.

"Mea..." I can't hold it in any longer. I think if I try, my chest will explode. "I ran into Grisham today."

I keep my back to Mea so she won't see how thoroughly I blush at the mention of his name.

"Grisham? Grisham Abbot?" She sounds shocked.

I nod. "Yep." My attempt at nonchalance is foiled by the extra octave my voice reaches.

"Does that have anything to do with the injury you haven't mentioned on your forehead?"

Now she sounds suspicious.

I busy my hands with adding the smothering ingredients to the tops of the chicken breasts. This time, I leave the lid of the grill open. "It's no big deal. I fell off my surfboard today and sort of ended up unconscious."

"What?"

She sounds agitated. *Time to turn around.*

"It's fine, Mea. Really. I was just being clumsy."

She frowns at me. "You're not usually clumsy when you're surfing."

"Yeah, but I was just blowing off steam after seeing Gabi in the hospital one more time. You know? She's got bronchitis again, and Mom brought her to the ER last night when she couldn't catch her breath. It's so hard to see her that way."

Mea leaps off the couch and hurries over to wrap her arms around me. At five foot eight, I'm a good five inches taller than she is. But she wraps me up like a burrito in her embrace anyway, and I rest my head on her shoulder as I fight the tears back.

We stay that way for a few minutes until I pull away, swiping at my eyes. "I know, I know. She's okay. But still...she's the toughest kid on the planet. She never complains. It's just not fair."

Patting my arm as I turn back to the waiting chicken, she sighs. "I know."

"So, anyway, there I am, lying on the beach when I came to, coughing up a lung like a beached whale. And there's Grisham, leaning over me. He'd just given me *mouth-to-mouth*. He freaking *saved my life*, Mea."

Her eyes widen. "You're shitting me. For real? Are you okay now?"

She scrutinizes me with a careful gaze.

"Yes, I'm fine. Grisham took me to urgent care so I could get stiches. Then he bought me lunch at a drive-through. Then he brought me home. Then he got one of his buddies to meet him back at the beach so he could bring me my car."

I shake my head in disbelief. I still can't believe the events of today really happened. Grisham literally rode back into my life like a knight in shining armor. It's enough to give a girl some kind of hero complex.

Especially when her hero looks like Grisham Abbot does.

Memories of his golden-tan body gleaming in the sunlight cause a gentle wave of warmth to flood through me. His body was *sick*. His wet suit was pulled down to his waist, and there were just ripples and ripples of abs. I mean, the things seriously went on forever. Right down into the uncharted waters beneath the wet suit. Which I unfortunately didn't get to see.

He was bigger than I remember, too. When I saw him last, it was right before he entered the SEALs training program. And he had a great body then, but not nearly as ripped and defined as he is now. At least it didn't look that way before.

Mea's giving me a slow, knowing smile. I can imagine that

my face rivals the color of a strawberry at this point.

Damn Irish skin. I can't hide anything I'm feeling when I blush like a maniac all the time. Why can't I have beautiful, toffee-brown skin like Mea?

"Uh-huh. And how is Mr. Grisham looking these days, Greta?"

I groan, forgetting about the chicken and leaning back against the counter. "The same way he's always looked. Only better. His hair is longer. Sexy-messy. Even when his focus was clearly on Berkeley last year, I always thought he was gorgeous."

Mea claps her hands together with wild glee. "I know! And now he's back! So did you get his number?"

My mouth drops open. "No, I did *not*. And he didn't ask me for mine, either. So that's that."

Mea's mouth goes all scrunchy, the way it looks when she's devising a master plan. Mea's master plans are notoriously devious, and I raise my hands for protection.

"Stop it, Mea. Just stop thinking whatever it is you're thinking, all right? Grisham isn't for me. He never has been. I could never be with a guy who doesn't put me first, and that guy was always all about Berkeley. Now he's a freaking Navy SEAL. Do you know how dedicated those guys are to their jobs? Just as dedicated as my father was to his. And look how great that turned out for my family. No way. Just turn your brain around and go back to start. I'm not playing this game."

My voice is firm. But all Mea seemed to hear was *Grisham*, *Navy SEAL*, and *game*. The girl rubs her two dainty hands together like a greedy little goblin.

"You always liked him, Greta. More than you would ever admit. I saw it. And I see it again now. Plus, you owe the man.

He saved your life *and* he bought you lunch. Don't you at least think he deserves a 'thank you'?" She shakes her hips, shimmying to demonstrate her point.

My mouth is working to let Mea know that I don't think this plan she's hatching is a good idea. But my heart is squeezing so tight in my chest I'm in danger of going into cardiac arrest. My heart is *happy* at the thought of seeing Grisham again.

It's a foreign feeling. I'm not sure when the last time my heart felt happy was.

"I did say thank you."

Mea throws her hands up in the air.

"It's like I'm always working with amateurs," she mutters. "Of course you *said* thank you." She tugs a piece of my long, inky hair with two fingers. "But now you need to *show* him thank you."

I cross my arms in outright defiance. "And how am I supposed to do that when I don't have any way to contact him?"

Mea smiles an extra devilish smile before skipping back into the living room.

Oh, God. I realize my mistake too late. *I asked a question! And that was her green light.*

"You just leave it to Mama Mea."

She tosses a smug smirk over her shoulder at me as she heads toward her phone. Before she makes it to the coffee table where her phone is sitting idle, my own phone dings a text alert on the kitchen counter. I grab it up, still wondering what dangerous machine Mea is about to set in motion.

Hey there. It's Grisham. Checking to see if you're doing okay?

A shiver runs through me just at the sight of his name on my phone.

What the...?

"Mea," I say, my words slow and succinct. "What did you do? And how did it happen so fast?"

She pauses, her hand midway to her phone. "What are you talking about?"

I point at my phone, frantic. "It's Grisham. How is a guy I didn't give my number to texting me?"

I'm simultaneously filled with panic and euphoria.

Mea's full mouth stretches into a slow smile. She bounces on her tiptoes, causing her array of lustrous dark brown curls to shimmy.

"Don't be silly. I hadn't even picked up my phone yet! What did he *say*?"

She flies over to where I'm standing, and I hold out my phone so she can see Grisham's text.

"See?" Her face is full of mirth. "Text him back!"

I hesitate, biting my lip as I think. Then I send Grisham a response:

I'm hanging in there. A little headache but nothing I can't handle.

Mea reads over my shoulder. Frowning, she huffs out a disappointed breath. "Boring."

My eyes widen as I stare at her. "Mea! Am I supposed to sext the guy during our first convo?"

Her nod is solemn. "Absolutely."

Now it's my turn to throw up my arms at her utter hopelessness.

My phone vibrates, and I glance down at it with eager eyes.

Glad to hear it. You gotta watch that pretty head of yours when U R surfing alone. Don't forget to have your roommate wake you up every couple hours tonight for the concussion.

Huh. I'd actually forgotten all about those doctor's orders. "Mea, can you—"

"Nope!" she sings happily. "Can't, sweetie. I'm staying at my cousin's in Wilmington tonight. In fact, I don't even have time to stay for this delicious dinner you cooked. I have plans."

I stare at her, my eyes narrowing into suspicious slits. "Since when?"

"Since right now."

I grab the dish towel and throw it at her head. "You little devil! I need you! I have a freaking concussion!"

She grabs my phone and runs to her room, slamming the door behind her.

"Mea!" I take off after her. My fist thuds against the wood of her door. "Don't do anything stupid! I am begging you!"

She opens the door a crack and hands me my phone. "I have to pack. You're welcome, babe." She closes her door again with a firm *click.*

"Ohhhhh, you little..." I pull my eyes back down to my phone and they widen at the text I supposedly just sent to Grisham.

Actually I'll be waking myself up tonight. My roommie is in Wilmington for the night ? You think I'll be OK?

Just reading that text is making my skin heat with a furious blush. Why...*why* is there no way to take back a text after it's already been sent? I stare in misery at my phone, waiting for his response. If he even—

My phone dings.

And my heart stops beating.

Mea is *amazing.*

Um, no. Actually that's not OK with me at all. I'm packing a bag. B there in 30 mins. U hungry? I can pick up dinner.

If he were here, I'd be stuttering my response. But even as my heart is beating a rhythm so rapid it could run right out of my chest, my brain finally kicks into high gear. I type out a response, telling him that I've already prepared dinner and that I have plenty to share. Then I hold my phone to my chest and try to tamp down the enormous smile that wants to crack my face in two pieces.

Grisham Abbot doesn't want me to sleep alone tonight.

He's on his way over to my apartment *this minute.*

My stomach sinks with dread at the exact moment that my heart takes flight.

3

Grisham

In my Jeep driving to Greta's, I'm arguing with myself like a crazy person.

So much for walking away, half of me is thinking.

But the other half is of a different opinion.

She needs you tonight. Just for tonight. You'd be a jerk if you didn't help her out.

My head bobs in a firm nod. What kind of guy would I be if I let a girl with a concussion sleep on her own? As someone who's had plenty of concussions before, thanks to football and active duty military service, I know a thing or two about concussion care. And she needs to be woken up so that someone can check her for signs that her condition is worsening. The doctor said that her concussion was mild, but still.

You can't take chances with these types of things.

I can't help it when my lips pull into a small smile at the thought of seeing her again. The last time I saw her in her sleepwear...*damn.*

That thought goes straight to my quickly hardening cock, and I reach down to adjust myself because that shit *hurts*.

There's no doubt that Greta is the most gorgeous girl I've ever laid eyes on. Any residual feelings I had for Berkeley died long ago, and I haven't thought of her that way since she's been hot and heavy with Dare. But thinking of Greta now...the way her dark hair contrasts so starkly with her milky skin. The way her eyes pierce mine, rather than just looking at me. The way her body is just feminine curves stacked on top of lithe limbs...

I hit the steering wheel lightly, trying to shake the image from my brain. I'm going to her place tonight for one reason and one reason only—to help her. Not to get into her pants like a fucking perv.

When I arrive, I sling my duffle over my shoulder and walk up the two flights of stairs to her apartment. I rap the back of my hand against the door and wait, my hands hanging on to the top of the doorjamb. My heart pounds a little harder when I hear the sound of soft footsteps approaching from inside. The door is yanked open, and I'm suddenly *this close* to the face that's been playing on repeat in my mind all damn day.

I'm frozen in place, because those eyes of hers have the power to hold me hostage. I don't even blink.

"Hey," she says, her voice like satin as a slow, shy smile crosses her lips.

She's fresh, her face free of makeup. I try to keep my eyes on her face, but they act of their own accord, making a languid trek down her body. She's dressed for the late-summer heat in a ribbed purple tank top that hugs her tight, lifted breasts and her slim midsection. Small white cotton shorts that send a zing of awareness straight to my cock leave miles of skin free for my amusement. When I pull my gaze back up her body, her eyes are wide, and there's an adorable blush dusted across her cheeks.

"Hey." I clear my throat.

"Um...come in." She scoots to the side so that I can move my large frame in through the small doorway.

I walk into the apartment. Expecting to be flooded with both good and not-so-good memories of Berkeley and the time I spent with her here, I let my gaze roam around the living room. Everything is decorated in shades of white and blue, with a beach theme. Navy-blue couch and oversize armchair, white wooden coffee table. Navy-blue drapes with vertical white stripes. Large white lamps on mismatched end tables with navy-blue anchors. It's so kitschy and girly that I smile.

But the expected flood of regret and memories don't come. Instead, Greta steps into my line of sight, and my gaze shifts to her with focused intent. I set my bag down beside the couch and crook my finger at her.

"Come here."

She doesn't hesitate; she walks straight over and stands, tipping her head back to look up at me. Something inside me twitches happily at her willingness, and it takes a lot of willpower not to grab her and let my hands roam over all of that exposed skin.

Instead, I cup her chin with one hand and brush featherlight fingers over her head wound with the other. "How is this feeling?"

She winces as my fingers touch it, and I pull them away. "It's fine."

One side of my mouth tips up. "Tough girl."

Grinning, she turns and heads through an arching doorway to the open-concept kitchen. "You hungry?"

I wasn't until she said that. Now, my stomach rumbles as the aroma of something delicious and homemade wafts under my nose. "Wow. Something smells amazing. What'd you make?"

"Smothered chicken, garlic mashed potatoes, and corn soufflé." She says it like she just made Hamburger Helper or something equally mundane.

"Holy shit. You really *cooked*."

She shrugs. "Yeah. I cook a lot. It's something I love to do."

Instantly, curiosity rushes through me, and I want to know what else she loves to do. I pull out a seat at the bar top facing her and watch as she works to prepare our plates. She piles one high with a mound of mashed potatoes and a huge piece of chicken, and my stomach growls.

"You do? Huh. I didn't know that. I guess we never really got a chance to get acquainted before, did we?"

She shakes her head, sending cascades of that thick, dark hair rippling around her shoulders. I'm betting it would feel amazing tumbling around my fingers.

Stop. Mind out of the gutter, Abbot. You're here because she needs your help. Not your dick.

"Not really. But...I'd like to get to know you better, Grisham."

Oh...fuck. When she says my name, something long and forgotten opens up inside my chest like an expanding balloon.

Like a dragon, waking up after a long, restful sleep. I reply automatically, before I can think better of it.

"I've wanted to know more about you ever since you first batted those long eyelashes at me a couple of years ago."

Wait...what? What the hell was I thinking, saying that out loud?

My gaze stays glued to her face. I watch a myriad of emotions chase each other through her eyes, and a warm blush spreads over her cheeks. Her eyes widen, and her plump bottom lip disappears between her teeth as if on cue. I can almost count the different ways her body reacts to what I just said, and that's only while I'm looking at her face.

I can't help the easy smile that creeps onto my own lips. It's just too easy to tease her.

"Do you not realize that you're hot as the freaking sun, Greta? Any guy would want to get to know you better."

She drops her gaze to our plates and finishes filling them with food. It's a physical thing...how much I want to get close to her right now and make her look at me.

She slides a plate across the bar top toward me and brings hers around to sit beside me. She climbs up onto her stool and I reach out a hand and place it on her lower back to make sure she's steady as she settles herself. The warmth emanating from her is addictive; I don't move my hand right away. I hear her quick intake of breath as my hand smoothes across her shirt, cupping her tiny waist. I pull her toward me, and her stool scrapes against the floor. When she meets my stare under long, dark lashes, I grin.

"Much better." She clamps down on her bottom lip, and my

eyes are drawn there instantly. God, she's sexy. It takes every-thing I have to tear my eyes away from her mouth and focus on my food.

I cut a piece of chicken and stick the bite into my mouth. "Oh...damn, girl. I haven't had a home-cooked meal in...I can't even remember how long. This chicken is delicious."

Her face breaks into a true, ungrudging smile that steals my breath away. "Thank you. That makes me feel good. Don't you ever go home and have dinner with your parents?"

I snort. "Yeah, occasionally if I can't avoid it. But having dinner with my parents means going out or ordering in. My mom doesn't cook."

She gasps, her fork frozen halfway to her mouth. "Never?"

"Never."

"I mean...nothing? Like, not even grits for breakfast?"

I burst out laughing. "Of all the things...grits? Is that some-thing you have to have? My parents are both originally from Illinois. So no grits."

She nods, quick and passionate. "Oh my *word*, yes. I need my grits. And I like to make 'em with plenty of butter. And cheese...ohhh, yeah. Definitely cheese."

Still laughing, I wipe my mouth with my napkin. "Well, aren't you just the cutest southern girl."

We eat in silence for a few minutes before I think about what she said and start laughing all over again. She smiles over at me, her face shining with pure light. I reach over and brush her cheek with the back of my hand, because I can't *not* touch her in that moment. Her pupils dilate at the contact, and I can see the breath hitch with a quick rise in her chest. I'm lost in the deep blue of her eyes for a moment, and the connection between us pulls taut.

"Grits." My voice is hoarse with lust as I chuckle, shaking my head.

"You won't be laughing in the morning when I make them for you." She fires it right back at me, which causes my grin to grow.

"No, I'm sure I won't. But I do like the idea of you cooking for me again in the morning."

I wait for it...and there's the blush.

This is going to be a really entertaining night.

After dinner, it's still pretty early, so we settle onto the couch. Greta sinks into the cushions on one end, and I settle down in the middle not too far from her. My body lists in her direction, itching to move closer, but I don't want to crowd her.

This isn't a date, I remind myself.

"Want to watch a movie?" she asks. Her voice is like velvet. I just want to wrap myself up in it.

Her mouth pops open in a yawn, and I laugh. "Are you sure you'll make it through a movie?"

"If I don't, my knight is here to wake me up in exactly two hours."

"Knight, huh?"

Her head tilts to the side, and she looks at me. Really looks. "Didn't you save me on the beach today?"

"Anybody would have."

Her bright blue eyes don't falter as she answers, "No, they wouldn't have. But you did."

A hard lump forms in my throat. Swallowing it down, I tear my gaze away from hers and hand her the remote. "Movie night is lady's choice."

One side of her generous mouth tilts up in a crooked smile. I want so badly to lean in and taste it, but instead I lean away from her and zero in on the TV.

"Why, thank you, *sir*."

I glance at her again, and we both burst out laughing.

It feels good, laughing. Growing up, laughing and having a good time were discouraged by my strict dad. I was taught that hard work is what pays off, not goofing off and having a good time. His harsh hand was always something I feared, and I never felt safe enough to laugh around him at all.

I laugh with my buddies sometimes when we're at work, trying to break a tense situation. Or when we're out having a few beers. But this is really laughing...letting go. Being loose. It's light, and for some reason, it makes me hopeful.

It feels different. It feels *good*.

We start watching a movie about a man and a woman who go back to their hometown for a funeral after being high school lovers. I'm not supposed to like it because it's a chick flick. But I find myself drawn into the story, wanting to know what's going to happen with the couple now.

Midway through, I have to stand up and stretch my leg. I can't sit for long stints like this anymore without feeling like I need to walk, exercise my good limb a little bit. It's something I've had to do ever since the explosion. I stand, flexing, trying to be as casual about it as I can.

I can feel Greta's eyes on me as I walk to the counter and do a couple of standing knee flexes. Knowing she's watching me sends a flush of embarrassment creeping up my neck. The last thing I want is for her to see me as weak. Or as less than what I was before.

When we first met, I was whole.

But I came back from the other side of the world with a piece missing. My imagination runs away, weaving the tale of what she must think of me now.

When I return to the couch, she reaches over and places a hand on the thigh of my leg that was partly amputated. My muscle tenses under her touch, the skin of my neck heats. I reach down and grab her hand in mine. It's warm and soft, and I squeeze it gently as I look over at her.

"Does it hurt?" she whispers.

I shake my head with a small smile. "No."

"Did it? Hurt? I mean...when it happened?"

I don't answer for a minute, and she misinterprets my silence.

"I'm sorry, Grisham...I didn't mean to...just forget I asked."

Her hair forms a veil around her face as she looks down at her lap. I lift her hand to my chest and tug until she looks at me.

"Please don't ever apologize for asking honest questions. People never do that. They stare and they wonder, or they obviously try *not* to stare when I know they really want to. No one, even my family and friends, comes right out and asks about it. My dad has actually never even bothered to have an honest conversation with me about what happened. Not once."

She nods. Her face is certain; there's not a hint of hesitation there. "I want to know."

I sigh and lean my head back against the couch cushions. Going back to that night...it's not something I ever willingly do. I had to talk to a therapist about it, and I opened up as fully as I could. I think the talking helped, but it's hard as hell to revisit what happened.

"An RPG hit our convoy as we were on our way in as support for a unit of Rangers. The hum-vee in front of us took a direct hit, but we caught a big portion of the explosion. It hurt, Greta. It felt exactly the way you'd imagine it would feel to have one of your limbs literally blown off your body. But when you're out there...in a situation like that, you can't focus on the pain. You have to focus on living. On surviving. So that's what I did. I focused on living and making sure my men were out of danger. And then I don't remember anything else until I woke up in Germany."

She sucks in a loud, hissing breath through her mouth. "I can't imagine. How did you adjust to having a prosthetic?"

I smirk at the memory of waking up in the hospital. "When I realized the leg was gone from the knee down, I was pissed. Really fucking pissed. I thought it would completely change my life. And it has...but prosthetics are really, really good these days. There's a lot I can still do. I probably won't be able to be active duty much longer, but I'm going to get to finish out this year with my team at least."

She nods. "And then what?"

Shrugging, I close my eyes briefly. This is something I worry about a lot, but I don't want anyone to know how much. "I don't know." As much as I attempt to keep it locked tightly away, my uncertainty bleeds through in my tone.

She turns her legs toward me, the right side of her face leaning against the couch. I open my eyes and stare right into hers. "You'll figure it out, Grisham. I have faith in you."

I give her a small smile. "You don't know me well enough to have faith in me."

She squares her shoulders and lifts her chin.

Ah. This girl has a stubborn streak. And I bet it's a mile long. For reasons still undiscovered, the thought makes me smile.

"I know enough." Her lips pull into a tight smirk, her eyes shining brightly as she holds my gaze.

The urge to kiss her is so strong I can't deny it. It's like I'm a poor fish caught on her line. With every sentence she utters, with every smile she so freely gives, she's reeling me in slowly, and I can't wriggle free. I don't even want to.

I lean in, and I see her lips part the slightest bit as she readies herself for my kiss. Her grip tightens in mine, and I use my other hand to grasp the back of her neck. The heat radiating off her skin scorches me, and all I want to do is drown in the flames. Her gaze darkens, and I know her expression mirrors the pure, inescapable lust in my own. Our eyes are locked and loaded, and all I have to do is close the remaining inches between us.

Greta's phone vibrates on the table. I close my eyes for a moment in frustration just as she jumps backward and reaches out to grab her phone.

She gives me a guilty glance as she checks the number. "I have to answer this. It's my dad."

I nod as I try to get control of the burning fire raging inside of me. *Why is everything so...*much *with her? So much more?*

I've kissed more girls than I can count. When I want to do it, when I feel it's right, I just do it. There's never much buildup or thought. It's the natural order of things. But with Greta, everything feels like a big fucking deal.

I zone out for the few minutes she's on the phone with her father. When she hangs up, she looks disgruntled.

"My father wants to see me."

"Now?"

She shakes her head. She's agitated, or irritated. I'm not sure which. I remember briefly that her father was the man who assisted in Berkeley's rescue last year when an enemy of her boyfriend's brother kidnapped her. Greta's father is some kind of security specialist. He owns his own company that Berkeley's boyfriend, Dare, now works for as his right-hand man.

Greta doesn't seem thrilled about the impending conversation with her father. If I had to guess, I'd say they aren't close. Either that, or Greta has an issue with him.

We can start a club. The I Can't Stand My Father *club.*

"In the morning." She flops back onto the couch and trains her eyes on the movie.

I reach for her hand again, gauging her expression. She's trying really hard to keep her face blank.

"I don't want to talk about him."

I nod, rubbing small circles with my thumb on the back of her hand. "Then we won't."

We watch the rest of the movie in silence. I can't stop thinking about how drastically different her headspace is now from where we were when our faces were inches apart.

And on top of that, the movie has a terrible ending. The main character dies, and the girl has to go on without ever knowing what could have been.

Fucking chick flicks.

4

Greta

Greta."

I don't recognize the soft voice calling my name, but I know its smooth, deep timbre makes me want to squeeze my eyes closed tighter and snuggle down deeper. A low rumble reaches my ears, a male chuckle. And then the soft brush of rough fingers against my forehead forces my eyes to fly open.

"Hey," whispers Grisham. He's leaning over me, his face directly above mine. I can feel the hard lumps of his thigh muscles tensing under my head, and the memory of the evening comes rushing back in the form of moving pictures in my mind.

"Grisham," I murmur in a voice heavy with sleep. "What time is it?"

"It's only eleven. You fell asleep near the end of the movie. I just wondered if you wanted to sleep here or if you want to go to your room."

I struggle to sit up and Grisham's hand is there, cupping my head and helping me to lean against the back of the couch. I swipe at my eyes.

"If I haven't been asleep long, why am I so wiped?" I groan, flopping back against the sofa cushions.

"Because you have a concussion." Grisham scoops me into his arms and stands. "I'm making an executive decision. Lead the way to your bedroom."

A sleepy smile tugs at my mouth as I look up at him. "I like the direction of this decision."

And then I promptly turn tomato red, because where the hell did *that* come from? I'm blaming the head injury for my forward remark.

But Grisham only smiles down at me, his green eyes darkening a shade and flaming with something even darker. "Be a good girl."

I tell him which room off the short hallway is mine, and he deposits me on my bed.

He kneels down on the floor beside me as I roll onto my side to face him. He places his chin against his folded hands as he stares at me.

"So," he says. "I'm going to wake you up in a couple of hours. You'll probably be pretty out of it, but I'm going to use a flashlight to check your pupil dilation, okay? Then I'll let you go back to sleep."

I sit up again. "I didn't get you a blanket and a pillow."

He pushes me back down with gentle hands. "Greta, you need to relax now. I can get it. Just tell me where the stuff is and I'll make a bed on the couch."

"No."

He arches one eyebrow. "No?"

I shake my head. "I don't want you to sleep on the couch. Will you sleep in here?"

I'm not sure what goes on in his head then, but it looks like a war. I adjust my prior request.

"On the floor. You can make a bed on the floor. Look at all these pillows on my bed. I think I can spare a few for you."

He smiles, gazing into my eyes as he nods his head. "Okay. I'm good with sleeping on your floor."

I tell him where the linen closet is at the end of the hall, and he retreats to grab a few blankets. After spreading them out across the floor, along with the pillows I offered, he leaves again to grab his bag and use the bathroom across the hall.

When he returns, my breath gets trapped somewhere between my lungs and my throat. Because Grisham isn't wearing a shirt. And Grisham without a shirt on is like watching a Greek god walking amongst us normal folk in the flesh.

I can't avoid staring. A white-hot heat lances through my core at the sight of his rock-hard chest, oceans of abdominal muscles that clench and flex as he moves through the doorway, and astounding absolute masculine beauty.

But it's not only the ripped perfection that has me staring. It's the scars that mottle his torso: clear evidence of a man who's been through something horrendous. They're littered among the beautifully drawn lines and epically graceful script of several tattoos along his chest and shoulders.

His eyes burn into mine, and I don't care that I'm staring. I'm pulled to my feet by some unseen force and drawn to him like a magnet. He stands there, watching me with rapt attention as I approach.

Halfway to him, I snap to my senses. *What am I doing? Am I really just going to attack him like a rabid fox?* Instead of stopping where he stands, I squeeze past him in the doorway, creating a path to the bathroom.

As I pass, the tips of my breasts through my shirt brush ever so slightly against his arm and I squeeze my eyes shut tight. Just that small, galvanizing touch was enough to send piercing shards of desire spiking through my body. It's a match to a gasoline. It's not just electricity or attraction that I feel for Grisham.

It's pure, primal *need.*

I freeze, trying to regain just a single ounce of control. And then he speaks. And his voice is enough to melt me where I stand.

"Greta." His voice is rough, like nails dragging across concrete.

It incites a shiver that starts somewhere deep inside me, some deep, dark place I've never explored. My body responds to his voice like an instrument only he knows how to play. Heat rushes to my core, starting an ache between my legs that pulsates with my racing heartbeat. My nipples harden instantly, straining against the material of my shirt. My mouth fills with saliva, and I swallow without pulling my eyes away from him.

For just a second, his expression is tortured. And it makes me wonder whether his body is reacting to me the way mine is to him. Everything about this man is hard, beautiful, and scarred. His eyes are dark, an eclipse that has shadowed their usual glow.

Could it be possible that he wants me, too?

Then he schools his face, donning an unreadable expression as he averts his eyes and clears his throat. He walks stiffly toward his palette on the floor.

I watch him only for an instant before I flee for the bathroom.

Locked inside, I lean against the counter, my chest heaving with every breath. If Grisham had made a move, if he'd taken even a step in my direction, I would have thrown myself in his arms. But that's obviously not what he wanted. I was like an animal in heat, and he turned away. Embarrassment colors my face as I lean over the sink with trembling limbs.

What the hell, Greta? You've gotta get it together. You're acting like a complete idiot, and he's going to think you're a total psycho. Don't have any illusions about this guy. He was never yours and that isn't going to suddenly change now.

My body has never betrayed me like that before. Never have I lost control of myself around a guy. Grisham does something to me that no one's ever done before, and that fact scares the shit out of me. I can't control it.

But I have to control it.

I splash some cool water on my face, brush my teeth, and take a deep breath before opening the bathroom door and trekking back across the hall to my room.

Grisham is lying on top of his blankets, his hands laced behind his bed as he stares up at the ceiling. I steal across the room and climb into bed, pulling my covers up to my chin.

Reaching over to the nightstand, I yank on the lamp chain, leaving us in darkness.

My breaths are just starting to even out when Grisham speaks again.

"So how long have you been surfing?"

I shrug before I realize he can't see me from his position and in the darkness. "I think I started when I was around twelve. We actually lived in Georgia until then. When we moved to Lone Sands, it was because my father was retiring from the army and this was where he'd always wanted to retire. He and my mom were fighting a lot, and I needed an escape. I found it in surfing."

He's quiet for a moment. "My mom and dad always fought a lot, too, but they didn't give me the relief of a divorce. I don't think my mom could ever find the strength to leave him. She should have."

His voice is bitter on the last sentence, and I find myself wishing I could see his face, read his expression. "Divorce is awful, Grisham."

There's a pause before he answers me. "Some marriages are worse."

I mull that over for a bit.

"We should surf together sometime," he says.

Smiling, I agree. "We should."

"But only if you can stay on your board. No more visits to urgent care."

Giggling, I throw one of my extra pillows at him. I hear his soft grunt as it makes contact. Then I laugh aloud as he tosses it back.

"Better me falling off my board than you. I wouldn't be able to save you. I faint at the sight of blood."

"Seriously?"

"Well, mostly my own blood, but yeah. It's not pretty."

His laughter stalls. "I'm pretty sure there's no moment in existence when you aren't pretty."

Warmth surges through me at his compliment, and I'm at a loss for words. I replay the nicest thing a guy has ever said to me repeatedly as my breathing evens out once more. When I feel my eyelids growing heavy, I turn on my side and whisper down to him.

"Good night, Grisham."

His response is immediate. "Good night, Grits."

When my eyes open again, the sun is streaming in through my apartment window. I stretch, and then sit up. The first thing I do is search for Grisham on the floor. The pillows are neatly stacked by my nightstand and my blankets are folded just as adeptly.

I climb out of bed and scurry to the bathroom to check my hair and brush my teeth. When I emerge, I venture down the hallway, through the kitchen, and into the living room.

Grisham is sitting on the couch, a mug of coffee in his hands. His profile is to me; I expect the TV to be on, but it's not. He's sitting in silence. Thinking?

"Grisham?" My voice escapes in a tentative squeak.

He turns toward me, aiming a beautiful smile my way. "Good morning, Grits."

I put my hands on my hips. "I'm going to make you some. Then you won't make fun anymore."

"Hey," he protests, "I'm not making fun. But the nickname fits, and I'm not dropping it unless you ask me to."

He waits, but I turn for the kitchen, hiding my smirk. I don't want him to ditch my new nickname, and he knows it.

He follows me. "I made coffee."

Sniffing the delicious aroma, I whirl on him. "Thanks. So, you didn't wake me up last night."

His eyes widen. "Damn. I knew you were sleeping heavily, but I didn't think you'd completely forget. I woke you up every two hours, Greta. Just like I said I would."

Surprise pulls my expression into confusion. "You did? I had no idea." Then I'm filled with apprehension. "Did I say or do anything stupid?"

He smiles, coming closer. When he's standing directly in front of me so that I have to look up at him, he taps my nose with his index finger. "You were completely adorable in sleep. Just like I'd expect you to be."

My skin instantly heats at his nearness. My breathing comes faster, and I'm reminded of how out of control I was last night. It isn't just his looks that do this to me. It isn't just the fact that I know exactly what sort of sculpted masterpiece is hiding beneath his clothes. All of that turns me on, sure, but it's everything that encompasses Grisham. It's his tenderness juxtaposed with his rough and manly job. It's his beauty, which directly opposes all of his scars. It's his consideration, taking care of me when it isn't his job to do so.

Blushing scarlet, I turn around and begin pulling out pots and pans. "Well, thank you for doing that, Grisham. You must be exhausted this morning. What time did you get up?"

He shrugs. "I'm always up at five. Old habits die hard."

"I haven't seen five o'clock in so long I can't remember what the day looks like at that hour. What do you do that early?"

"I work out, usually. And make coffee. And then I go to work. How do you like your coffee?"

He meanders over to the full, steaming pot and I watch the view from behind. His low-slung jeans are hanging exactly right on the tight cut of his hips, and his plain white T-shirt hugs his sinewy biceps deliciously.

I need a fan.

He turns around and quirks an eyebrow at me, totally catching my stare-fest.

He gives me a slow, sexy smile. "Coffee?"

"Oh. Um...give me about an inch of half-and-half at the bottom. And a teaspoon of sugar."

He makes a face. "That's sweet."

I shrug. "I like sweet."

He loses all trace of a smile, and his expression grows so intense, so scrutinizing that I want to take a step backward. I don't, though. I just stare right back.

"Grits...you know that I'm not sweet, right? I'm...damaged. In more ways than the obvious one."

I'm struck silent by his comment. We don't break eye contact as he waits for my response, and I finally give him an honest one.

"I only know what I can see, Grisham. I see a guy who pulled me out of the ocean when he hadn't been in the water in months. I see a guy who took me to the doctor and found my number to check up on me the same night. I see a guy who, when he realized I was going to be alone with a concussion, showed up on my doorstep with a duffle bag and a smile. If that's not sweet...I don't know what is."

I drop my gaze, studying the countertop. But the fact that he doesn't even know how awesome he is...it gives me the courage to look him straight in the eye when I speak next. "You've been through a lot, Grisham. So you have a story. We all do. It doesn't mean you're not good enough for someone else."

He averts his eyes. His voice comes out in a ragged whisper. "You don't know what you're saying, Greta. You don't want...this."

He gestures toward himself.

Still keeping my eyes locked firmly on his face, I shrug. My attitude screams "carefree" but my heart is hammering a violent rhythm in my chest. "Why don't you let me be the judge of what I want?"

"There's no room in my life for a partner. Not anymore. I've dedicated myself to saving other people...to making sure they're safe from harm. I gave up the illusion that I could do that any other way than alone a long time ago."

It feels like I've been punched in the gut. If Grisham really feels that way, that he needs to be alone in order to fulfill his purpose in life, then I'm just setting myself up for a broken heart. This broken, beautiful man has dedicated his life to making sure other innocent people have one. How can I take that away from him?

But now that I know him, how can I let him go on thinking that all he can ever be is alone?

5

Grisham

Seven...eight...nine...ten!"

The bar clatters back on its anchor and I sit up on the bench. I'm out of breath and my biceps are burning.

"Damn, bro. You've been intense this morning. Five reps of ten with two-forty? Shiiiiiit, Ghost."

I smirk at Lawson's use of my combat nickname. "It was a hard road coming back from the amputation, Laws. My upper body functioned the way it was supposed to, so I worked the hell out of it. It was therapeutic or something."

Lawson nods as he reaches for a pair of dumbbells and begins a set of bicep curls. "I ain't mad atcha, Ghost. But..." He pauses in his lifting.

Here it comes.

I rise from the weight bench to grab my towel and my water bottle. I stand, waiting for him to spit out his question, wiping my dripping forehead with the navy-issue towel. We work out for the first two hours of every shift. It's my favorite part of the day, unless we're working on training exercises and maneuvers in the afternoon. We aren't today. It's mainly an admin day, and I have paperwork lined up on my desk I want to put off for as long as possible. Planning for the next mission my team will embark on without me is just depressing.

"Ben and I got your text yesterday morning that you weren't gonna make breakfast. But then you missed pizza Wednesday. You never miss pizza Wednesday. What the hell kept you so busy yesterday?"

And there it is. I've been wondering when I'd have to bring up Greta. Knowing Lawson, he'll rag on me until I let him meet her. And I'm conflicted about when or if that'll happen. What would I introduce her to my buddies as? A friend? The way my body reacts to Greta is way more than friendly. But I haven't made any type of commitment to her, either. Do I even want to?

And what if I introduce her to the guys, and one of them decides to make a move on her? Just the thought of anyone else getting close to Greta sends a sizzling jolt of anger ripping through me.

"I ran into a friend on the beach who needed help. I ended up needing to hang out with her for a while during the day yesterday and then again last night."

I leave it at that, but on the inside I'm cringing, because I have a feeling Lawson "Sleuth" Snyder is going to ferret out the meaning behind the words I didn't say.

I groan and turn away as a slow, suspicious smile dawns over his face. "So you didn't go grab waffles with us because you 'ran into a friend.' And that *same* friend kept you busy for most of the day, and then again after dark. So I'm assuming this friend is hot, and you had her panties lying on the floor by the end of the night."

I whip back around. Anger builds up inside me until I imagine I look like a cartoon character with steam pouring out of my ears. "I said she's a friend. Get your fucking mind out of the gutter."

Lawson drops the weights and holds up his hands in defense. "Whoa, whoa, whoa, Ghost. I didn't mean any disrespect. Does your friend have a name?"

I blow out easy breaths through my mouth as I bring my heartbeat back down to a more normal pace. "Her name's Greta. She used to room with that girl I told you about...Berkeley. I hadn't seen Greta for a while, that's all. We were catching up."

"I bet you were," mutters Lawson. When he catches my death glare, he picks his weights up again with a chuckle. "Sorry. If she's just your friend, then I guess she can come hang out with the guys this weekend at your barbecue."

Shit. That's right. This weekend is a long one, ending in Labor Day on Monday. I'd told my buddies we would do the end of summer up right and celebrate the fact that we'd all come back from Syria alive and well. They'd be ready to deploy again early next year, but I'd likely be sending them off without me for the first time since we'd been a unit. My leg can only take me so far from this point on. My SEAL days are over.

An overwhelming feeling of sadness and anxiety washes over me at the thought.

"You gonna bring her?" asks Lawson with another sly smile.

"I said we're just friends, L. I might ask her and her room-mate to stop by. Berkeley and Dare are coming, so I don't want her to find out about it from them."

Lawson scrutinizes my face as he finishes his third set. His normally cinnamon-brown face is morphing into a dark shade of red, and he hisses out a breath as he lets the weights drop to the ground. "Yeah. Act all nonchalant if you want to, Ghost. But I see it in your eyes. You want this chick to be there. So ask her to be there."

I pretend to think about it. Then, moving quicker than Lawson expects, I snap his bare chest with my towel and take off, running as fast as my fake leg will allow me to go before he can give chase. Our workout ends with him cursing me as he follows me to the showers, while I howl with laughter.

I sit in the Jeep, my parents' enormous Lone Sands home looming like a majestic beacon before me. It's been months since I've been here. My mother flew to Germany when I was hurt. She stayed with me during my month-long hospital stay, and the entire time we were together, I could forget about my father and the way we'd left things the last time I'd seen him. She was there for me and me alone, and that felt good. For once.

But when we flew home, there he was. Back in control, try-ing to manage my medical situation professionally. He was sure he could still make a desk job at the base happen, and all of my protests fell on deaf ears. It was when my CO came to me with the transfer papers that I finally lost my mind and told my father exactly where he could shove his meddling manipulations.

So, sitting here now in the hot, late-August sunshine doesn't feel too good. It feels wrong. But I know I have to go inside and at least invite them to my barbecue.

They're my family. The only family I have. Regardless of the way I feel about their marriage and the way my father's control issues have fucked up my life, I won't ever stop trying to be there for my mother.

Ever.

I shove the Jeep door open and climb out. Before I reach the bottom of the impressive staircase leading up to the three-story home, the front door swings open. My mother stands there, a huge smile on her pretty face.

"Grisham, honey! Oh, I've missed you so much!" She hustles down the steps to grab me into a bone-crushing hug.

I hug her to me, a large lump forming in my throat as I realize how thin she is.

"Mom, it's good to see you, too. How are you doing? I'm sorry I've stayed away."

When she pulls back, her eyes are shining. "I'm glad you're here now. And just in time for dinner!"

I glance up at the house, wary. "I don't think I'm staying, Mom. I just wanted to talk to you and Dad for a minute. Okay?"

Her face falls. Upon closer inspection, I can see that her makeup is flawless, as usual. The tiny creases around her eyes and mouth are cleverly hidden with whatever miracle product she's currently using. Her blond hair is perfect, placed in a short style, and even at five o'clock in the evening, when most people are changing into comfortable clothes to wind down the day, she's still wearing a skirt and heels.

"Come in, then, sweetheart."

She leads me up the stairs and into the house.

My parents' Lone Sands home has been a second home ever since my father reached two-star admiral status and was stationed to the base in Brunswick County just under his long-time friend Admiral Holtz. Berkeley's father.

Just off the gray slate-tiled foyer, Mom walks into her front sitting room and sits on the sleek, white couch. She pats the cushion next to her. Her eyes monitor my progression as I move to join her.

"How goes it these days with your foot?" she asks, all trace of a smile gone from her tone.

If anyone knows the frustration I endured while fighting my way back from an amputation, it's my mother. She was there at the beginning. She saw the circuit of emotions I traveled, from denial, to red-hot anger, to mourning. The loss of a limb is a living, breathing journey from one end of the emotional spectrum to the other.

"I'm all good," I assure her. "Regular workouts with the team and everything."

She nods with genuine mother happiness. "I knew you'd get there, Grisham. Now, what's this you need to talk with me about?"

I open my mouth to speak when the heavy thud of boots on the stairs freezes us both.

"Katie? Do we have company?"

My father.

My mother stiffens beside me, and my hand shoots out to rest on her arm, reassuring her that I'm here. It's funny; it doesn't matter how much time you spend away from your family, the habits ingrained in you don't ever change or fade away. They're permanent, like the sunrise or the way the leaves change color in autumn.

"Yes, dear. Grisham's here."

Her voice is completely different when she talks to him. When she's talking to me, her voice is clear and confident. Loving. She's my mother, and she throws herself into that job fully. During my recovery, there wasn't an ounce of uncertainty in her the entire time. She knew I'd make it back to full usage of my leg, and she made sure I never forgot her faith in me.

But when she talks to *him?* She's unsure and tentative. She walks on fucking eggshells. Anger roils inside my gut, threatening to overtake me.

Chill out, Grisham. He hasn't done anything. This time. Just get the invitation out. You're here for Mom.

I stand and wait for Admiral Michael Abbot to enter the room.

And enter he does, with a gigantic presence that envelops every room he's in. Our heights are identical at six foot one, and our faces are complementary. But I get my dark blond hair from my mother, whereas my father has a thick head of salt-and-pepper locks. His sun-weathered, tan skin stands out today in his white golf polo and crisp khaki pants.

"Ah. The prodigal son returns. What can *we* do for you, Grisham?" His tone is smooth, detached. In his opinion, we had it out once and that was all he needed to cut me off emotionally.

I avert my gaze from him and focus on my mother. "I'm having an end-of-summer barbecue. At my house. It's going to be Sunday afternoon and evening, so that everyone can still wake up and sleep in the next day. I'm extending an invitation for you two to come."

There. I've done what I came to do.

Silence stretches across the room, and rather than enduring it, I turn for the door.

"Grisham!" My mother stands and reaches for my arm. "We'd love to come."

Her voice is strong and sure.

My father clears his throat, and we both eye him with practiced caution. "We actually have plans, Katie. Remember? The church is having a barbecue that day. You're supposed to make potato salad."

Her lips tighten, the fine lines around them deepening as she tries not to frown. "I'm sure we could do both, dear. Grisham's barbecue is going into the evening. I could bring a dessert."

I feel like a kid again, caught between them. My eyes bounce back and forth from one parent to the other during their exchange.

My father narrows his eyes at Mom. "We'll talk about this later. When we're alone. Grisham, thank you for the invitation."

And he's done. He strides from the room without a backward glance, most likely headed for the dinner table. My mother takes a deep breath, and I glance at her. Guilt floods through me, a dousing wave to remind me that I haven't been here for her enough. She needs me.

"I didn't mean to make trouble, Mom. Just wanted to make sure you guys knew you were welcome."

She reaches up and wraps her arms around my neck, squeezing me tight. "I love you, honey. I'll try to convince him to come."

I nod as we make our way toward the door. "Would like to have you. But there's no pressure. Maybe you and I could grab lunch sometime soon, okay?"

Her eyes light up. Just the sight of it makes me want to punch my father in his overbearing face. "Yes. Lunch would be wonderful. I...I miss you, Grisham."

It's gut-wrenching when your mother, who lives in the same town you do, tells you she misses you.

It lets me know that I'm messing up, and something needs to change.

"I love you, Mom. Take care."

With that, I'm walking back down the steps and climbing into my Jeep. I let out the breath I've probably been holding since I arrived, and send a thankful prayer up to the sky. I've done what I came to do.

Now there's another invitation I need to extend. This one should be no less complicated, but much more pleasant to deliver.

6

Greta

Strolling through the nondescript industrial steel front door of my father's firm, I enter his lobby and glance around. My father doesn't employ a receptionist in his office; there aren't a lot of walk-in visitors. Most of his clients have appointments, and those visits, as well as the light administrative paperwork that occasionally piles up, are handled by his assistant.

Kyle Wessler looks up from a desk in the corner of the glossy, gleaming lobby, and his face breaks into a huge smile. I return his smile fully and throw my hand up in a small wave.

"Hey, Kyle. I've been summoned."

He comes around the side of the desk and folds his arms across his chest. His bespectacled brown eyes are jovial, his clean-shaven face sculptured and handsome. Kyle's look is very buttoned-up and conservative, but his nerdy appearance is belied by a toned, chiseled body under his collared shirts and pleated pants.

"Well, I guess you must have been. It's the only reason you show that beautiful face around here."

Kyle crooks a finger so that I'll come close enough for a hug, and I do just that.

"It's been awhile," I agree. "Sorry about that, Kyle. You know, life gets crazy."

He holds me at arm's length and scowls. "Too crazy for old friends you went to high school with?"

I nod, glancing down at my feet. "There's no excuse. Especially since you started working for my dad after school, huh?"

He glances at the stacks of papers on the desk. "Being his assistant keeps me busy. It's not exactly what I had in mind when I started here, but it's paying the bills."

My dad's private security firm is extremely successful. Jacob Owen, owner of Night Eagle Security, Inc., is well known in the world of privately contracted security and protection services, and he's done a damn good job expanding his reach throughout the country. He's got another office in Dallas, and the home branch is here in Wilmington, North Carolina. Most of the work my father does is out of his home office, but he's always thinking bigger, especially when it comes to his baby.

His company.

"So, is part of your job as my dad's assistant to pump iron on a daily basis?" I tease Kyle, prodding his noticeably larger bicep with my index finger.

His face reddens, and I giggle at his reaction.

Despite his good looks, Kyle has never been a ladies' man. He's just a tiny bit awkward with girls, and much too shy for his own good. So I'm filled with surprise when he meets my gaze head-on and takes one of my hands in his.

"Pumping iron is for recreational purposes only. Your dad won't let anybody in as a security team member unless they've got Special Forces on their résumé, and that's not ever going to be me." He gestures toward his glasses.

I nod with a sympathetic smile. "Tell me about life, Kyle. You must have a pretty serious girlfriend by now with all those muscles."

Kyle glances down at his feet, shaking his head. "Nope. Pretty busy with work here."

I wave my hand in the air, dismissing the thought. "That's silly. You can always make time for a personal life. Work can't be your whole world, Kyle."

His face brightens, and he meets my gaze again. "Well, maybe we could catch a coffee sometime soon. Catch up a little bit."

I nod, smiling. "Absolutely. And my roommate is single. You never know. Next time we're hanging out, grabbing a few drinks, I'll let you know. Sound good?"

Kyle chuckles as my father's office door opens and he fills the doorway.

At six foot three, 275 pounds, my father is a formidable man. His hair is cut in a short, graying buzz like he never got out of the army. I try not to roll my eyes at his stern expression.

"Wessler!" he barks. "Were you going to tell me that my daughter was here, or were you attempting to keep her to yourself for the entire afternoon?"

Kyle hesitates, and I can see the wheels turning in his brain, so I step quickly forward.

"He was just coming to get you, Dad. Do you want to go into your office and talk?"

He nods, extending his arm through his doorway and keeping an eagle-sharp eye on Kyle as I walk into the large room with the wall of windows overlooking the blue-green ocean.

My dad closes the door behind me with a sharp snap, and then he stiffly pulls me into his arms.

He's not stiff because he doesn't care; he's stiff because he's so damn big and ferocious that hugging is like a foreign language for his body. I flash back to all the times I wanted nothing more than to have him wrap his big, strong arms around me when I was still a little girl terrified my daddy wouldn't come home. How many nights my tears dampened my pillow and the song that serenaded me to sleep was my own weeping.

As much as I try to hide it, I'm still that little girl inside who just wants her father to hold her close.

I pull back after a moment, and he looks into my eyes, concern weighing on the corners of his.

"How's your sister? I heard about the hospital this week."

I nod wearily. "Is that why you called? I mean, I'm glad you're concerned about Gabi, but you could have actually just paid her a visit. She's back home now. I'm sure Gemma could also do with some father-daughter time."

I'm beyond sick of lecturing him on how to be a good dad. I feel like I'm in a topsy-turvy fairy tale; I'm always in the opposite position with him than where I'm supposed to be. The daughter isn't supposed to act like a parent.

He holds his hands up in front of himself defensively. "I know, I know. I've called her. I'll stop by this weekend. I just wanted to ask you, because I know you were there and have firsthand knowledge."

My head bobs, and I sink into one of his oversize chocolate-brown leather chairs. The seating in his office is comfortable, clustered around a rustic wooden coffee table. My dad's desk is in the center of the wall of windows, but when he's consulting with a client, they almost always use this more comfortable seating.

"Okay, let's get down to business."

He sits down across from me and leans back in his seat, steepling his fingers together.

"I asked you to come in today, Greta, because I need your help."

I sit up straighter. "My help? With what?"

He gestures around his office. "Kyle's a good assistant. He does solid work with scheduling and dealing with clients when I'm on an assignment. But the company is growing by leaps and bounds. I'm hearing from new potential clients every day. I'm going to need an office manager."

I open my mouth to speak, and then snap it shut again. "You want me...to *work* here? Dad...you know my plans for my future. I cook. I want to be a chef."

He frowns. "Yes, I know. I offered to pay for culinary school, remember? You turned me down."

I stare at my folded hands. My voice sounds muffled. "I don't need a handout. I can do it on my own."

It's not exactly true. My mom pays for my rent. I know

the money comes from her alimony, which comes straight from my dad. But accepting it straight from him feels different somehow.

He sighs in frustration. "It wouldn't be...I'm your father, Greta! Part of my job is providing for you."

Yeah, you've always been a great financial provider. But don't you understand there's more to fatherhood than that?

But then my thoughts slowly turn in a warmer direction. My father asking me to share a workspace with him is like giving me a tightly wrapped hug. His company—his work—is his life. He always put it before his family; that's why he and my mother's marriage failed. That's why his relationship with his three daughters suffers.

But inviting me into his world? That's the same as asking me to share his heart.

I study him. "I'd have a normal salary?"

He nods emphatically. "Yes. And you could save it up so that you can send yourself to culinary school one day, if that's what you want. I only want to help you, Greta. You're my baby girl."

My eyes begin to mist over before I can stop it. "I'll think it over."

He smiles, a gruff twist of his lips: a Jacob Owen classic grin. "Sounds good. That's all I can ask. Along with Dare and I, we have a team of five other guys here. We could use someone like you to keep us in line."

I laugh in spite of myself. "Yeah, right. Like I can keep a bunch of ex-soldiers in check."

He frowns. "You know, if you're going to work here,

you're going to need to complete a bit of training."

My eyebrows lift. "Training?"

He grins again. "Yeah. Like PT. I'll get one of the guys on it, okay? Call me and let me know after you've thought about it over the long weekend. And then we'll talk if you agree."

I stand, a strange sense of excitement fluttering in my belly. "Okay, Dad. I'll call you after the weekend."

He pulls me into another awkward hug. "I love you, honey. I'll be waiting for your call."

I drive home in a daze. My father has his flaws, but inviting me into the professional fold was a big move for him, and it spoke volumes. Could I turn something like that down? Because it's not just a job.

It's an opportunity.

I'm so preoccupied that when I let myself into my apartment I realize I haven't even looked at my phone since before my meeting. I flip it out of my purse and check the screen.

Missed call from Grisham?

Warmth floods my belly again at the sight of his name on my phone's lit-up screen, but this time the feeling has nothing to do with fatherly love. This feeling is all about the elusive butterflies that have been missing from my life ever since Grisham went MIA more than a year ago.

I press the green call key and listen to the ringing.

"Hello?"

Grisham's voice from the other end of a phone is the chocolate coating over a delectable piece of caramel. All of the rough embers of masculine goodness smoothed out over the cellular waves. I shiver with excitement.

"Grisham? Just got out of a meeting with my dad and saw that you called. What's up?"

"Hey, Grits. How did it go with your dad?"

I flop onto the couch and put my bare feet up on the coffee table. I watch my wiggling toes as I think of how to tell Grisham about my father's job offer. For some reason, the entire story wants to pour out of my mouth.

And I let it.

After I'm done, Grisham whistles. "That's quite the offer. I get the feeling your relationship with your dad is kind of strained. Am I right?"

I nod before I remember he can't see me. "Yes. It's definitely that."

He chuckles darkly. "Trust me, I get it. More than you know. You gonna take it?"

"That's the thing! I'm not sure. I told him I'd take the long weekend to think it over. But...I kind of want to, you know? If for no other reason than he'll pay me well and I can put money away for culinary school."

His voice is full of something I can't quite pin down when he answers. Admiration, maybe? "It's a good plan. It's smart to at least consider it."

"Yeah. So, what were you actually calling me about before I spilled my guts?"

His outright laughter sends a pool of desire splashing through my core. How does he do that to me with just one sound?

God. Imagine what he could do to me with his hands. Or his mouth.

Oh, hell. The thought of Grisham's big, strong hands on my body...or his hot, sweet mouth connecting with my skin...

"So how does that sound? Greta?"

Damn. My runaway imagination made me miss what he'd asked me.

"Um, I'm sorry, Grisham. Can you run that by me again?"

Sounding amused, he repeats his question. "Do you want to come to my Labor Day cookout? You can bring Mea. I'd...I'd like to have you there."

I decide to play coy, rather than standing up and shouting "Hells, yes!" at the top of my voice. "Why? Why would you like me there?" I let the teasing show in my tone.

"Because if you don't come, who else is going to cook up some potato salad in my kitchen?"

I gasp, and his laughter rings out through the phone.

"I'm kidding! Can you come? Please?"

On the last request, his voice drops an octave, and I'm putty in his hands. I'd probably say yes to just about anything he asks if he uses that deep, sexy tone again.

"Sure. And I'll bring potato salad."

My voice is breathless when I accept.

"Yes! Mission accomplished."

Laughing, I stick my tongue out at the phone. "And if you're good, I'll bring you a special dessert."

Silence stretches across the line, and a hot blush creeps across my face as I wonder if my flirting went too far.

"Um, chocolate pie tarts. That's what I meant."

Grisham's voice is sand rolled in my palm when he answers, rough and coarse. "Damn. The dessert I'm picturing doesn't have anything to do with chocolate. But it's still really fucking sweet."

Oh, Lordy in heaven above. I fan myself with one hand while I tuck the other between my knees as hard as I can. Tension is building fast and hard in my belly, and I squeeze my eyes shut as I silently count backward from five.

"That image might stay in my head all night." My voice is just a whisper. "Good night, Grisham. I'll see you Sunday afternoon."

His low, sexy drawl will be repeating long after we hang up, I just know it. "'Night, Grits. Yeah...Sunday."

With a squeal, I throw my phone down on the couch and run to the bathroom for a nice, long, *cool* bath.

7

Grisham

When Sunday afternoon rolls around, I figure it's finally happened.

I've lost my goddamn mind.

"Dude. I just want to know one thing. Have you always had a rug...on your deck?" Ben stomps his flip-flops a few times to emphasize his point.

I brush past him, carrying a bag of ice. "Bought it yesterday."

"But *why*?"

When I drop the ice beside the cooler and look over at Ben his expression is so bewildered that I have to laugh.

"I just want everything to be good. This is a party. I'm gonna have chicks here. They judge."

He nods, as if that makes total sense. "Gotcha. Well, this shit is kinda nice."

I toss a bottle of beer at him before I dump the ice into the cooler. Then I carefully place some of the beer bottles deep inside the cold depths.

"You could use this more than me right now." Ben pops the top of his beer and takes a long swig.

"Hey!" calls Lawson from the fire pit in the yard. "I could use your help puttin' the wood in this thing, Cowboy. Get your ass up."

Ben heaves himself off the lounge chair he'd just chosen and lumbers over to where Lawson is working to make sure we'll have a good fire after dark.

After I finish putting some nonalcoholic drinks in the second cooler, I stand back and survey our work. There's seasoned meat chilling in the refrigerator in the kitchen, and my gas grill is clean and ready to go. It stands beside a stone bar area where a pub table is set up with three stools. My backyard is probably the nicest part of my house. It's a beach house, so spending time outside is mandatory. But knowing that Greta will be here today and that there's a chance my mom will stop by made me step up the decor just a little.

I strung small white lights over the pergola overlooking the wooden deck and arranged all of the lounge chairs in a way that promotes conversation. Just beyond the patch of grass off the deck is a walkway to the beach, and I placed two tiki torches on either side of it. Two more torches stand proudly on either side of the bar.

The rug I bought matches the deep green cushions on the lounge chairs, with green and turquoise stripes. I just hope everything looks good enough that the girls will be impressed by my decorating skills.

The slider leading into the kitchen opens, and I glance over to see Berkeley leading Dare outside by the hand. Her whiskey-colored eyes scan the deck and then she looks at me with approval in her gaze.

The first thing I realize when I see Berkeley is that this is the first time I'll be with her and Greta in the same place at the same time since being back home. Even though Berkeley and I were never an actual couple, unease gnaws at my stomach. The last thing I want is for the friendship between me and Berkeley to make Greta feel uncomfortable.

"Nice job, Grish!" she exclaims. "You stepped it up a little bit, huh? Who are you trying to impress?"

Shit. Despite the fact that Berkeley and my relationship with her have changed a lot since she got together with Dare, she still knows me too damn well.

I shrug, attempting to stay casual. "No one. Everyone. It's a party, so I bought some stuff. You know how it is."

Her eyes narrow as she watches me. "Sure. I know how it is." She scrutinizes me, but I head over and hold a hand out for Dare.

"What's up, man? Glad you could make it. Where's Drake?"

Drake, Dare's best friend and old roommate, was an army buddy from Dare's Ranger days. I don't know him well, but he seems like a good guy. I'd told Berkeley when I invited her that Drake was welcome, too.

We shake, and Dare tilts his head toward the beach. "Said he'll be here later. Sweet view, man. I like your place."

"Thanks. It's pretty cool. I can walk right outside with my board in the morning if I want."

Dare's eyes drop to my leg and back up again. "You been back on a board yet?"

Shaking my head, I turn my eyes to the ocean. The place I've always felt the most at peace, the most at home. It's rolling gently against the shore today, no big waves crashing against the sand. "Not yet. Working up to it."

Berkeley hugs me. "You'll get there."

"I know I will."

We're silent for a moment, and I know Berkeley is mourning the loss of my leg like she's done the handful of times I've seen her since returning stateside. "You two grab a drink. I've got chips and dip in bowls over there."

"Awesome. I brought homemade salsa." Berkeley drags Dare to the coolers just as Lawson and Ben head over to greet them.

I head back into the house to hunt down Berkeley's salsa. As I'm searching the contents of my dark cherrywood cabinets for a bowl, the doorbell rings.

"Should have put a note on the door that says 'Come Around Back,'" I mutter as I jog to the door.

When I pull it open, Greta is standing there. She's all I can see for the first couple of moments because she's such a knockout. She's wearing a short, blue sundress that does crazy things to the color of her eyes. Her long, dark hair is pulled up with some pieces hanging down around her fresh, clean face. Her cheeks dimple slightly as she nearly lays me out with one of her sweet smiles.

My body strains to be wrapped around her right then. She's a total vision, and I shift my feet with the excitement I feel at being able to show her off to my friends.

"Hey," she greets me.

I step back so she can step inside, and Mea and a guy I don't know follow her. My radar springs up instantly, circling the guy with startling intensity. Because, why the hell did she bring a guy?

I rein in what can only be jealousy and pull her into my arms. "Hey back. You brought friends."

I pull back from her and reach out to grab Mea into a friendly hug. "Long time no see, Mea. You doing okay?"

She nods, her small stature almost brimming with hyperactivity. She bounces on her toes as she scans the living room. "I'm great! This place is super nice, Grisham. You did good."

Smiling, I do a quick scan of the room. "I did okay, huh? Thanks."

Greta also gives the room a favorable once-over. "I like the white brick fireplace. That's so different and cool."

Pride is a helium balloon in my chest, puffing it out a few inches. "Thanks. Painted it when I moved in. It was this weird light brick color before. It looks better now."

She nods and then gestures toward the guy. "I hope it's okay I brought another friend."

When she says the word *friend*, I relax a little bit. I hadn't realized how tense my muscles were until she said the magic *F* word.

"This is Kyle. He's my father's assistant at Night Eagle."

Kyle shoves his hand in his pockets. Glancing up at me, he holds out a hand for me to shake. I eye him with keen curiosity.

"Greta's about to become my new coworker." Kyle slides her a small smile.

"Not yet," she says firmly. "I haven't accepted yet."

"You still thinking about it?" I look from Greta to Kyle and back again.

"I'm gonna leave you guys to chat for a minute. I gotta go find Berkeley! You coming, Kyle?" Mea disappears from the room, and I hear the slider open and close in the kitchen.

Kyle glances at Greta and me, but I can't keep my focus off of her long enough to be friendly with him. "Better follow her outside. Catch up with you later, right, Greta?"

She nods, a gorgeous dimple appearing in her cheek and her eyes shining bright with what can only be pure kindness. She radiates goodness, and I want to step closer so I can be captured by the glow.

"I'm going to talk to you about the job more tonight. I need you as a sounding board." Greta's shy gaze slides up to mine, and my body responds with a painful rigidity. I want to take her into my arms and disappear with her, so she can tell me all the pros and cons she's considering. I'll gladly be her soft place to fall. And then I curse myself inside my head.

How can I be anyone's soft place to fall? I'm all hard edges and sharp points.

Greta jerks her head toward the door. "I brought some stuff so I could make potato salad, Grisham. Want to help me get it out of the car?"

I smile at her. Of course I'll get the stuff out of the car. And then I'll monopolize her attention while she cooks. "Sure, Grits."

She follows me onto the front porch

"So, Kyle is just a guy who works at Night Eagle with your

dad?" I ask casually as we walk toward Greta's RAV4. She pops the back hatch and I grab two grocery bags from the trunk.

She gives me a sideways glance. "Jealous, Abbot?"

Pretty sure I'll be jealous of any man standing close enough to touch Greta. The feeling rests in my mind like an anchor, sinking deep. Realization slams me hard.

When did I turn into the jealous type?

Chuckling, I shake my head at her. "Should I be?"

She blushes, which drives me crazy. The pink tinge that sweeps across the tiny, delicate freckles dusting her cheeks is intoxicating.

"I've known Kyle for a long time. We went to high school together. But he's always just been a friend."

Good enough for me. I can keep an eye on Kyle, but if Greta says she's not interested in him, I'll take her word for it.

Greta closes the trunk and we're strolling up the driveway when it happens. A souped-up car engine rumbles; it's close, no more than a block away. The sound doesn't just bounce off of me, it travels *through* me, burrowing deep and taking hold. I stop, freezing in midstep, my head turning toward the sound. The car roars onto our street, and my head jerks toward Greta. When the car backfires, I jump a fucking mile, dropping the bags from my hands and changing my stance to a crouch. I want to yell for Greta to get down, but then the car zooms past us.

It's harmless. Just a car.

Not a military hum-vee. Not a man-driven steel frame serving as a missile to destroy me and my team.

Just a car.

I'm trembling, my entire body shaking, as if I've just walked off a battlefield. A thin sheen of sweat coats my forehead, and I swipe it off. My heart beats wildly against my ribs, and I give a heavy sigh. Hanging my head, I reach down and grab the grocery bags, which are thankfully still sitting upright.

When I glance at Greta, her gaze is shrewd. She's looking at me, but that clear blue expanse stares straight through me. I know, instantly, that she realizes what just happened.

"Is it over?" she asks, her voice like the gentlest caress. It curls around me, wrapping me up in everything sweet.

I nod, blowing out a breath. "Sorry if I freaked you out."

She shakes her head, dark locks flying in the breeze. A light, fresh floral scent wafts under my nose, and I'm immediately calmer, more collected. "Don't be. I know exactly what that was. How often does it happen to you?"

I begin walking toward the house again, and she falls into step beside me.

How often does it happen?

I want to laugh, but I know there's nothing funny about feeling the aftereffects of a trauma. It happens when I least expect it. Not as often as it did before. But there are times when I'm just walking down the street, and I see something or hear something that brings me right back to hell.

"Not often." I want to keep Greta out of that dark place if I can help it. She's everything light, beautiful, and happy. She's sunshine. The last thing I want to do is cover her with my dark clouds. Stain her with all of my gray.

I lead her into the kitchen, and she gets to work finding a big mixing bowl and my sharp knives. I sit on a barstool to watch her chop up potatoes, onions, celery, and some kind of leafy green spice. She glances at me every so often, and I can almost see her thoughts turning back to my moment of weakness. It makes my stomach clench, my toes curl with regret.

"Want some help?" I ask.

She looks suspicious. "What can you do?"

I glance around at her array of supplies, thinking. "I'm a good stirrer."

She pushes a bowl of something creamy into my hands, and I use the spoon inside to begin stirring.

"So when did you buy this house?" she asks.

"About a year ago."

Nodding, she continues preparing the ingredients in front of her. "It's awesome. From what I remember, your parents live in town. Right? They must be so proud of you."

I drop my gaze, concentrating extra hard on my stirring duty. I give a noncommittal nod.

"Last night, on the phone...you said you understood about my strained relationship with my dad."

She pauses until I finally look up and meet her gaze. Her blue eyes are laser-focused on mine; she tilts her head to the side, as if she's seeing straight through the front I'm putting on.

"Maybe sometime we should compare notes."

The idea of sharing what I went through—what I still go through—with my father is less than thrilling. But there's also a sense of companionship there I don't expect. Talking to her is easy, warm. Her voice, her gaze...everything about her wraps me up tight and soothes out the rough edges of pain and apprehension.

"You want us to share? I did enough of that with my therapist. And he wasn't as pretty as you. You might be able to get me to share too much. You're dangerous." I wink at her.

She laughs, the tendrils of hair around her face drifting into her eyes. I step closer, and when she stops laughing abruptly, I can't help but invade her space. Standing right in front of her, I brush the nearly raven hair away from her big, gorgeous pools. She blinks, staring back at me.

"Better?" I whisper.

Electricity sizzles between us, like we're connected by a live wire. My arm wraps around her waist, and I snake my hand around to the small of her back, pulling her against me.

Damn, that feels good.

Her full breasts press into the top of my rib cage, and my heart thuds faster. My head dips toward hers, my body moving of its own accord. When I'm around Greta, I feel like I don't need to think. It's like muscle memory; my body just knows what to do. It needs to connect with hers.

I want to kiss her. More than I want to breathe right now, I want to take her perky pink mouth as my own personal treasure. But if I do that...will I ever be able to stop?

8

Greta

He's going to kiss me. Every part of my body is buzzing with desire at his nearness; the scent of him envelops me. He smells like fresh, clean musk with a hint of the salty ocean. I want to lean in and inhale him, but at the same time I want to pull back and run.

Running from Grisham would be the smart thing to do. It wasn't a year and a half ago that he was hung up on one of my best friends. He's a wounded warrior, his head is a mess.

But more than anything right now, I want to make him *my* mess.

I want his lips on mine.

The back door opens, and I jump backward like I've been caught doing something illegal. We both look to the door as Mea bounces in, a devilish smile on her face.

"Sorry. Am I interrupting something?" Her feigned innocence earns a glare from me.

Grisham clears his throat and takes a step back while my face turns an embarrassing shade of red.

"Of course not. What do you need, roommie?"

As Grisham perches back on his stool, I pull the bowl of potato salad ingredients toward me so that I can add the chopped potatoes and vegetables. Then I slide the bowl in front of him once more.

"Stir," I instruct without meeting his eyes. I'm pretty sure that if I look at him right now I'll drag him somewhere dark and quiet where we won't be interrupted.

"Yes, ma'am."

"I just came to see if you needed any help with the potato salad. But it seems like you two have it covered."

I nod. "Yep. All good here."

We hear the front door open and close, and we all turn expectantly toward the arched doorway where kitchen meets living room.

Drake enters the room, stopping and turning sideways to fit through the doorway. He's huge, the same height as Dare but broader and with bulgier muscles. He scans the room with a furrowed brow, his eyes stopping momentarily on Mea before finding the rest of us.

Grisham stands and goes to give Drake a bro hug. "Glad you could make it, Drake."

"'Sup, man? Glad to see you back in one piece."

Grisham shrugs. "Mostly one piece."

Drake nods, his expression somber. "Must be tough comin' back from that. I know a couple of guys who dealt with amputations, too. You're one tough son of a bitch, Abbot."

They turn and look at us.

Drake's eyes land on my roommate first. Again. "Um, hey, Mea. How are you?"

I glance at my friend, and she's gone rigid and tense. She crosses her arms and narrows her eyes into slits. She's always been a little weird around Drake. If I didn't know better, I'd think they'd known each other before Berkeley and Drake met. But Mea won't cop to it, and she never wants to talk about Drake.

"Hello, Drake. I didn't know you'd be here."

A frosty silence falls on the room until Grisham clears his throat. "Why don't you head on outside, Drake? There's beer in a cooler, and I'm about to fire up the grill in a few."

Drake nods, his eyes never leaving Mea's. "Sounds good. Thanks, man."

When he's gone, I whirl on Mea. "You've got to be nicer to him, Mea. What's up with you? Every time he's around, you turn into Mrs. Frost. You're never that cold toward anyone."

She shrugs, dropping her arms by her side. "I've never met anyone who irks me as much as he does."

My mouth falls open. "What? Why? What'd he do?"

Grisham looks concerned. "Did he hurt you, Mea?"

She shakes us both off. "No. It's nothing like you're thinking. Listen, don't worry about it. I'll try to be civil, okay? I wouldn't want to ruin your cookout, Grisham."

She flounces out the door, leaving me completely flabbergasted.

"I've never known her to give someone such a cold shoulder," I muse. "I hope she's okay."

"Maybe she'll tell you about it when she's ready."

Maybe she will. But I have a feeling that when it comes to Drake, Mea's never going to share her true feelings. And I'm really starting to wonder why.

Grisham and I finish preparing the potato salad while keeping a healthy distance from one another. The banter and the joking, however, continue at an alarming rate. Things are so simple and easy between us. Every time he calls me "Grits," a shiver of delight runs through me.

When he heads outside to start the grill, I place the big bowl of potato salad into the refrigerator to cool. There's two large trays of meat: a big platter of chicken breasts and an equally large plate of hamburgers occupy one, while the other is full of hot dogs and bratwursts.

I smile.

We're going to end up with way too much food.

Outside, there's upbeat music playing from someone's phone hooked up to a speaker. The afternoon is waning, and the sun is hanging low on the dimming horizon. I can hear the waves whispering gently against the shore, and the entire scene is the picture of relaxation. The end of summer always gives me a sad sense of loss, but I'm happy to be spending it like this.

Grisham and his buddies are horsing around in the yard. I grin as I watch them. At this moment, he appears carefree and happy. He dips his head low and goes to tackle his friend Ben, charging forward to throw Ben backward. A snarl escapes him as Ben curses, and my body is immediately aware of him in each nerve ending. That sexy growl hits me right in my core, and I'm instantly aroused by his extreme manliness at that moment.

Ripping my gaze away from Grisham, I survey the deck and yard. When my eyes land on Berkeley, my heart sinks.

It's such a strange sensation for me, feeling disappointed to see one of my best friends. But I know that Grisham used to have feelings for her, and the thought makes me feel territorial. My stomach clenches almost painfully tight as the oily emotion takes root...I'm still frowning as Kyle comes to stand beside me. He hands me a beer, which I gratefully put to my lips.

"You have a good group of friends here," he remarks.

"Yeah. I do. You having a good time?"

He nods, looking at me sideways. "Thanks for inviting me."

"You're welcome, Kyle. Anytime."

My eyes lock with Grisham's from where he stands at the grill. One corner of his mouth tilts up in a half-smile, and I can't look away. He's a vision of hot male perfection, standing there in a pair of board shorts and a plain white T-shirt. The tattoos that stretch across his chest and shoulders peek out from below the cuffs of his sleeves like colorful wisps of smoke. His jaw is covered in a fine layer of two-day scruff, and his messy hair is sticking up in a million different directions.

Gah. He's gorgeous.

Gorgeous doesn't even begin to cover Grisham's manly beauty. He's strong, and he's a leader. He's kind to his friends, yet he wears a distinct air of "don't mess with me or you'll regret it." When he speaks to me, he looks at me like he's listening, really listening. Like everything I say is a matter of severe importance to him. And now, with Berkeley sitting at the same cookout, his eyes are on me, not her. He makes me feel special.

And all I want to do is figure out a way I can spend more time with him.

"Do you want me to come back later and get you?"

Mea stands at the front door with my car keys dangling from her fingers. Kyle is already standing beside the car, waiting patiently for Mea to drive him home.

I glance at Grisham, who shakes his head.

"I can drive you home, Grits. Thanks for staying to help me clean up."

I look back at Mea. "Guess I'm all good."

Mea grins. "*Yeah* you are."

I sigh and push the door until it's only open a crack with her on the other side. "Shut up and get going!"

All I can hear is her giggle as I shut the front door.

Grisham and I start cleaning up debris from the cookout, grabbing bowls and stray red Solo cups from the deck and putting all discarded plates into a big, black trash bag. Then I get to work filling the dishwasher with dirty dishes while Grisham takes out the trash and recycling.

When he comes back inside, he joins me at the sink, rinsing dishes.

"So, how're you feeling about your dad's offer?"

I sigh, finding it hard to turn my tumultuous feelings into proper sentences. As I try and explain, Grisham listens carefully and silently, giving the occasional head nod as I release all of the mixed emotions that have been tumbling around in my brain since the meeting.

"And so I kind of want to do it, you know? It'll definitely help us become closer. But at the same time, I'm scared. My dad has disappointed me a lot over the years."

I look down at the counter I've been repeatedly scrubbing with a sponge for the past five minutes. It's gleaming. I swallow around the ball of feelings lodged in my throat.

Grisham's quiet voice makes me bring my head up to look at him. "I know it's scary. But I think you already know what you're going to do, don't you? Or else we wouldn't be having this conversation."

Sighing, I nod. "I can't say no to this."

Grisham gives me his small, rakish grin. "Then this is a good thing. You have a new job. At a private security firm. Fancy."

I swat him with the dish towel playfully. "It's not fancy. It's just for my dad."

"Ohhhh, the boss's daughter," he teases, grabbing the towel out of my hand. "Even better."

Giggling, I back away from him. "Don't snap that at me. It'll hurt."

His eyes darken as he stares at me, and I stop moving. He licks his lips, and I'm so transfixed I forget that he's wielding a dangerous dish towel as a weapon.

Then he moves forward. The man sure can move fast on a prosthetic foot, and I squeal and turn to run. I make it about two steps before I feel the sharp, sweet bite of the towel snapping against my ass. I yelp and turn to glare at him, my hands resting on my hips.

He's chuckling as he assesses my anger. "All in good fun. Forgive me."

How can I not, with that face and that body?

He holds out his hand to me. I step toward him and take it. He leads me into the living room, turning on a lamp as we pass it. We both settle onto the couch and lean back against the cushions.

"So when do you start?" he asks.

I pull my legs beneath me. "Not sure. I have to call him tomorrow and tell him I accept the job. And he wants me to do some combat training if I'm going to work there. You know, just hand-to-hand stuff. He says I need to be able to defend myself if I'm going to be working for a security firm with a bunch of ex-Special Ops soldiers."

Grisham sits up a little straighter. "That makes sense. I can teach you."

I pause, staring at him. "You would do that? Dad said he'd get one of the guys at the firm to teach me."

Shaking his head, Grisham squeezes my thigh just above my knee. The contact sends tingles radiating outward from his warm fingers. He stares down at the place where his touch is doing something wild to my heartbeat, running his fingers first up my thigh and then back down again. I bite my lip so I don't do something completely embarrassing, like moan in delight. "I want to teach you, Greta. Let me."

Not ever going to be able to say no to you, Grisham Abbot.

Aloud, I whisper, "Okay."

His face breaks out into a wide, little-boy grin. "Awesome. We can start tomorrow."

9

Grisham

I'm off work the following day, so I drive out to Greta's dad's firm, where she says he has a small training facility.

The building is located in Wrightsville Beach, and compared to the glossy surrounding homes and offices, Night Eagle is pretty nondescript. It's a three-story, tan stucco building across from the oceanfront sitting between two grandiose beach houses. There are a few other businesses on the block, but driving in I noticed they sold things like insurance and surfboards. Greta's dad's building is perfectly placed, because no one would ever suspect what really goes on inside: the strategic security of high-profile organizations and government-contracted missions.

When I walk inside, a strange shiver of familiarity runs through me. I've never been to this place before, yet somehow it feels…like I'm where I'm supposed to be. The sensation tingles along the back of my neck and I grab the spot, rubbing my hand over it. I shake the odd feeling off and look around.

I recognize Greta's father right away from his involvement in Berkeley's kidnapping rescue. He's standing against a desk in the corner and looks up when I enter. He comes around the desk, his hands in his jeans pockets.

"Good morning, sir," I greet him formally. "My name is Grisham Abbot."

He nods, watching me carefully. "I know who you are. My daughter told me you volunteered to help teach her some combat moves. She tells me you're a friend of Dare and Berkeley's?"

I nod. "Yes, sir. I've known Berkeley for a long time. But I'm also a friend of Greta's."

His eyebrows shoot up. "Is that right? Well, I would have had one of my guys teach her. But she's insisting you do it. Seeing as how you're a SEAL, I guess you're qualified enough."

He says the last part gruffly, and I smile inside, knowing his ex-army training is telling him I'm not nearly good enough for this job.

"I'm honored to do it," I say with a straight face. "I want her to be as safe as possible."

Jacob finally reaches out a hand to me, and we shake firmly. He squeezes my hand a little too hard, but I keep a straight face as he stares me down.

"Then we want the same outcome, son. Greta's upstairs in the training room."

"Yes, thank you, sir."

I head in the direction he pointed and find a door at the end of the wide-open front room that leads to the stairs. When I open the door at the top floor, I see that the "training room" is an enormous, open space with training equipment, mats, and gym machines. It's state-of-the-art stuff, and I realize that Night Eagle Security, Inc., is nothing to be messed with.

Greta, previously sitting in the center of one of the gray mats, scrambles to her feet.

Fucking hell.

She's wearing workout gear, but her workout gear isn't what I expected at all. Her tight, black leggings fit her like a second skin, and I realize that her long legs and hips have curves for days. My eyes travel from her purple sneakers up her legs, to her tight, toned stomach. Which is exposed, because her top is just a sports bra. A purple-and-gray-patterned sports bra that gives me a peek of the lush tops of her breasts.

"Damn, girl." I stagger toward her. "What are you trying to do to me?"

Confusion clouds her gaze. *God, I love how clueless she is about her own hotness.* "What? Am I not dressed right for training?"

I blow out a frustrated breath and close my eyes. When I open them again, I'm a little more composed and better able to handle the sight of her in that outfit. "You're fine. Sit down with me and let's stretch. I want to tell you about what you're going to be learning."

We take a few moments to limber up, and then I direct her to stand in the center of the mat. I circle her, assessing her from all angles before I stop in front of her.

"Greta, if you have to fight someone in this business, or just as a woman out on the street, it's likely going to be a man. A man who is bigger and stronger than you are. I have to teach you some strategies to weaken him, bring him to a level where you can effectively get him fumbling, and then how to kick his ass."

As I prepare to teach her the first sequence, I observe her closely. Taking in her inexperienced stance, I figure she's never been in a fight. This is going to be her first experience with combat, and a strange sense of pride gathers in my chest.

I get to be the one to teach her.

"If someone comes at you from directly in front of you, like this"—I pantomime reaching an arm out toward her throat—"then you can apply a wrist peel."

I show her how to bring her arm up and over mine, grabbing a hold of my wrist and bending it painfully. As I retreat from her, I fold over at the waist.

"There, now," I explain. "Once his head is below your waist, you use your knee to strike his face as hard as you can." I nod, and she demonstrates the motion I just explained. When I rise, I smile. "That's it. Let's try it again."

I pretend to come at her again several times with more force each time, allowing her to render me harmless as I double over and she fake-knees me in the head.

"Now, let's try for real. I'm going to really come at you, Greta. I want you to try to hurt me. Okay?"

She bites her bottom lip; it's obvious she's suddenly nervous. She doesn't want to try and hurt me. It's written all over her face as her expression turns sickly. I shake my head at her.

"Pretend it's not me. Pretend I'm just an asshole who wants to hurt you. Dig deep, Grits, and take me out."

I don't give her any more time to think; I accelerate forward. Her muscle memory kicks in, repeating the moves she just practiced moments ago. When I double over in pain from my wrist, she grips the back of my neck with both hands and jams her knee upward. She slows herself down just in time, before she actually slams it into my head.

We both stand up straight again, breathing heavily.

"How was that?" she asks.

My grin is wide and warm. Looking at her sends tingles of energy through the center of my body. "That was perfect, Grits. Really good job. Let's do the next move."

She beams with pride, and my heart lifts with joy at seeing it. *She did it.*

"What's next?" she asks eagerly.

"Okay. Most of the time, if a man makes a move to attack a woman, he's a complete pussy about it. He'll try to take you from behind."

I move behind her. She peeks over her shoulder at me. The look in her eyes is so open, so pure, that I can't help the desire to dirty her up a little. I move in close, bending my head to inhale her intoxicating scent. My lips graze her neck slightly, and she trembles in response. Damn, I love the way she reacts to me.

"Now, your attacker may come at you like this." My voice is rough as I drop my arms down over her shoulders and use them to trap her arms by her chest. "What do you do?"

She takes a deep breath. I'm glad she feels the need to gather herself, because I'm bordering on the edge of losing control. Then she struggles against me, trying to drag her arms out from underneath mine.

I let go immediately. "That doesn't work. Struggling to free your arms first will just expend your energy, giving him the advantage. As soon as you feel his arms make contact with you"—I drop my arms over her again—"you need to take a step to the side. And squat down low. When you lower your center of gravity, he will lose some of his power over you. One of his arms will loosen, or drop altogether. Then you head butt the shit out of him."

Her eyes widen as she peers over her shoulder. "Head butt him? Won't that hurt?"

I nod, my gaze level with hers. "It'll hurt him more than it hurts you, though. The back of your head is a powerful weapon. You could break his nose if you use enough force. You'll have to aim back and up, because he's going to be taller than you, most likely."

I have her practice the two moves a couple of times.

"Step to the side, squat, and head butt. I think I've got it." She nods confidently. "Now what?"

I come at her again. "Then, while one of my arms is incapacitated and I'm yelling in pain from the head butt, you take the opportunity to twist to the side"—I indicate which way I want her to turn her body—"and use your elbow to jab him in the stomach or groin."

She does so, and I can't help the smile in my voice. "Good job. Want to try it?"

She nods. Her steely, determined expression tells me that all of the nerves are gone. "Ready."

I dart at her suddenly, dropping my arms over her shoulders. For an instant, she stiffens as panic overtakes her. Her arms are trapped by her chest, and her hands are useless. I suck in a breath as she struggles vainly.

"Stop, Greta. Remember what I told you. If you struggle, you're only using up all of your energy."

She stills, and her chest stops heaving as her breaths slow. I softly repeat the instructions I gave her earlier, and wait while she steps to the side and squats down.

"That's it. Now use your head. Go!"

She jerks her head backward, making contact with my face. The burning sting only fuels me, because she's succeeded in her task.

"Ouch."

Alarmed, she looks over her shoulder. "Oh, my God. Are you okay?"

"Keep going." My teeth clamp tightly together and I nod my head, urging her forward.

She uses her left elbow to jab me in the stomach. She doesn't hurt me, but I double over as if in pain. When I do, she's free to turn around and face me.

I stand up and face her. "And then, you run. Got it?"

She frowns. "But I want to finish him."

I put my hands on my hips and laugh. I'm not mocking her; I'm proud.

"Down the line you'll learn to take them out. But for now, at the beginning of your training, you only need to be able to incapacitate them and get away."

She puffs out her lips and scuffs a sneakered toe on the floor. "So this is really more like self-defense, then?"

I cup her chin in my hand, staring deeply into her eyes. I

forget for a second that I'm supposed to be amused with her irritation and instead lose myself in the endless ocean of her gaze. I step even closer, and my heart picks up the pace in my chest. I wish I could force it to slow down, because the fact that she can surely feel how ridiculously fast it's racing is embarrassing.

"Self-defense and combat are the same thing. You're always trying to defend yourself in a fight. And most of the time, it's either your life or the other person's on the line. So I want to teach you to take them out. I just want to make sure you have a few initial maneuvers down pat first, okay? Your safety is really important to me, Grits."

A shiver runs through her as I drop my voice. All the blood rushes to my cock, and her eyes darken with something stormy and certain.

"Why?" she whispers.

I hesitate, my gaze dropping down to her lips. My mouth is suddenly as dry as desert air, and I swallow audibly.

"Because I care about you."

Before I went into SEAL training, Greta was Berkeley's roommate. We knew each other only through our mutual friendship with Berk, but there was an attraction there I never felt comfortable exploring. It just wasn't the right time back then.

It might still not be. But as her eyes glisten, staring at me with an expression of pleased surprise, I find myself wondering if this is a moment I should seize. Greta's the kind of girl who makes me want to capture every single second I spend with her, saving them up like a chest full of treasure.

The door to the training room opens and she takes a step back from me, forcing me to drop my hand from her face. We both turn to face her father, who's standing there with his arms crossed over his chest.

"Lesson over?" he asks without amusement.

"Almost." I clear my throat. "Greta's got a couple of moves under her belt, but I want to make sure she knows one more before we leave today."

Greta's father's eyes float toward her, and she shrugs. I feel like I've been caught with a girl in her room, which is absurd because we're adults. But his presence has the ability to shrink me down to size. He's her father, and I'd respect him for that fact alone. Not to mention his size and his credentials.

"Are you tired, Greta? You two have been working for about an hour."

She shakes her head. "I'm good, Dad. I'm going to let Grisham finish his lesson."

Her father nods, taking one last look at us before he steps out of the room.

When I glance at Greta again, her face is heated. She spreads her legs apart and crouches into a fighting stance. "What's next, sensei?"

Her lips turn up at the sound of my chuckle and we get back to work.

It's another thirty minutes before I decide we're done for the day, and we both grab water bottles from the stocked fridge in one corner of the room. I let her lead the way back downstairs, where her father is on a call in his office.

"Even though Night Eagle is technically closed for the holiday, I'm not surprised he's putting in hours. That's what Jacob Owen does. He puts work first."

Her tone is half bitter, half amused, and I quickly assess her facial expression. She's staring wistfully into the office.

We haven't talked about how deep our issues with each of our fathers go, but I can read deeper into her feelings about Jacob nearly every time I'm with her. It seems like she's missing something important from him. Something she wants him to give but never actually receives.

We wave good-bye on our way out, and Jacob lifts his hand in a dismissal.

"So your dad's pretty intense. He's exactly what I expected him to be like." I glance at her as we walk.

She laughs as she walks to her car, which is parked in the lot directly beside the building. My Jeep is parked right next to her car.

"He is, yeah. Work is his life, you know? So I guess if I'm going to be working here, he's pretty serious about me learning to fight."

Thoughtful, I nod. We reach her car, and she uses her key fob to unlock her doors. I lean against the driver's side as she throws her small gym bag into the backseat.

"Work is his life? You really feel that way? Where does that leave you and your sisters?"

She shrugs. "Out in the cold. I'm so used to it that it barely registers anymore. And now I'm going to be part of his work life, so..." She sighs. "I still feel really bad for my sisters, though. Gemma and Gabi are still young, teenage girls who need their dad. My mom and I aren't substitutes for that, even though we try. Did I tell you that Gabi has CF?"

I frown. "Cystic fibrosis?"

She nods, leaning against the car, right beside me. "Yeah. She's a tough kid, but it's really rough sometimes, you know? For all of us."

I whistle low as shock and sympathy slam into me. "Damn, Grits. I didn't know. I'm sorry to hear that." I'm stabbed with a prick of acute pain somewhere inside me at the aching look that crosses her face when she mentions her sister's disease.

"We handle it. But my dad has never really been there for her and my mom the way he should have been. I mean, he pays for everything. Which is helpful, of course. We'd be up shit's creek in medical bills if he didn't. My mom's a nurse, but she only works part-time so she can take care of my sister if she's sick. So her salary wouldn't cover all of that."

Her voice breaks on the last word, and I don't hesitate. I pull her into my arms. She rests her cheek against my chest, and I think she's glad I can't see her face.

"I just wish he'd realize that throwing money at a problem doesn't actually fix it. Gabi and Gemma want *him*, not his money."

I stroke her incredibly soft hair and brush my lips across the top of her head. "What about you, Greta? What do you want from him?"

"N-nothing." She sniffs.

"I think you need to be honest with yourself about that. You feel like you're missing something. You brush it off as sympathy for your sisters, which I'm sure is partially true, but he's just as absent from your life as he is from theirs. Working with him might be the first step to changing that, right? This is going to be a good thing for you two."

She nods. "I hope so."

And then we just stand there while I hold her. It feels amazing cradling this girl in my arms. She's soft and warm. She feels like if I hold on tight enough, I can be whole again. Greta's like a tether from the darkest place inside me, from all the scary, dirty things I've seen and done a world away, to the light. She draws me further into her sunshine each time I'm with her. With her, I believe I can be important to someone again. I can start over once my SEAL days end. She's my glimpse of the future, and she feels perfect standing against me.

She feels like home.

10

Greta

I can't remember the last time I talked about my father with someone. I've talked to Mea about him and the way my relationship with him makes me feel, but Grisham is pulling emotions out of me I thought were dead and buried. I don't cry about Jacob Owen anymore. What's the point?

It could be worse. Some people have never met their father. Some people have lost theirs. Mine is still here, he's just not here in the way I'd want him to be in a perfect world.

I know it's not a perfect world.

For the remainder of that week, I'm unable to see Grisham because of how busy he is at work, helping his team prepare for another mission. He hasn't said much about it, but I know he's devastated about the fact that he's not going with them. I'm not sure what to say to help him through it, though. We haven't reached a point where I can offer him any type of encouragement where his job is concerned. I'd like to be there for him, but I'm equally as busy learning the ropes at Night Eagle.

On Friday morning, I arrive at the office before my father. With a little whoop of triumph, I use the key card he gave me to let myself in. I turn on the computer at the front desk, which is now my desk, and head to the little lounge to make myself a cup of coffee. My father cleaned out a secondary desk in his office for Kyle, and I know it won't be long before he arrives.

There's a knock on the office door, and I check the giant wall clock hanging in the front lobby: 7:45 a.m. We don't even officially open until nine. Who would be knocking?

I hesitate, wondering whether I should just ignore it, or open the door and inform whoever it is of our office hours. The visitor knocks again, and I curse under my breath.

I walk to the front door. Right now, I really wish this was a retail facility and the doors were glass, rather than the dark steel so that I can have a view of who is standing on the other side.

Suck it up, Greta, I tell myself. *The boogeyman doesn't come out this early in the morning.*

I pull the door open to find a bike messenger standing there. He hands me a large white box, and nods. "Have a nice day."

"Wait!" I call as he mounts his bike.

I want to know why the hell a bike messenger is delivering to us so early on a Friday morning. But he ignores me, riding away before I can say another word or ask him a single question.

Shaking my head with confusion, I sit down at my chair and inspect the white box. My name is labeled on the front, but nothing else. Just my first name.

When I open the box, I gasp, one hand flying to my mouth. Lying in the box are a bunch of long-stemmed bloodred roses.

"What the..." I dig around in the box, searching for a note.

I've never been sent flowers before in my life. I rack my brain, trying to think of who would even think to do such a thing. Just then, I hear the buzz of a key card being used and Kyle walks in through the front door.

"Hey, Greta," he greets me cheerfully. Our eyes meet, and his eyebrows shoot up curiously. "What's wrong?"

I glance down at the box, unable to speak, before looking back at him helplessly. He comes over to the desk quickly, walking around to where I'm seated, and peers into the box.

"Wow," he says quietly, fingering the bud of one perfect rose. "From your SEAL, I'm guessing?"

Well, crap.

I hadn't even thought of Grisham until Kyle referred to him as *my SEAL*. Would he send me flowers? A heated smile crosses my face without my permission before I beat it back down with pure willpower.

"First of all," I retort, "Grisham isn't *my SEAL*. We're friends."

Kyle looks doubtful. "A friend who makes sure he's the one teaching you combat moves instead of the well-trained guys who work here? A friend who sends you roses?"

I gaze down at the box of roses in my lap again. Fingers of pleasant surprise walk across my skin, paralyzing me. "I have to send him a text...thank him."

Kyle shrugs. "Hop to it, then. You want me to find something to put those in? You can keep them on your desk all day."

Now a real, unhidden smile breaks out, and I don't bother to try and hide it. Looking at flowers sent by Grisham all day is going to make this the best Friday ever.

"Thanks, Kyle."

He goes off in search of a vase, and I pull out my phone to thank "my SEAL." I know he's in a workout, and I don't want to interrupt him with a phone call. I figure he'll text me back when he's finished.

> Hey Romeo…thanks for the flowers ?

There. That should do it. Not too sappy, even though I feel like gushing.

I've just put my phone back in my purse when I hear the *ding* that signifies I have a text. My spirits soar, realizing that he texted me back during a workout.

Grisham and I have spoken or texted every night this week. Our conversations have been easy and flirty, but every single time we talk, I get off the phone with tingly limbs and a racing heartbeat. He just makes me feel…lifted. Like I can fly. I'm excited about the prospect of hearing from him every single day after work, and when I do, it's like I've just come in first place in a race. It's euphoric. And it's scary.

When I read the text, my confusion ratchets up again.

> Hey beautiful. I know I should just take the credit but…I didn't send you flowers. Yet!

He didn't send them? Then who on earth did?

My gaze is flipping between my phone and the flowers when Kyle comes back into view, holding a water jug that he's cut the top off of. He smiles apologetically. "This will have to do, yeah?"

I nod numbly. When my phone dings again I startle before glancing at the text.

Should I be jealous? So who DID send you flowers??

I shake my head to clear it, and then I type back a quick response.

No clue. They're pretty though.

I put my phone down on my desk, place all of the roses in the jug, and settle in to get some work done. My dad's schedule is kind of a mess, so I'm putting all of his appointments and conference calls into an Excel spreadsheet and exporting it to a cloud so that he can access them from any device or computer at any time. I shake my head as I work, in disbelief that this hasn't been done before.

Over the past week I've realized that although my father is the best at what he does—running a private security business, effectively acquiring and successfully completing government contracts, and protecting people—his office skills are seriously sucky. I've made it my personal mission to help him with that and make this office a smoothly running operation, just as efficient as his field missions are.

I'm working so hard that lunchtime comes and goes. My father, Kyle, Dare, and the other members of the team have been locked in the office all morning, going over the particulars for a new project they're working on. I haven't been briefed on the details yet because they're still hammering them out. But next week, my father will let me know what they'll be doing for the project, because he'll need me to input data into his computer system and make travel arrangements for the team as needed.

Early in the afternoon, I'm finished with my administrative tasks. The list I set out to accomplish by the end of the week is done, and it's a freeing feeling. I didn't expect to like this job, but it actually suits my skill set. I'm good at organizing things, with keeping details in order.

I'm good at this. The thought brings a smile to my face. I sit back in my chair, realizing my stomach is grumbling. I head to the lounge to grab the sandwich I'd stuck in the refrigerator this morning and bring it back to my desk. I don't want to be away in case someone comes in for a consultation.

The door opens, bringing in fresh, salty air, a seaside breeze, and Berkeley Holtz.

"Berk!" I exclaim, standing as she lets the door swing closed behind her.

"Hey, Greta!"

We meet in the middle of the room, pulling each other into a tight, squeezing hug. Berkeley and I grew pretty close while she lived with Mea and me, and now she lives with Dare. The fact that she's not around all the time, thought, makes my feelings for Grisham a bit easier. Even though my head tells me that he and Berkeley never actually dated, my heart sometimes protests that I'm breaking some kind of girl code.

"What are you doing here? Your man's in a meeting."

She flips a chunk of her long, curly blond hair over her shoulder. "I know. I brought him a smoothie." She indicates the drink in her hand. "He always needs a pick-me-up at this time of the day, and he didn't have time to make one this morning."

She suddenly turns crimson, and I give her a slow, knowing smile.

"He didn't *have time*? Were you keeping him *busy*?"

She swats at my hand, giggling as she heads toward the lounge. "Oh, shush."

I sit down to continue eating, and when Berkeley returns she perches on the side of my desk.

"So, how's the new job going?"

I sigh happily. "It's good. I thought I'd get to see more of my dad, but he's a pretty busy guy. I'm keeping busy with all of this, though." I gesture toward my desk and computer.

Berkeley smiles. "And...how are things with Grisham?"

My mouth drops open. "What? What are you talking about?"

"Don't play dumb, my friend." Rolling her eyes, Berkeley crosses her arms over her chest. "I saw you two together at the cookout. It was adorable. You were all shy and covert flirty, while he was all 'can't-keep-his-eyes-off-you.'"

"Really? You thought we looked..." I can feel my face heating, but it's not embarrassment that causes my blush this time. It's hope.

"Girl, he wants you bad. Like, *bad*. And he's Grisham, so

he'll right it as long as he can. He's a good guy, you know? He won't push you. Especially after everything he's been through."

I'm soaking in every word she says like a thirsty sponge. Any tidbit of knowledge she has about Grisham is precious to me. She's known him for a long time, and I trust her judgment. If she thinks Grisham's into me...

"Well, I thought he sent me flowers this morning." I sweep my hand toward the jug of roses sitting prettily on my desk.

Berkeley's whiskey-colored eyes widen. "Did he?"

Shaking my head, I frown. "No. And there was no note, so I have no clue who would have sent them."

Unable to help herself, she moves closer, inspecting the flowers. The designer inside of Berkeley inspires her to begin arranging them, turning them this way and that in the vase. Her face lights up. "You have a secret admirer!"

Just the thought makes me cringe. "No, I don't."

"Yes, you do!" she says, clapping her hands. "And as soon as Grisham finds out, he'll probably go all alpha-male on your ass." She continues arranging the flowers, but then she frowns. "You only have eleven. Your secret admirer got gypped."

I don't care about how many flowers there are. But I immediately lock on to her comment about Grisham. I consider him for a minute. I think of the sexy, colorful tattoos covering his chest and shoulders, of the single-minded determination in his eyes when he's teaching me a combat move. I think of the way he saved me from the ocean the day he came back into my life, and the way he growled when he was horsing around with his buddies at the cookout. A flare of heat rises inside of me, and I close my eyes briefly.

"I think he's already an alpha male."

Berkeley laughs. "Maybe he is. But the thought of another guy going after you is going to make him plain old crazy."

I'm flooded with liquid want, and I squeeze my knees together.

Time for a subject change. "Did you know he's teaching me to fight? Well...to defend myself, at least. My dad wants me to learn how to for this job."

Berkeley nods. "Dare told me. How's that going?"

"We've only had one lesson so far, but it went really well. Grisham's a good teacher."

"I'm sure he is," she says with a knowing grin. "I like you two together. I hope you guys make it happen." She snaps her fingers. "Hey! Let's get everyone together for drinks tomorrow night. Sound good?"

I nod. "Sounds good to me. Want me to ask Grisham?"

"Hell yes, I want you to ask him. And make sure Mea comes, too. I hardly ever get to see her anymore now that she's getting ready to open her own yoga studio."

"I think she's a ways from the 'opening' stage. She's still planning. But yeah, she's been super busy with it. I'm proud of her." And I really am. Yoga is something Mea is passionate about and really skilled at teaching. She's going to have a kick-ass studio once she gets it off the ground.

"Me, too. Anyway, I've gotta get back to my own job. When Dare comes out, will you let him know his smoothie is in the freezer?"

I walk with her to the doors. "See you tomorrow night, Berk. Text me what bar you want to go to."

She gives me another quick hug before stepping out into the sunshine. "Will do!"

As soon as she's out the door, my phone dings again. When I glance at it, a big smile crosses my face at the sight of Grisham's name.

Want to grab some dinner tonight?

The line of text is so casual and flippant, but it stems big feelings inside of me.

Did he just officially ask me out on a date?

I don't want to jump to conclusions. This could just be a friendly fast-food meal between friends, right? We've had dinner together before. But something about this text just feels different.

I miss him. I haven't seen him all week. The fact doesn't surprise me at all. In a short time, Grisham has become a part of my day. I expect to hear from him in some capacity, and if I didn't, I'd be heartbroken. So then will getting closer to him when he's made it known he isn't ready for a relationship be a stupid move?

Probably.

But I'm feeling pretty damn stupid, so I send him a return text.

I'm in.

Not only am I in, but I'm in over my head when it comes to Grisham. But I don't care. Because letting go and having fun with him feels good.

Everything about Grisham Abbot feels good.

Later, I'm still smiling about my upcoming date as I head for my car after work. I'm pulling out my key fob to unlock when the keys slip from my fingers and clatter to the ground. Bending down to retrieve them, I continue to my car and open the back door. I set my bag down in the backseat, close the door, and open the front. That's when I realize that I never actually unlocked my car doors.

"That's strange. I always lock my doors."

Great, now I'm the crazy girl who mumbles to herself in the parking lot.

Shaking my head with a rueful smile, I prepare to sit on my seat when a flash of red catches my eye.

"What the hell?"

It's the rose. The twelfth rose from my bouquet is no longer missing.

It's sitting on the driver's seat of my car.

11

Grisham

I know why I did it. I asked her to dinner because I missed the hell out of her this week. I missed the way her long, raven hair feels when it tickles my skin. I miss the way her full lips poke out in a pout when she doesn't get her way. I miss the strength that emanates from her in waves. I miss her gorgeous face and her soft, feminine curves that *will* fit so perfectly in my hands. I miss her sunshine.

I'm completely fucked.

I'm doing exactly the opposite of what I promised myself I would do. I said I was going to walk away from her, and yet all I keep doing is pulling her closer. It's like I can't help myself. Something about Greta makes me want to stand up and be the kind of man who's put together enough to deserve her. Like I can even stand up and be *her* man if I work for it. All my life I've defined manhood by rank, by physical strength, and by military caliber. I've embodied that in my professional life now as well. And even though I still think those things are important, Greta is giving me a new perspective. Being there for her during this transitional time in her life, teaching her to protect herself, and bringing smiles to her face make me want to beat my fists against my chest, throw her over my shoulder, and shout "Mine!" to the world.

But do I have the guts to actually make her mine? Right now, sitting across the table from her in a classy Mexican restaurant just off the beach, I can't stop thinking about taking her home with me tonight.

About making this thing with her, whatever it is, official.

I've never had a girlfriend. A night with a girl here and there was all I ever needed. Hell, at one point in my life I thought I'd be spending forever with Berkeley, my childhood best friend. So what did I need to date for? I never learned the ropes about how to be a good partner, about how to be the other half of someone else. Maybe with Greta I can learn.

I shake my head to clear it as I watch her order chimichangas. She also orders a bottle of Dos Equis, which makes me smile. After I put in my order of tomatillos and Mexican rice, I turn to her with raised eyebrows.

"You drink Dos Equis?" My awe for her is growing with every new revelation she shows me, and I can't stop it. The raw, primal feelings that are forming for Greta come from somewhere deep down inside me, somewhere I've always kept hidden away. No matter how hard I try. Greta is a woman with a thousand different facets, and I want to uncover every single one of them.

"I always pair Mexican beer with Mexican food." Her tone is matter-of-fact. "You should have one, too. It's delicious."

Laughing, I nod. "Sounds good. Order one for me when she comes back, okay?"

"Okay." She clasps her hands together and leans forward, her gaze locking intently on mine. She doesn't say anything else, though, just looks at me. And I'm in danger of drowning, lost in those eyes of hers.

"So." I clear my throat. "Tell me about those flowers you received today."

She shrugs. "Just got a dozen roses. Wait, not a dozen. Eleven."

A strange look crosses her face and her voice trails away. "What, Greta? What's that look?"

"Well, it's just...something happened after work that kind of creeped me out."

I straighten in my seat, leaning forward slightly and narrowing my eyes. "What happened?"

She begins fidgeting, toying with her long, slender fingers. "It was the weirdest thing. I thought there were a dozen flowers, and then Berkeley pointed out that there were only eleven. I didn't think anything of it."

She pauses for a second, and I want to reach across the table, grab her hands in mine, and urge her onward in the story. I need her to finish. But without pushing, I wait patiently for her to go on. Right now, I think she just needs me to listen until she gets it all out.

"I didn't think anything else of it. And then, after work I went to my car. I was so excited to get ready for this date..." She stops suddenly and looks at me with wide, startled eyes. "Shoot. I didn't mean to say the *D* word."

I stare at her, confusion making me frown. "Why? This isn't a date?"

A huge smile breaks out across her face, and I'm in danger of pumping my fist into the air, knowing I put it there. "Is it?"

Unable to stop myself this time, I reach for her hands and clasp them tightly in my own. "Do you want it to be?"

She nods, her chin dipping low and her eyes meeting mine. "Yes."

"It's a date," I declare. "What happened when you got to your car?"

"Well, I wasn't really paying attention because I was thinking about our dinner, and I just opened the door and got right in. Once I thought back, though, I realized that my car door was unlocked. That's strange, because I always lock my car door. It's habit, I hit 'lock' on the key fob every single time."

I nod, but my stomach is sinking. I don't like where this story is going. In fact, I fucking hate where it's going. "Was there someone waiting for you in your car, Greta?" My voice is so low it barely registers with me that I asked the question aloud, but she hears me.

Shaking her head quickly, she rushes on. "No, no. Nothing like that. But the twelfth rose was in there."

"Excuse me?"

"The missing rose, from the dozen? It was in my car. Someone had pulled the petals off and spread them over the driver's seat. The stem was lying right on top of the petals."

My hands tighten on hers, and I pull them away so I won't hurt her. Someone invaded her space. First, someone sent her flowers. That was one thing, but then thinking about the fact that someone broke into her car and touched her personal property like that...that sets my blood into a rapid boil.

"I guess someone picked the lock. Or something? I don't know. Anyway, it freaked me out. I looked around, and then I tossed the stem and petals on the ground and got the hell out of there." Her forehead wrinkled in the middle as she frowned.

"Did you tell your dad?"

"No! Are you crazy? He'd flip out. I want to keep working there, Grisham. I've really enjoyed my week. I don't want him to worry and do something drastic, like lock me in the house forever."

I want to lock her in the house forever. As long as I'm there with her.

Our server brings out Greta's beer, and I order one as well. When she leaves, I take Greta's hands again. They tremble in mine, and I rub soft circles on her skin with my thumb. Her wide eyes shine with the subtle fear she's probably feeling at having her space invaded that way.

"Do you promise to let me know if anything like this happens again? I'm not comfortable with it, Greta. On the one hand, it could just be someone you know pulling a prank. But on the other hand, it could be something more sinister than that. Just promise you'll tell me if anything else happens that you think is strange or makes you feel creeped out. Anything at all. Okay?"

She nods, one corner of her mouth quirking up in a tiny smile. "Okay."

"Why are you smiling?"

"Because you're going all alpha male on me."

I can't fight the smile that springs onto my face. "Alpha male?"

"Never mind."

"You didn't promise yet, Grits."

She nods automatically, pulling one of her hands out of mine to give me a mock salute. "I promise. Sir!"

Laughter rumbles inside of me, bursting out the way water does from a geyser. I can't help it. Greta teasing me for taking myself too seriously is freaking hilarious.

The server brings our food and my beer, and we sit and enjoy a delicious dinner. I can't remember the last time I felt so relaxed, unwound. She's light and funny, even though she has tough family issues. Greta's a breath of fresh air in a world where I felt like I couldn't inhale enough oxygen. I watch her as she laughs at something one of the guys on her father's team at the office said today, and just the airy, tinkling sound is enough to pull my manhood to rapt attention. She's sexy as hell in the most unassuming way. A fact that makes her even more alluring.

She's right; the dark, full-bodied Mexican beer pairs perfectly with our food. There's a lot she's right about, I'm starting to notice. Across the table, Greta puts the dark brown bottle to her lips and sips. Her eyes meet mine, and I'm pretty sure it's written all over my face how turned on I am. The bottle pauses just at the entrance to her mouth, her deep, knowing eyes pinning me down.

I swallow, shifting in my seat.

"Greta."

She lowers the bottle an inch. "Yes?"

"Do you want to come back to my place after dinner?"

She nods slowly. "Yeah, Grisham. I do."

Oh...shit. The blood rushes straight to my cock, and I can't think straight anymore. Without breaking eye contact with the sexy seductress in front of me, I raise my hand into the air. Like magic, our server appears.

"*Sí, señor?*"

I'm still caught in Greta's fixed stare. My pulse is pounding each rushed beat like a drum in my ears. "Check, please."

The server scurries away and makes quick work of our bill. The tension at the table builds to a thunderous level; I can almost feel the thickness of it pulling the air between us tight. As soon as the check arrives, I throw a large bill down on the table, hardly even looking at the amount. My chair scrapes against the floor as I shove it backward and stand, extending my hand to Greta. She jumps up, grabbing on tight.

Without another word, I tow her toward my car.

The cool breeze stirring up the night air does nothing to cool off the heat radiating off me. I stalk toward the Jeep, unable to slow my pace. Checking beside me, I see that Greta's keeping up just fine. I throw open the passenger-side door of the car, pulling Greta toward me at the same time.

Her body collides with mine, and my arms automatically go around her. That soft, supple body shapes to mine instantly, and I can't ignore the sparks setting fire to my blood. Our eyes meet; the second her plump bottom lip is sucked between her teeth I react. Turning her so she's pressed firmly against the side of the car, I brace myself with my arms on either side of her head. She barely has time to grab a breath before my lips are devouring hers.

I kiss her like she's my last breath. I don't bother to take my time to explore her; there will be time for that later. Right now? Right now I just need to taste her.

She opens for me almost immediately, causing a growl of approval to rumble deep inside my chest. She reacts to it beautifully, arching her back and pushing her breasts against me.

God, I want to touch her so bad.

But again...later. I lick and nip at the bottom lip I wanted so badly to taste, then delve deeply inside her hot mouth again. She's greedy, raking her hands up into my hair and tugging me closer.

My phone vibrates and chirps in my pocket, but I'm so into her I barely hear it. She tastes like my own personal version of heaven, and I can't stop kissing her. Finally, she pushes against my chest, but I don't let her go far. Leaning my forehead against hers, I attempt to catch my breath and force my racing pulse to slow.

It doesn't work.

Looking at her swollen lips, her mussed hair, the way her dress strap is hanging off of one shoulder, I just want to pick her up and throw her into the backseat.

"You. Are. So. Damn. Hot." I punctuate each word with a squeeze of my hands on her ass, and she giggles, letting her warm breath trickle over my face.

"Your phone...it's ringing again. Must be important."

Groaning, I pull back from her and retrieve my phone from my pocket.

"Better be real fucking important," I mutter as I check the screen.

My mood sobers and I answer the call immediately. "Mom?"

"Grisham? It's happening again." Her voice is shaking, a sure sign that she's scared shitless, and my heartbeat slams to life, this time for a completely different reason.

"I'm on my way."

Greta must hear something in my voice, because she hurries to clamber into the Jeep. I close her door behind her and jog around to the driver's side. Climbing in, I gun the engine before pulling out of the parking spot.

"What's wrong?" asks Greta, her voice full of breathless anxiety.

I don't look at her; my focus is on the road. "I hate to do this, Greta, but I need to bring you with me. I've got a situation I need to handle at my parents'."

She nods. I can feel the heat of her gaze on me, but I can't focus on her the way I had just seconds ago. All I can see now is the way my mom's face looks when she's scared.

I just need to get there.

The mantra repeats over and over again in my head the entire fifteen-minute drive to my parents' beach house.

Get there.

Get there.

Get there.

12

Greta

Something is very, very wrong. I can tell by the tiny muscle I see twitching on the side of Grisham's neck as he hauls ass to his parents' home. I'm not sure who was on the other end of that phone call, but it clearly scared the religion out of him. The set, determined look on his face, lying just on top of a thin layer of fear, reminds me of the way I feel when I receive a call from my mom about Gabi.

Someone he loves is in trouble.

Glancing down, I see the knuckles of the hand resting on the gearshift are white. I lay my hand gently on top of his and don't let go as he shifts the manual transmission. A piece of blond hair is falling over one eye and I want so badly to reach over and brush it away. But at this point I think it's best to keep the physical contact between us to a minimum.

I push the feelings about the most spectacular kiss in the history of kisses down deep, promising to revisit it later. Right now I'm just worried about him and what he might be about to walk into.

We pull into a short driveway leading up to a three-level beach house. Under any other circumstances, I'd be gawking about the size of the place. His parents clearly aren't hurting for money, though I figured a navy admiral and his wife would be living well.

Grisham throws open his car door and climbs out.

"Stay here." He tosses the words at me and is off running toward the front door. I flinch as the Jeep door slams soundly behind him.

I know I should listen to him; *I know I should.* But the little voice living inside my head tells me I can't let him walk into this situation alone. So I slide out of my seat and steal silently through the humid night to follow him.

Grisham's already entered the house, where I can hear things shattering and banging inside. When I cross the threshold I don't see anything, but I hear the commotion coming from the back of the house. I creep down the ornate hallway, decorated with all kinds of seaside knickknacks and beautiful, glossy ocean art. The place is so beautiful, but every few feet there's something broken on the floor or a picture is hanging askew. A growing feeling of dread threatens to take over, but I will it away and keep going.

The sound of raised voices is coming from just around the next corner. When I peek around the driftwood-paneled wall, the scene before me makes my mouth go dry.

Grisham is standing in front of what must be his mother, his hands on her shoulders. He's crouching so that he's eye level with her, asking her repeatedly if she's all right. She's clearly not all right. Her short blond hair is flying all around her head, and her bare arms are covered in bruises. Her tear-streaked face is stricken, and her wild eyes are focused on the man standing a few feet behind Grisham, shouting obscenities at his wife and son.

"Mom! Look at me. Not at him. Do you need the hospital?"

She finally shifts her focus to Grisham and shakes her head. "No, I...no."

"Listen to me, Mom. We're not brushing this under the rug like the other times. He's going down for this."

Grisham's father raises his voice even louder. "You little piece of shit! Do you know who I am? How dare you threaten me! Don't talk about me like I'm not in the room; I'm your father, you fucking idiot."

Grisham turns his back on his mother, and his fist flies, landing a solid punch in the wall beside him. A crack forms in the plaster, and my hands fly to cover my mouth.

"You sick son of a bitch! No more. No fucking more. You'll never lay another hand on her, do you hear me?" Grisham's face is turning a frightening shade of garnet as he advances on his father, his hands balled into fists at his sides. The expression on his face reads pure fury, unbridled and unrestrained. His breaths are coming fast and hard, and I almost don't recognize the man standing before me.

I flinch at the harshness of their words.

As dysfunctional as my relationship is with my father, never has he ever spoken to me or my mother or sisters in this way. Never has he cursed at us or belittled us. My face must reflect the horror I feel, and I can't help the startled cry that escapes me.

Freezing midstep, Grisham glances my way, and I see the flash of pain in his expression when his eyes land on me. But he quickly turns his attention back to his mom.

"Mom, look. My friend Greta is standing over there. I want you to let her take you outside. Okay?"

His mother's face looks panicked as her gaze flickers from her husband to her son and back again. "No, Grisham. I won't leave you alone with him."

His voice grows soft and tender. "You're done protecting me. And we're both done protecting him. Now, go!"

He gives her a little shove, and with a sob, she stumbles in my direction.

My brain switches to autopilot as I catch her in my arms and hustle her back the way I came and out the front door. She immediately crumples to the steps and begins to sob. I pat her shoulder and sprint to the car, retrieving my phone. Then I run back to the porch steps where Mrs. Abbot sits. With one arm wrapped tightly around her, I use my other to pull my phone out of my pocket.

I dial 9-1-1.

The military police car pulls away from the curb with Admiral Abbot inside.

I watch as Grisham guides his mother into the passenger seat of his aunt's car. His aunt has driven an hour from a different part of the state when she heard her sister needed her. Then he turns and has a few words with his aunt, who, in turn, hugs him tightly. He taps the roof of the car with a fist just before it pulls out of the driveway.

My heart twists painfully as he stands still in the driveway long after the car is gone. I can't imagine the turmoil that must be tearing him up right now. How long had his father been hurting his mother? How long has he had to bear the weight of the secret that just tore his family apart?

My feet carry me to where he's standing before I realize I'm moving. I stand beside him and grab his hand, entwining our fingers together as I stare off into the darkness in the same direction. Grisham remains still, but his large palm squeezes my hand tightly.

"Come on, Grisham," I whisper gently. "Let's go."

He nods absently, and we turn toward the Jeep. He opens the passenger door and grabs my waist to help me up before closing my door and walking around to the driver's side.

When he starts the ignition, he sits for a moment, his head resting against the back of his seat. He looks heavy, defeated, like he's carrying the weight of fifteen men on his shoulders. My heart breaks for him, over and over again.

"Grits...I understand, after everything you just saw, if you want me to take you home."

I turn in my seat to face him completely, trying to show him how open I am. "What do you want? Do you want to be alone?"

His reply is automatic. "No. I really don't."

"Then take me home with you."

His deep green gaze holds mine for a moment, and I'm trapped there, the startled doe to his harsh headlights.

Without saying a word, something passes between us. A sense of understanding, maybe, or the assurance that we both come from pretty fucked-up families, but we can find comfort in the other's commiseration.

Finally, he throws the Jeep in reverse and backs out of the driveway. The drive to his house is quiet; we're both tucked deeply in our own thoughts. When we walk into the house, Grisham closes the door behind us as I stand, waiting in the entryway.

"Do you want something to drink?" he asks, walking past me toward the kitchen.

"I think we could both use something stiff," I suggest. "Wine?" Following him toward the kitchen, I stop beside the fridge, leaning against the kitchen counter.

He shakes his head and gives me an apologetic smile. "Sorry, I'm all out. Beer, or I can bust out a bottle of Jack."

It only takes a moment before we simultaneously blurt, "Jack."

With a tiny smile that kicks up just the corner of his full lips he grabs the bottle and pours the thin amber liquid into tumblers. He adds two ice cubes to his and raises his eyebrow to me in question.

Shaking my head, I sip the whiskey, letting the comfortable fire burn a path down my throat. I smack my lips together a few times as I adjust to the heat.

"Nope. I like my whiskey neat."

Watching me, Grisham knocks back his own large gulp without blinking. "You're full of surprises, you know that, Grits? I'm pretty sure that most girls, after seeing the shit show that happened at my parents' house tonight, would have called a cab midway through. But you...you stayed."

I down my drink, never taking my eyes off of him. I walk over and grab the bottle beside him, filling up my glass again.

"Of course I stayed, Grisham. You needed me."

He pours himself a second glass. "Losing my temper like that...the way I was back at my parents'? That shit never happened before my accident. Sometimes I have trouble getting control of my temper. I hate that you had to see that side of me."

He drops his gaze, and I shake my head. "You had every right to be pissed. The things he was saying...I don't expect you to be perfect, Grisham. I don't know why you expect it of yourself."

I watch him sip, mesmerized by the way his Adam's apple bobs when he swallows. A small drop of whiskey escapes his glass and drips down his lip and onto the rough stubble coating his jaw. The strongest wave of lust I've ever felt overtakes me, making me blush. I want nothing more in that moment than to use my tongue to follow the trail that drop of whiskey is taking.

"I...I've never been able to help her, you know?"

I snap back to attention at the serious tone in his voice. His eyes are so sad, I want to wrap him in my arms and never let go.

He takes another gulp of his drink before continuing. "It didn't happen too often, you know? That I was aware of. But when I was little, there was nothing I could do. Then, as I got older, my mom would stand in front of me to make sure I didn't step in. Or she would send me away before it started. He never touched me...he only put his hands on her. It pissed me off even as a little kid. I knew it was wrong for a man to treat the woman he loved that way. But I still knew...and I could have told someone."

"Why didn't you?" The question slips out before I can stop it. I shake my head, angry with myself.

Stupid, Greta. So freaking stupid.

Grisham's hand on my arm stills me. "No, it's okay. It's a fair question. I didn't tell because in the military, domestic violence isn't always handled with the vigilance it deserves. Especially when its offenders are as high up in rank as my father. No one knew, you know? He let me know in no uncertain terms that if I told, no one would believe me. And that I'd be separated from my mom for lying. I didn't want to leave her."

I'm horrified. "He lied to you. He used your love for your mom to scare you into silence."

His face is crestfallen. "Yeah, he did. And I bought it. But after what I saw tonight...I couldn't take it anymore. I haven't been living with them for a while now...I hoped it had stopped. She told me it had, when I asked her."

My gut twists with sympathy. I can't imagine not being able to protect my mother from something so violent. Not being able to protect my sister from her CF nearly kills me, and that isn't something anyone can control. What Grisham has gone through, watching his mother hurt and not being able to stop it, must have eaten a hole straight through the inside of him.

"You did the right thing tonight...he's going to be prosecuted."

He nods thoughtfully. "Yeah, he is. But I don't know what the outcome will be. I'm going to try my damnedest to make sure this doesn't get swept under the rug."

I nod emphatically. "You were her hero tonight. You'll do what needs to be done."

That tiny smile pulls at his mouth once more. "You know, with my leg...sometimes it feels like I can't do it anymore. Save people, I mean. It's all I've ever wanted to do, probably because I couldn't ever save my mom. But after the accident...I thought my ability to help people was gone."

Unable to stay away from him any longer, I turn toward him and wrap my arms around his neck. My fingers find the soft hair there, rubbing gently and feeling each and every sensation they make on my skin. Gazing up at him, I attempt to speak truth right into his soul.

"Grisham, your ability to help people is just beginning. Don't you remember how we came back into each other's lives? You saved me from the ocean. And you just saved your mother from the person who's been hurting her most of your life. It's tragic that he's your father, but you did what needed to be done. You save people...it's what you do. And I have no doubt you'll continue to do it. God, I wish you could see how amazing you are."

Something shifts in his gaze, something that was previously dark becomes light, and a ragged breath escapes him. He also downs the rest of his whiskey, and then he cups my face with one large palm. The rough pads of his fingers brush against my skin, and a shiver runs through me in response. Seeing it, his eyes darken once again; this time they're flooded with desire.

"You're kind of incredible." His voice is nothing but a caress, and I close my eyes and lean into his palm. Something warm heats up my insides; whether it's from the whiskey or the lust pooling in my core I can't decide. My breathing comes faster, harder.

Suddenly, his hands encircle my waist as he lifts me onto the granite countertop. My butt lands hard against the stone, sending a jolt of electricity coursing through me. His touch is light and sensual on my thighs as he strokes from my knees upward, pushing my dress with it. Feeling the heady effects of the whiskey combined with Grisham's clean, musk-and-ocean scent, my head falls back and a small sound of need escapes me when his hands meet the creases between hip and thigh.

He leans forward, nipping at my exposed collarbone with his teeth. His lips close around the tender bite as he sucks the small sting away. The juncture between my thighs burns and pulsates as my body craves more of his touch.

His hands slide up my back, bringing my dress up over my hips. I raise my arms, and he lifts the cotton easily over my head.

I can't explain how exquisite his hands feel when they're grazing my skin. It's like Grisham knows exactly how to touch me, where to stroke, so that I'm completely enthralled by his touch. Anticipation pools between my legs, which squeeze him tighter between them as his fingers skim around my sides to fully cup my breasts.

I cry out as his thumbs brush sensuous circles around the tips of my breasts.

"Fucking hell, Grits," he murmurs as he buries his face in my neck. He's yet to taste my lips, but I'm a wanton mess of liquid need in his arms.

"You're so responsive," he says with awe in his voice. "Your body reacts to my touch like it's the answer to every question you've ever asked."

It's never been like this with another man.

Never.

I don't know where this is going with Grisham; I don't have the first clue. We haven't discussed a future, or even given a label to what we're doing right now. But I'm throwing caution to the wind, because being in his arms is as natural as breathing.

It all might go up in flames tomorrow, but tonight all I want to do is burn for Grisham until there's nothing left but a pile of ashes.

13

Grisham

I'm not thinking straight...I can't. Her body feels like heaven against my fingers. She's all soft curves and long limbs, the better to wrap around me. I'm completely blown to pieces by the way she surrounds every last one of my senses by just *being*. I can't get enough of her; whether it's her sweet taste, her sexy sounds, her silky touch, or her intoxicating scent...I want more.

Fucking *more*.

Breaking through my hazy thoughts, a distant voice of reason attempts to reach me.

She's not just another girl. She's not here to get a piece of a man in uniform. She's here for you.

If I use Greta this way...it'll all be over before it begins. I haven't made her any promises, haven't had a conversation with her about a relationship. Yet, I know this girl, and she's more than just a good fuck. She's the kind of girl you keep close to you, because if you let her go you'll regret it for the rest of your life. But am I ready for that?

I just sent my father to jail for beating up my mother. I just put my mother in a car to stay with my aunt so she can have some distance from the shitbag she calls a husband. A few months ago, I lost a limb in a secret part of Hell that most Americans will never know about.

The exact wrong thing for me to do right now is bring a sweet, albeit sexy-as-sin, girl like Greta into my bed. It'd stain her.

I jerk backward, feeling the sting of my lips leaving her skin like a jab to the gut. Taking a healthy step away from the temptation of her body, I turn away.

"Grisham?" Her voice is uncertain. "What's wrong?"

Clearing my throat, I shake my head. "Nothing."

Everything.

I turn back to face her, seeing that she's still completely naked save a tiny pair of sky-blue lace panties. My mouth going dry, I reach down to the floor to gather her dress in my arms. Thrusting it at her, my voice sounds raw when I ask her to please put it back on.

Her eyes widen slightly, her mouth drops open, but she complies, slipping the thin garment over her head and hopping down from the counter so that it falls neatly over her hips. The loss of the beautiful view makes my stomach hurt, but I focus on her eyes.

They're filled with pain.

Fuuuuuck. I want to wrap her legs around my waist and erase that look from her eyes. I want to kiss every inch of her until it's gone. It's going to haunt me in my sleep. By trying to prevent myself from making a mistake, I've made a mess of things.

I extend my hand to her. She looks down at it, and then folds her arms across her chest. "Greta. You didn't do anything wrong. Can we just go sit down and talk?"

A tear slides down her cheek, and I'm in her space again in an instant. "Don't, Grits. Don't cry. It's not you...I swear. You're fucking perfect. Too perfect. I don't want to mess shit up by taking advantage of you when I'm an emotional wreck and you've been drinking. This isn't going to be the night I make love to you...not when we've been through hell together tonight."

She looks at me then, really looks at me. It's like she sees straight to the heart of me, even when I'm trying to shutter myself off. She heard everything I *didn't* say.

She allows me to lead her to my bedroom. I still want her to stay with me tonight, and I'm hoping that by skipping the couch and coming straight back here, she'll be more likely to listen to what I have to say and then stay.

God, I want this girl in my bed tonight. Any way I can have her there.

I kick off my shoes and sit down on the king-size mattress, swinging my legs up onto the bed. Then I pat the spot next to me, inviting her to join me.

I lean back against the headboard as I watch her crawl up and onto the bed beside me. My cock stirs inside my black slacks, but I ignore it and focus on Greta.

She turns expectant eyes to me. "So you're saying you're planning on making love to me at some point?"

Holy... "I guess that's a decision we'll have to make together. But damn, girl. The way you were just now...it was hot. You're hot. And being with you does something crazy to me...every time we're together. So, yeah, I plan on getting physical with you at some point. But not like this. I'm a fucking disaster tonight."

She nods slowly. "Of course you are. Back there, in the kitchen, I wasn't thinking. I was just reacting to you." Her voice drops down to a whisper. "Your hands feel so good on my body."

My head falls back against the headboard and a groan escapes me. "You're killing me, Grits."

She giggles softly.

"I wish you knew how much more I want to do to you with these hands. And I will."

Yeah, I definitely will. Just not tonight. I'm going to give her one last chance to save herself.

I gesture toward her dress. "Do you want to sleep in that?" Jumping down from the bed, I indicate my dresser. "Or do you want me to lend you something?"

"Lend me something. I'll just run to the bathroom to get ready for bed."

I rummage around in my drawer, trying to find something small enough for her to wear. I settle on one of my white undershirts and a pair of gym shorts with the navy football logo on the front. She thanks me, grabbing the clothes, and disappears into the bathroom adjoining my bedroom.

While she's gone, I strip down, replacing my slacks with a pair of lightweight cotton shorts and deciding to go shirtless.

I sit down on top of the covers and am just looking at my prosthesis, trying to decide something, when Greta walks back into the room.

Which sends a whole new wave of desire rippling through me, because she's not wearing my shorts. Her long legs are all exposed, with my white shirt ending at the tops of her thighs. She's taller than a lot of girls, and the shirt doesn't hang to her knees the way it might on some people.

She stops short when she sees me staring, and then gazes down at her bare legs. "Sorry. I would have worn the shorts, only they were hanging off me even when I tried to adjust them."

Yeah, I guess that makes sense with her thin frame. Swallowing the need making a power play inside me, I pat the bed once again. "This is your spot."

She gives me a crooked little smile, crawling into bed. She looks at me, sitting with my amputated leg propped up on the bed. "So, do you usually sleep with that on?"

Leave it to Grits to get right to the heart of the matter. Shaking my head, I nod at my prosthetic foot. "I usually take it off. It's not the most comfortable to sleep with it on. But if it makes you uncomfortable in any way—"

She cuts me off. "Nothing about you makes me uncomfortable, Grisham. This is your house." Squeezing my thigh, she scoots a little closer and rests her head on my shoulder.

I take a breath. I've never done this. No one, except for my doctors, my mother, and my SEAL team, has seen my leg ending in a stump. The last thing I want her to do is get freaked out and bolt.

But if that's going to happen, I guess it's better we get it out of the way now, right?

One step at a time, I pull my prosthetic foot from my prosthesis, and then remove the sock and liner. I'm shaking as I sit back and release the breath I've been holding, staring down at what used to be my foot. I can feel beads of sweat breaking out on my forehead. This revelation is something I've never done before. My leg was blown off just below my knee, above my calf. At first, I could still feel the limb there. I almost couldn't believe it was gone unless I was looking directly at my leg.

Someone with a prosthetic these days can pretty much live the way they did previously, unless they're expected to put their life on the line for a living. I can walk, run, jump, and climb in this thing. I just can't have other people, namely the guys on my SEAL team, depending on me when they could end up dead if I can't perform.

When I feel the warmth of Greta's hand on my leg, every single muscle in my body tenses. I'm not expecting her to touch me...there. My gaze slides toward hers, and her expression is fiercely burning into mine.

"You're still *you*, Grisham. You're still the same guy I met and crushed on two years ago. You just have a bit more of a story to tell. That's all."

My breath catches as something in my chest shifts, sliding back into place. I hold her gaze as a million different thoughts and feelings wage war for the top spot in my brain. Finally, I lift a hand and cover hers with my own. My fingers curl around hers, holding on tight.

"Thank you."

She slides underneath the covers, pulling me with her and we lay on our sides, staring at each other.

"You don't need to thank me, Grisham. It's the truth."

Pulling her face toward mine, I kiss her. Our lips are tender at first, but when I delve my tongue inside her warmth to stroke hers, she moans. With a growing sense of need and hunger, I deepen the kiss, our mouths moving rapidly over one another. I memorize the contours of her lips, the feel of her tongue against mine. The sweet taste of her does nothing to curb the appetite she's whet. Pulling her closer, I think I kiss her until I fall asleep, because the feel of her lips on mine is the last thing I remember.

I become alert before I actually open my eyes. I can tell it's still dark outside, the way it always is when I wake up in the morning. Even though I don't still need to be up before the sun, like when I was in the academy and in SEAL training, old habits die hard. But before I can stretch and sit up, a strange sensation makes me freeze.

My arms are locked around something soft, warm, and sweet smelling. I inhale deeply, realizing the floral scent belongs to a woman.

Greta. The previous night comes rushing back to me, and I'm immediately rock-hard underneath the sheets. I open my eyes and glance down at her, and the sight brings a stupid grin to my face. She's facing the same direction as me, and I'm spooning her from behind. The curves of her body fit like puzzle pieces into the long, hard lengths of mine. She's so close we're sharing the same pillow, and her rivers of thick, onyx hair tickle my nose when I move. I wish I could see her face, because I'd bet my Jeep it's breathtaking in sleep. But there'll be time for that the next time I wake up beside her.

Whoa, dude. Slow down. The next time? Like, this is going to happen again?

I mull it over even as I squeeze her a little tighter. She hums softly in her sleep but doesn't wake.

Do I? Do I want this?

I know the answer, but I'm not yet willing to admit it. Right now I just want to enjoy the fact that she's here, and that waking up to her feels…insanely good.

For the first time in months, I don't get out of bed before the sun is up. I nuzzle my face into Greta's neck, sigh contentedly, and fall back to sleep.

The next time I wake, it's to the scent of coffee and bacon. I open my eyes to see the sun is now streaming bright yellow light through the window. I stretch and yawn, an immediate smile plastered to my face.

"Good morning, sleepyhead." Greta's voice comes from the doorway of the bedroom, and I turn over in bed to see her standing there. She's wearing my T-shirt, her bare legs going on for miles underneath.

Sitting up, I try to keep my eyes off all of her creamy, exposed skin and focus instead on her flawless face. "Damn. I was supposed to be up before you this morning. But the first time I woke up, you were snuggled up next to me and I didn't want to move."

A gorgeously shy smile creeps across her lips. "I'm glad you stayed in bed with me, then. I haven't been up long. But I did make some coffee, and there's bacon frying on the stove. Want to come make the eggs?"

Instead of waiting for me to answer, she turns and heads back out of the room. It's a treat to watch her ass sashaying away from me, and the sight draws me out of bed. I quickly attach my prosthetic foot and hurry into the bathroom to take care of business before exiting my bedroom. I follow the delicious morning aromas to the kitchen, where Greta stands barefoot in front of the stove.

I could get used to this. The sight of her standing in my kitchen every morning like this? Hell, yeah.

I can't help myself. I cross the room to stand behind her and wrap my arms around her waist. I squeeze her against me, letting her feel the evidence that the red-hot chemistry between us last night was no fluke. She gasps, her head falling back against my chest. It gives me the perfect access to her neck, where I plant my lips and suck softly. She's sweet and succulent, exactly the way she tasted last night.

My hands play at the skin underneath the shirt she's wearing, sliding up her flat stomach to rest just against the curve of her full breasts.

"I want to touch your hot little body all over right now," I whisper into her ear. She removes the pan of bacon from the heated burner right before pushing her ass back against me, maybe to show me she's right there with me, and I groan. "Is that what you want?"

Her breath is coming faster, I can see how rapidly her chest rises and falls and feel the quickness of her thudding heart against my hands. She wants this. I want this. So...

"No," she rasps. My hands still, and the blood running through my veins turns to ice. That one little word is as effective as a bucket of icy water thrown on my head.

"No?" I ask, confusion evident in my tone.

"I mean, yes. Gah, Grisham! Yes, of course I want this. But I don't think you're sure about it...or about me. And I'm not the kind of girl that can just use my body and leave my mind and my heart out of it."

She turns in my arms, a sad little pout dancing across her mouth. "I wish I was...because you and me together in your bed would be really fucking amazing."

It's the first time I've ever heard her say the word *fuck* and somehow it's the sexiest thing I've ever heard. I smile. "That needed to be punctuated with the *F* word?"

She nods emphatically. "Definitely." She leans forward and brushes her lips against my throat, and my hands immediately squeeze her plush ass. "I want you, Grisham. And when you know that I'm what you want—really want, and not just for a night—then I'm all yours."

All kinds of promises want to spill from my lips at that moment. And if I were a bastard, I'd use each and every one of them just to get this girl back to my bed. But I knew from the minute Greta opened those baby blue eyes on the beach and blinked up at me that she would never be just another girl in my bed. She's more. I knew it then and I know it even more completely now.

"You're right. I'm a fucking wreck inside my head, and my heart's even worse. I don't know when I'll be ready for what you're asking."

She shrugs, her mouth still connected to my neck. "I'm not asking for anything from you, Grisham. No more than you're willing to give. Maybe we can just keep getting to know each other better." I feel hot wetness against my throat as her tongue darts out to stroke my skin.

My fingers dig into her soft flesh in response. "Getting to know each other sounds good."

There's a whole other side of you I want to know really fucking well. I keep my dirty thoughts to myself.

"I'm kind of messed up, too, you know? My dad...I have my own set of trust issues with men to deal with. Probably not the best idea to just jump into bed. Even if it is with the sexy SEAL who saved my life once already."

I back her up against the counter beside the stove, déjà vu from the night before striking hilarious irony in my brain. How many times would I have her up against some surface in my kitchen before I was actually claiming her body as my own?

"I'd save you again ten times over. It led to you and me here like this, so it's hands down the best decision I ever made." My tone is teasing, but the words are dead serious. "I'm glad I was there that day, Grits."

She sighs softly, laying her head on my chest. "Me, too."

We stay like that for a moment, neither of us talking. Then I lean back so that I can look down at her. "You ready for more fighting lessons this morning after breakfast?"

Smiling up at me, she gives a slight nod. "I'm ready for you, Abbot."

I smile wickedly down at her. "That's what you think."

14

Greta

I leave Grisham's house on a natural high the likes of which I've never experienced. Something had changed between us last night, something big. The fact that I was there with him during what was probably the most gut-wrenching experience of his life brought us closer together. Seeing how lost and hurt he was after the scene between his parents made me want to be there for him, pick up the pieces when he fell apart. Something about Grisham tells me that I could help him.

Helping people is something I do effortlessly. It's as easy as breathing, because I've been doing it for as long as I can remember. It's when the tables are turned, when I need to allow someone to help me, that I struggle. Maybe Grisham can help me, too.

My thoughts are still lingering on Grisham and the night we spent together when I pull up at my apartment complex. On Saturday morning, the lot is pretty full, so I have to park farther away than usual. I'm walking toward the door, still wearing Grisham's big shirt and a pair of his shorts rolled twice. My feet are bare, and I'm carrying the clothes I'd worn yesterday in a bundle.

Halfway to the apartment, the skin on the back of my neck begins to tingle, raising the hairs there. I pause, automatically searching the parking lot around me. No one is around, everyone still in their apartments doing whatever they do on a Saturday morning. Frowning, I continue walking toward the sidewalk leading to the stairs.

But the feeling doesn't dissipate. In fact, it increases as I walk, becoming stronger and stronger until I want nothing more than to break out into a sprint. I resist, though, because I feel silly. I've walked from the parking lot to my apartment a million times, and it's bright, sunny daylight. There's no reason for me to be afraid.

Then why does it feel like someone is watching me?

When I reach the stairs leading up to my floor, I huff out a sigh of relief. Hurrying upstairs, I let myself in and slam the door behind me.

And I run smack into Mea, who is standing just inside the threshold with arms crossed, tapping her foot.

"Seriously?" she hisses. "You decide to stay out all night with a hottie like Grisham, and all I get is a text message saying you'll see me in the morning?"

Laughing off my nervous energy from the walk up, I hug her. "Good morning to you, too, roommie."

I walk past her down the hallway toward my bedroom to drop off my clothes. Mea follows me, sitting on my bed and folding her legs up underneath her. "Spill, girl."

I shrug. "There's nothing to tell."

Mea merely arches one perfectly tweezed eyebrow. "Bullshit."

I giggle. "Okay, I spent the night with Grisham. We didn't have sex, but we did make out and it was freaking *hot*. Then we made breakfast together this morning, and now I have to shower and change so I can go get hot and sweaty with him all over again."

Her mouth falls open farther and farther as I talk until finally she squeals and claps her hands together. "So now you guys are like, together?"

I shake my head firmly. "No labels, Mea. We're just getting to know each other."

Mea's eyes narrow. "If you don't make the man you're bangin' stamp a label on it, Greta, he'll assume you're in it for the sex. And he'll be fine with that. Is that what you want?"

Gasping, I swat at Mea's leg. "Mea! I didn't have sex with Grisham last night."

She scowls. "Well, still. Make him label it."

I shake my head at her, smiling. "We'll label it when and if we're ready. Until then...no labels and no bangin'."

I head toward the bathroom as she shrugs. "Suit yourself. Don't say I didn't warn you."

I stop short, just inside my bedroom door. "Why do you sound like you're giving me firsthand advice? Is there something you want to talk to me about?"

Mea and I have been friends since we met in college at East Carolina University years ago. She's always been a bit of a wild child. Being my first time away from home and my too-adult responsibilities, combined with her unstable upbringing and wild nature, we'd been two peas in a pod in the party scene in college and had become fast friends. The more I got to know Mea, the more I realized that beneath her fun-loving, party-girl demeanor was a very closed-off, scarred girl who never shared too deeply what was going on inside of her.

There were very few people in the world Mea opened up to: me, Berkeley, and her younger brother, Mikah. But I knew there would always be things about her past and present life she'd never open up about. I always want to be there for her, just in case she decides to spill her guts.

She hops off of my bed, and I can almost see her walls rising so she won't have to answer my question. As I expect, she deflects. "We're not talking about me. We're talking about you and your hot SEAL." She flounces out of my room, leaving a light whiff of honeysuckle behind her. Her signature scent matches her sweet nature, but not her sassy personality.

I watch her go, silently wondering what she isn't telling me. Then I shake off the questions I have regarding my roommate and head into the bathroom to shower. Grisham will be waiting for me at Night Eagle in a little over half an hour.

"Try it again," Grisham instructs, his chiseled face set in serious determination.

I gaze at him, momentarily distracted. *Guys shouldn't be allowed to be that beautiful.*

We've been working together in the training room at Night Eagle for a little over an hour as Grisham patiently teaches me fighting moves that will help me defend myself and gain the upper hand if the situation ever arises where I'll need it. Grisham started off today with a lesson in mixed martial arts. He told me that along with self-defense tactics, MMA would give me all of the resources I would ever need in a fight. So from now on he'd be training me in MMA as well as teaching me basic self-defense moves.

At first, I was thrown. I've never been in a fight in my life, and learning to use my feet and my fists to hurt someone is such a foreign concept to me that my brain fought against it. But Grisham's firm-yet-gentle coaching put me in the correct frame of mind. Working for Night Eagle could very possibly place me in the range of some dangerous people and sketchy situations, and the men in my life want me to be able to handle myself.

First we reviewed the three sequences he taught me during our last lesson. Grisham made sure I was really comfortable with them before moving on to fighting with my fists.

"You've got this, Grits," he encourages. His arms are covered with punch pads. "Remember: jab, cross, and then switch your feet quickly. Keep your hips forward while you immediately jab that knee upward."

I suck in a deep breath as I nod, bouncing lightly on the balls of my feet the way Grisham taught me earlier. My eyes zero in on the punch pads he holds in front of his face. I try to focus, telling myself that today Grisham isn't a super-sexy man of action who causes my heart to flutter dangerously in my chest whenever he's near. Today he's an attacker, and my life depends on whether or not I'm able to fend him off.

"Go!" he shouts.

Reacting to the intensity in his voice, I jab my left fist forward. It's covered in the sparing glove Grisham fitted me with at the start of today's lesson. My fist connects with the pad, but before I allow the jolt to rocket through me I'm crossing over with my right fist and it slams into the other pad. Then I hop lightly, switching the position of my feet, and immediately throw my right knee up. I hear the swift crack of its connection with the pad.

"That's my *girl*!" Grisham cheers for me, raising one arm in the air and pumping it in victory.

"I did it." I'm amazed that my muscles just remembered what to do on their own, after practicing with Grisham. "Holy shit."

The buzz of empowerment that runs through me at the completion of today's lesson is all-consuming. I'm elated, feeling so high from the pride and joy of my success that I feel like I could float off the ground. Grisham throws the punch pads on the ground and comes toward me, sweeping me off my feet and into a bear hug.

"I knew you could," he says, his voice gravelly in my ear. "I'm so proud of you. You rock at this, Grits."

A hot flush of pride sweeps through me, and I curl my arms up around his neck. "Thank you. For teaching me this."

He inhales, his nose planted against my neck. "It's my pleasure." He breathes.

When he puts me down, I slide down the front of his rock-hard body nice and slow, dragging sparks of heat and electricity with me as I go. I stare up at him, my arms still loosely entwined around his neck, my fingers playing in the short hairs at his nape. His eyes darken, and then his lips are on mine. His hands squeeze my ass until I'm flush against him, and I can feel the hard length of his erection pushing into my stomach. It's electrifying, feeling how much a man like Grisham wants me. My body's response is immediate and carnal as a flood of heat pools in my core.

I whimper softly as his tongue teases my lips open, invading my mouth to stroke mine. He squeezes my ass in response, a low growl emitting from his chest.

I'm not sure how long we stand there, making out while our hands explore and roam over our clothes, but I'm winded when he finally pulls away.

"Like I said." He gives me a rogue grin. "You're kinda good at this."

"I thought you were talking about the fighting," I whisper, slightly dizzy from our connection.

"I'm talking about *everything*." The meaning behind his words doesn't escape me, and a hot blush captures my face. He smiles.

"Oh, my gosh!" I clap a hand over my mouth. "I completely forgot to tell you. Berkeley stopped by here yesterday to bring a smoothie for Dare."

"And she wants us all to go for drinks tonight," he finishes with a wry smile. "She called me this morning."

Suddenly feeling shy, I peek up at him through my lashes. "Do you want to go?"

He pushes a lock of hair that has fallen out of my ponytail back behind my ear. "I'll take the excuse to go have some drinks with my friends and also spend the night hanging out with you."

A giggle bubbles up. "Uh, okay then. I guess we'll go home and shower..." My voice trails off when I realize what I've said. "I mean, not together, of course. You'll go to your home and shower, and I'll go to my home and shower..."

"I think the joint shower sounds like a good idea," he offers, smirking at my faux pas.

I smack his chest. "Stop it! God, why do you make me so nervous?"

He catches my hand and brings it to his lips. "Don't be nervous. I want to hang out with you tonight. I'm just going to tolerate the fact that everyone else will be there, too. Okay? Can I pick you up? Or will you be riding with Mea?"

I sigh in relief, watching the way his thumb strokes the back of my hand and feeling the sizzle all the way down to my toes. "I'll text you and let you know. I'll check with Mea when I get home to see what she wants to do."

He nods, releasing my hand, and we both walk out of the training room and down the stairs. "Sounds like a plan."

When we arrive in the lobby, Dare and my father are seated around the low coffee table in a couple of chairs, poring over a large map spread out over the sleek wood.

"What are you guys doing here on a Saturday?" I ask in surprise.

Both men glance up.

"You get a good training session in?" asks my father. He stands up and shakes Grisham's hand.

"She did some sparring today, and was excellent." Hearing Grisham brag on me is something I think I can get used to.

My father beams, the pride evident on his face. "Of course

she did. You keep working on it, okay, sweetheart?"

I nod. Gesturing toward the map and the electronic notebooks spread in front of them, I ask, "What's all this?"

My father sits down in his chair, leaning back while Dare stands up to stretch and greet Grisham. "We're trying to strategize. We have a new client."

The inner office door opens, and two men walk out. I recognize them as the Night Eagle team, but my father introduces them to Grisham.

"Grisham Abbot, these men are part of my team here. This is Ronin Shaw and Jeremy Teague."

Jeremy is a tall hunk of a guy with an olive complexion and dark hair to match. It's cut short on the sides and longer on top. His locks curl around the top of his forehead, and large dimples dent his cheeks whenever he smiles. He's in his midtwenties, just like Ronin.

Ronin is a lighter version of Jeremy. They both have similar builds, made of solid muscle, although Ronin is a little taller. His dirty-blond hair falls to just below his collar, but he usually wears it pulled up into a ponytail. Ponytails have probably never been as sexy on a guy as they are on Ronin. His hazel eyes twinkle with mischief half the time, like he's up to something no one else knows anything about. He'll pull his share of pranks in the office if given half a chance.

They both give me big, teddy-bear grins that make me smile back at them with affection. Both young men have become like big brothers to me in the short time I've worked in the office. They're sweet, even if Jeremy is gruff and Ronan's a goofball.

"Jacob kind of poached Shaw and Teague from the police force after they helped with Berkeley's rescue awhile back," explains Dare. He grins at my father.

My father shrugs. "How could they refuse? Private work pays better than public service."

"Yeah, and we still get to do what we love. Help people and kick ass." Jeremy crosses bulging biceps over his broad chest. He glances at me and winks.

I nod toward the office. "So you guys were working in there on the same tactical strategies while Dad and Dare are figuring out entries and exits out here?"

My father nods. "We decided to split up for a bit, because something about this situation is throwing us off."

Grisham leans closer to look at the map Dad has laid out on the table. I look, too, but I can't understand what they're talking about at first.

Dare explains. "This map is of the wooded area outside of Wilmington, farther away from the coast. There's a compound there where our client fears someone is keeping his wife. The FBI is involved, but he has hired us to help because he has the money and he's worried the person keeping his wife there will hurt her or worse."

A pang of sympathy shoots through my chest. "That's awful."

My father nods grimly. "We're trying to figure out the best way to approach the compound. The terrain is rough, and we have to expect that the owner of the compound will have eyes all over his property."

Grisham focuses intently on the map, stroking his chin

while he concentrates. "What if you did something like this?" He points to a spot on the map and leans in. "Dropping in from the sky would be a dead giveaway. But coming in at night in stealth mode on foot, right in this spot, might give you a chance to have the element of surprise. From what I can see on the map, this is where his security would be the weakest. There's the least chance of him having a visual on you entering the property."

My father looks sharply at Grisham before leaning in to take in what he'd pointed out on the map.

"That could work," says Dare thoughtfully.

I take a step back, glancing around at the five men as they pore over the materials in front of them. They're all so absorbed in what they're doing they've probably forgotten I'm here. I shake my head, amused at how quickly Grisham's been pulled into the fold, and head to my desk. I might as well get a little bit of work done while they're busy. I turn on my computer and pull up a schedule I'm planning to work on next week. I can get an early start on it for a half hour or so and then go home to shower before a night out with my friends.

I pull open my desk drawer, reaching in without looking to grab a pen. When a sharp prick stabs my finger, sending a jolt of pain through my hand, I let out a small cry of surprise.

"What's wrong?" asks Grisham.

When I look up, five pairs of eyes are staring intently at me.

"Um, it's nothing. I just hurt my finger." I put the offending finger into my mouth, tasting the coppery metallic tang of blood. I look at my finger and notice a small wound.

Feeling dizzy, I quickly pull my gaze away.

When I lean down to check my drawer, I see the offending weapon. The thorn of a single white rose.

A chill crawls up my spine and down again.

How did this rose get in my desk?

I stare at it a moment before I realize that Grisham is standing in front of my desk. Concern is etched on his face.

"Are you okay?"

I nod numbly, not sure what to make of the rose in my desk. "Yeah, I...I pricked my finger on a thorn from this rose."

Grisham's eyebrows shoot up toward his hairline. "That rose was in your desk? Just now?"

I nod. "I don't know how it got there."

Frowning, Grisham picks up the flower and turns it over in his hand. "I don't like this."

I shake my head. "It's weird."

"Who has access to your desk?"

I gesture. "Just these guys, I guess. But none of them ever touches my desk. And none of them would leave me a flower without telling me it was from them."

Then I remember Ronin's affinity for pranks. "Unless...hey, guys?"

The men look up at me again.

"Have any of you given me flowers lately?"

Genuine expressions of confusion cross their faces, and I know immediately that none of them have pulled a fast one on me. "Never mind."

Grisham studies the rose. "Do you want to report this?" He keeps his voice low.

I snort. "Report what? The fact that someone is giving me flowers?"

He frowns. "You're right. There's nothing to report. But I want you to keep your eyes open, okay? First the bouquet and the red rose in your car, and now this. It's strange, and I don't like it."

I nod glumly. "It's strange, all right. I'll keep an eye out. But I'm sure it's nothing."

He nods thoughtfully. "I'm sure it is."

Dare calls out, "Grisham, come here. Let me run something by you."

I shut down my computer and stand. Suddenly, I'm no longer in the mood to work. "Hey, guys, I'm out of here, okay? Grisham, I'll text you later."

He gives me a warm smile. "Looking forward to it."

I keep the warmth from his smile with me on my way home, helping to ease the anxiety the white rose brought me. But the throbbing in my finger keeps it at the forefront of my thoughts.

15

Grisham

I don't know why or how the path through the woods to the compound jumped out at me so easily. It just did. As I'm sitting with the Night Eagle team poring over the map and the digital notes they'd taken during their initial meeting with their client, it occurred to me that someone who's hiding something big enough to need an entire compound in the woods to themselves would have aerial coverage of the sky surrounding their land. But maybe it would be much more difficult to survey every acre surrounding their home.

"I thought about going in on foot," mused Jacob thoughtfully. "Actually, I was thinking that'd be the way we'd have to do it, but how'd you find this route so damn fast? You only looked at the map for about a minute."

"It just jumped out at me," I answer honestly. "My brain works that way with maps and data. I can see things other people can't...that's why I was able to lead my own SEAL team at twenty-four."

Dare grins at me, impressed. "Respect, dude. That's something to be proud of."

I glance down at my foot. "It was."

Jacob fixes me with a stern stare. His eyes are intense in their gaze, and he makes damn sure I can't look away. He holds authority the way most soldiers hold their weapons: with firm ease. "No, it *is*. You seem to move pretty damn well on that foot of yours, Abbot. Now, I figure the navy has given you your walking papers, am I right?"

With the sinking feeling in my gut I get whenever I think about leaving the job I thought I'd do until I died, I nod. "Yeah. The end of the year, I'm out. Honorably, and with some medals, yeah. But I still have to go."

Jacob gives me an assessing look, and the other guys are looking me up and down, too. I hold up under their scrutiny, though, because there's no way in hell I'm backing down to a bunch of ex-Rangers. As a SEAL, I'm proud of my branch and of my service, so if they don't think I measure up to them, they can all go to hell. Dare gives me a minimal shake of his head, almost as if he can hear what I'm thinking. I focus my attention back on Jacob.

"What are your plans after you're out?"

This is the question I've asked myself a hundred times and haven't yet been able to answer. How am I going to go from saving lives, putting myself on the line with each mission I'm a part of, the adrenaline rush that is being a SEAL, to all of that being completely absent from my life? How do I go from something like that to a desk job or something? I have a college degree, I know there are other avenues for me when I retire from the navy. But none of them have appealed to me so far.

"I don't know, sir."

Jacob pauses, mulling something over in his brain as he keeps his stare locked on me. I can almost see the gears turning, until he finally speaks.

"I have a proposition for you. I like how quickly that brain of yours read this situation, and I'm interested in having you on the team here at Night Eagle. We're growing, and I need to be able to split some assignments between a few men each here at the Wilmington office. If you're interested, I'd like to give you a PT test that I use for my guys here, and then I'd like to try you out on this assignment, since you already weighed in on it. Are you interested?"

Fuck, yeah...I'm interested! I want to shout it at the top of my lungs.

My heart is kicking up dust in my chest just thinking about his offer. I can't believe my luck...I literally just walked into a possible future for life after the navy. And I hadn't even seen it coming.

Kind of like Greta.

It's not lost on me that it's because of her that I'm now in the position to possibly start the rest of my life with a new, rewarding career that can give me the same sort of satisfaction being a SEAL does. So far, being around Greta has done nothing but bring me up, out into the sunshine where previously there'd been only darkness.

"Yes, sir," I finally answer Jacob, a wide grin crossing my face. "I'm damn sure interested."

Jacob breaks into a tiny smile, and the other three guys take a turn clapping me on the back. "Welcome to the team, Abbot."

Dare speaks up. "When we work together on a mission, we never use our first names. We use the nicknames we earned in the uniform. They call me Cujo, Jacob here is Boss Man. Teague over there is known as Brains because he's a tech guru, and we call Shaw Swagger. Because he's arrogant as shit, but he can always back it up. What about you, Abbot? What do your guys call you in the field?"

My smile comes slow and sure. "They call me Ghost."

"Because of all that blond hair and white skin?" suggests Teague.

Dare and Ronin laugh outright at his joke, but my smile is gone.

"No," I answer with a straight face. "Because the assholes we're after never see me coming."

Later, sitting around a local Lone Sands bar with my SEAL buddies, my new Night Eagle team, and my closest friends, I'm feeling good. Better than I have in a long time. The prospect of a new job where I don't have to worry about my prosthetic holding me back has lifted a huge weight off my shoulders. Greta is sitting beside me at the table, having arrived with Mea and her brother, Mikah. Berkeley and Dare are here with Drake, and the night is young and full of promise.

I sip my beer, feeling light as a fucking feather. Wrapping an arm behind Greta's chair, I scoot it closer to mine. She squeals in surprise, turning her legs so that her body is facing mine and her knees graze the side of my thigh. I glance down at where our legs are touching, a trail of heat sizzling through my black jeans.

"You want to tell me what happened today to put you in such a good mood?" she asks me coyly.

I smile, knowing the Jack in her Coke is making her bolder than usual. Her blushes are fewer and farther between tonight. I like that she's comfortable enough with me to relax in my presence. When I saw her order her Jack and Coke, I decided right there that I'd only be having two beers tonight. I want to be the one to make sure she gets home safely.

"Yeah...actually, you're not gonna believe this. Your dad kind of offered me a spot on his team today."

Her mouth falls open. I expect to see joy and excitement in her eyes, and she eventually does shoot me a quick smile. But before it, there's a shadow that crosses her expression. It immediately sends my radar into overdrive trying to figure out what caused her hesitation.

"That's...wonderful. You showed a lot of initiative today when you looked at that map. Stuff like that really impresses my dad. Are you...going to take it?"

She looks away, toward the next table where a bunch of college-aged patrons are getting loud and rowdy.

"Hey." I use my finger to ease her face back toward mine. "Do you have a problem with me working at Night Eagle?"

I drop my voice a little, wanting our conversation to be between her and me.

She shakes her head firmly. "No, Grisham. I don't. I want you to be happy, and this obviously makes you very happy." She offers me a brave smile.

Confusion is making my brain feel foggy. *What am I missing?* "Then why don't you sound happy?"

She tries to look away again, but I follow her gaze with my head, staying right in front of her. "Tell me."

She sighs. "It's just...I like where this is going, you know? You and me...it's kind of awesome. And things with my dad have always been strained, and it's because..." She trails off. Understanding clicks into place for me, like a puzzle I worked hours to solve.

"Because of his job. First the military, and then Night Eagle. And you're worried that if I start working there..."

She shakes her head ruefully. "I realize I'm being ridiculous. This is an amazing opportunity for you and of course you're going to take it, Grisham."

Suddenly, I pull her out of her chair and into my lap, not caring how many of our friends are sitting there to watch. I focus on her and her only as she stares uncertainly into my eyes. "Listen to me, all right? You and me getting to know each other is really fucking important to me right now. I'm excited about the job, sure. But don't think for a minute that my work will come before the people in my life. It won't happen. Especially if I'm lucky enough to have someone like you by my side. Okay?"

She nods, relief washing over her face. "Okay. We don't have to say any more about it."

"No, we have to say one more thing about it. Me taking a job at Night Eagle means we work at the same place. Did you realize that?"

She slowly shakes her head. "No...but now that you mention it..."

I smile, mischief brewing inside as I trace the line of her slender jaw with my index finger. "It means that I'll get to see more of you. And that we might make good use of that break room in the back."

She giggles, squirming on my lap. My cock is in instant beast mode, wanting to make sure she knows it's there. "I like the sound of that, Abbot."

"Stop moving like that, angel," I whisper darkly in her ear. "You're gonna make it really fucking hard for me to stand up."

She stills. "Sorry." Her telltale blush moves across her cheeks and flushes her chest, and *damn* I want to bury my head between her breasts and feel her heat. My hand slips up her bare thigh. Her skin is burning under my touch.

Someone at the table clears their throat. Greta and I both look up, having forgotten anyone else was with us.

"So, this is happening," says Berkeley amid a burst of giggles. She moves her hand between Greta and me, gesturing. "Should the rest of us, um...leave?"

Beside her Mea is grinning widely. The guys at the table are all trying to pretend they see and hear nothing, which I appreciate. Until Shaw leans over to tell me in a stage whisper: "I took a picture with my phone. Planning to send it anonymously to the Boss Man."

I lean back over. "If you do that, you bastard, I will make you pay. Repeatedly."

He holds his hands up in mock surrender. "Just jokes, Ghost."

I glare at him in response.

Greta buries her head in the crook of my shoulder and my

neck, embarrassed. All I want to do is get her out of here. The previous night with her is replaying over and over again in my head, mocking me.

I can't believe I didn't make love to her sweet ass when I had her in my bed. I could fix that tonight...

I lean into her, inhaling her sweet floral scent and feeling her soft skin against my lips. "I want to go pay our tabs. And then I want to take you home."

She pulls back slightly. "To your place?"

I nod slowly, meeting her gaze and feeling myself molding into her hands like putty. There's a real chance I could end up completely gone for this girl. It's a chance I'm willing to take because the way I feel when I'm with her is a high I never achieved, even when jumping out of a helicopter.

"Yeah, Grits. To my place."

She smiles, a slow curling of her lips that's somehow both shy and sexy at the same time. I take it as a sign she's ready to leave with me, and I start to vacate my chair and head for the bar, just as the first thumping strains of Luke Bryan's "Country Girl" sounds from the stage at the front of the room. The band throws themselves into the song, and there's a mass upheaval as girls all around me leap from their seats.

Including Berkeley and Mea. Mea places a vise grip around Greta's arm, pulling her behind them to the dance floor. Greta throws me one last longing glance before she disappears into the crowd.

I throw a look around the table. The guys are grinning, and Dare is shaking with laughter.

At the sight of my scowl, he shrugs. "I've been there, dude.

But girls and that song...you can't fight it. She'll be back soon."

I sigh, heaving myself up from the table. I'm going to go pay Greta and my tabs, so that we'll be ready to go when she's done shaking her ass.

Standing at the bar, I get a glimpse of her through the crowd. She's standing up near the front with Berkeley and Mea, but I barely see the other two. Greta is dancing, shaking it for all she's worth, her long, dark hair flying all around her. She's got moves, her lush body rippling and twisting to the beat. I watch, frozen in place, as she dances.

Then the crowd shifts again, and I lose sight of her. Shaking my head dumbly, I turn to flag down a bartender.

Yeah. I could definitely be gone for this girl.

When the song finally ends, I'm back at the table, waiting for Greta. The girls return well into the next song. Berkeley takes a seat in Dare's lap and Mea plops down in her seat, pristinely sipping her drink like she hadn't just been showing a bar full of dudes exactly what her hips are capable of.

"Where's Greta?" I ask, glancing the way they'd just come.

Berkeley glances around. "Wait. Where *is* Greta, Mea?"

Mea gives me a pointed grin. "Outside. Said she was gonna wait for you by the door because she needed some air."

I shove my chair backward and barely glance back as I head out. "That's my cue. See you guys later."

There's chuckling behind me as I go, but I don't look back to see who it is. I book it for the bar's entrance instead.

Outside, the cool sea breeze hits my face and I see why Greta wanted to get out into it after the way she'd been moving inside. She must be hot and sweaty, a thought that only makes me want to get to her faster. She's not standing by the front door, though. So I glance both ways outside before walking through the parking lot toward where I'd parked my Jeep. Anticipation at having her all wrapped up in my arms makes me move faster than I normally would.

But when I arrive at the Jeep, Greta's not there, either. A sudden jolt of panic swirls through me. Thoughts of what happens to girls who are left alone at bars flash through my head, and I'm running back toward the bar.

And stop short when I see Greta standing there, just outside the door.

She smiles. "There you are. I stopped by the table on my way back from the bathroom, but they said you were already outside waiting for me. Ready to go?"

My heart still slamming a rapid beat against the wall of my chest, I grip her shoulders. "You're okay?"

Her eyes widen. "Yeah...why?"

My breathing is too fast and I can't shake the fear. The fear that something bad is going to happen to someone I care about on my watch. My vision is blurry; I can't straighten the jagged line of my thoughts. Not knowing where she was, worrying that something had gone horribly wrong while she was so close...just the very thought tears me open inside.

Soft, warm hands cup my face. Greta's voice breaks through the darkness I never want her to see. I blink, focusing on her angel face.

"Breathe, Grisham. Just breathe." Her voice is nothing but a soft brush across my face. "I'm right here. I'm okay."

Blue, blue eyes. Long, raven hair. Small, perky nose.

Sunshine.

Sunshine.

Sunshine.

Letting out a pent-up sigh, I lean my forehead against hers and take a deep, shaky breath.

We stand for a moment like that, her standing in the shadow of my darkness and me standing on the edge of her light. Finally, her hands begin to stroke my face gently. "Everything okay now? Do you want to go?"

I wrap her in my arms. God, I don't want her to see this side of me. Wanted to keep her away from it at all costs. But damn if she doesn't have the ability to take it away with everything in her that's sunny and light. "Yeah, Grits. I'm more than ready to get out of here."

She shivers, and I pull her in tighter, thinking she must be chilly. The air is a little cooler than normal for Carolina in September. "Let's go."

16

Greta

You still haven't slept with him?" Mea and Berkeley stare at me in open shock.

The beginning of October has come and gone, and Grisham and I are following our plan to get to know each other and take things slow.

"But that night a few weeks ago when we all went out for drinks...you two were so hot and heavy at the table. I was sure he was taking you home to..." Berkeley trails off, tact making her end her sentence there.

The same tact hasn't yet gotten ahold of Mea, though.

"Bang your back out," she finishes matter-of-factly.

"Mea!" I scold her, choking on my Sprite. "Bad form."

She shakes her head, her dark brown curls bouncing everywhere. "I disagree. I tell it like it is, and I'll never apologize, my friend."

"We know," Berkeley and I say, our voices merging into a simultaneous chorus before bursting into laughter.

My friends and I have decided to take a girls-only spa day. We're sitting on the rooftop deck of an upscale spa in Wrightsville Beach, under the bright October sun, hot towels wrapped around our necks and clothed in white, fluffy spa robes. Our toes are bare, and each of us holds a glass of champagne.

I can't afford to take days like this with my girlfriends on a regular basis. Actually, I can't remember the last time I had an actual spa day. But Mea convinced us to splurge, claiming YOLO as her lifelong motto.

"No, we haven't. It's not like we didn't want to, especially that night. He's coming from a really messed-up place, and so am I. Especially now that he's working for my dad. I can't stop thinking that at some point, the other shoe is going to drop and he's going to choose the job over me. Like my dad always did."

"But you get to work with your dad now," Berkeley pointed out. "And Grisham is showing you how much he wants to be with you. I mean, I've known him for a long time, and there've been girls. But it's never been like this."

Her words send glowing pleasure radiating through me, but something still holds me back from giving myself over completely to Grisham. Whenever we're together, I can sense him holding back from me as well, and I'm not sure what he doesn't want me to see.

"I can't believe that the entire time our families have known each other, his father was such a monster behind closed doors." A shudder goes through Berkeley. "My heart goes out to his mom. How is she, by the way?"

"She's coping. She's going through therapy, and Grisham goes to Jacksonville so he can go with her sometimes. I think it's helping them both."

Berkeley nods, sympathy written all over her face. "Good."

Mea stretches out, her perfectly bronzed body not needing an ounce of color from the sun. Berkeley and I stare at her with envy.

"I hate you, Mea," I scowl, holding out one alabaster leg. "I really, really hate you."

"How's the training going, Greta?" asks Mea with interest. Mea has been asking me repeatedly to teach her some of what I'm learning, but whenever I try, her peaceful yoga-loving approach gets in the way of her learning how to kick serious ass.

"It's kind of awesome," I admit. "I didn't expect for it to be so...normal for me, you know? Grisham says I'm a natural." I can't help boasting about Grisham's praise.

Every time we get together for a sparring session, I get better and better at the MMA style. I have more than a handful of moves under my belt now that I can execute flawlessly, and the time I spend training is making me more toned and limber than I've ever been.

"I'm jealous," mutters Berkeley. "I want to look as lithe and muscly as you. But every time Dare points out that he's willing to teach me, too, I just end up eating a doughnut."

We all burst out laughing. Berkeley's figure is lush and curvy. There are no complaints from men in that department. If it weren't for Dare, she'd be beating them off with a stick.

My phone buzzes with a text, and when I pick it up I gasp at the time. "Shit! I have to go, you guys. Today is the day Grisham gets back on his board. He wants me to be there."

Mea snorts. "So you basically just did all this spa work for nothing, because you're about to get all sandy in the ocean."

Berkeley smiles. "Tell Grish I'm cheering for him!"

I call over my shoulder as I leave my chair and head for the exit to get changed. "I will. Love you girls!"

Then I haul ass to get myself to Grisham's favorite surfing spot.

It's one of my favorite times of the year to surf, because by October all of the tourists are gone. Not that many of them find our spot anyway, but a few trickle in during the summers. Our spot is mostly reserved for surfers who live for it, just like Grisham and I both do.

He's sitting on the beach, knees drawn up to his chest and his bright blue surfboard lying beside him. My steps stutter at the sight of him, and for a moment I just stand and take him in.

He hasn't yet pulled up his wet suit, so his broad, muscled back is exposed and tanned in the autumn sun. His back is riddled with scars, similar to his chest and abdomen, but it's clear of ink. When he moves, I can see the wiry muscles bend and shift under his skin, and the sight is amazing.

He's amazing.

His dark blond hair is messy as usual, and the sunlight glints off of him like a Greek god here on earth. I take a deep breath and continue walking until I'm standing right beside him.

"Where are the guys?" I ask, bending down to kiss his cheek and hitting the sand beside him.

He glances at me, his face warm and inviting as he leans in to press his lips against mine. He tastes minty and fresh. "It's just me and you today, Grits."

I pull back in surprise. "Really? You don't want Lawson and Ben here, too?"

He shakes his head slowly, holding my gaze hostage in his own. "Just you. That okay?"

I nod, feeling my heart pick up speed as I stare right back. I thought this would be an event he'd want to share with his friends, but he only wants it to be him and me. It dawns on me that this will be one of the defining moments of Grisham's life, and I'm the one he wants to share it with. It feels big for us.

Monumental.

I tug on his wet suit and indicate his board. "I'm ready when you are."

He kisses me one more time, his lips hard and warm and sweet, before pulling back and standing up. I watch as he pulls his black wet suit into place on his torso, and I stand and gather my board in my hands.

With a wordless signal between us, we jog toward the ocean.

The spray is shockingly cool as we enter the water and splash in until we're waist deep. Then we're on our bellies on our boards and paddling out into deep water.

"You okay?" I raise my voice so he can hear me over the sound of the ocean. He looks at me and smiles, letting me know he's just fine.

When we're deep enough so that the waves are just swells rising and falling beneath us and the sound of them crashing against the shore is distant, we stop paddling and straddle our boards.

Waiting.

"How does this feel?" I ask Grisham, curious about how he's handling his first time on a surfboard in months.

"It feels...right," he admits. His expression is relaxed, calmer than I've seen it when he's not in the water. He truly loves the ocean and being on his board; it's written all over his face. He's completely lit up. "I'm glad I waited...to do this with you."

I beam at him, reaching out to grab his hand. He squeezes mine tightly before letting go. "Me, too."

We both spot it at the same time. It's the perfect A-Frame wave, rolling toward us at a clip. Out of the corner of my eye, I see Grisham's biceps flexing as he readies himself to paddle.

The wave approaches, and just before it's upon us, we begin paddling as fast as we can toward shore. Just as my board begins to rise beneath me, I brace my hands against it and hop to my feet, gathering my balance. I can see Grisham doing the same a few feet away, and then we're both up and standing as we ride the center of the wave toward the shore.

I can hear his roar of triumph, and as I glance at him, he's pumping a fist into the air. He's so breathtaking that I almost lose my concentration, turning back quickly to focus on the impending shoreline.

The wave breaks perfectly and we both hop off our boards onto the sand. Tears are streaming down my face because not only did Grisham surf again, he rode the *hell* out of that wave.

He collides into me, grabbing me in his arms and thrusting

me into the air above him. The happiness on his face is complete, and it steals my breath.

"You did it!" I shout, happiness rolling off of me in forceful waves.

"Yeah." He's breathless as he lowers me back down to stand in front of him, and then his lips are on mine. He kiss me hard and long, and I'm nearly dizzy when he finally pulls away.

"Thank you," he murmurs against my lips. "Thank you for being here with me for this."

"You're back, baby. Like, all the way back."

He leans his forehead against mine. "Say that again."

I wrinkle my nose in confusion. "You're back?"

Shaking his head slowly, his eyes lock on mine and his lips curl into a sexy smile. "You called me baby. I liked it. I want to hear it again."

I gasp as his hands slide up my sides, grazing my breasts lightly. "Okay, baby. Do you want to go again?"

He jerks me to him. "Maybe one more time."

Planting a hard kiss on his lips, I pull away and grab my board. "Head start!"

Then I take off, giggling and running into the sea with Grisham chasing right behind me.

The stinging hot needles of Grisham's shower feel heavenly as they wash the sand and salt off of my body. I smile to myself as I run my hands through my wet hair, remembering how amazing the day was. I'm also remembering how hot Grisham is on a surfboard. He's such a natural out there, dipping low on his board when he needs to and riding each wave in effortlessly. He never once lost a wave.

It was an incredible day.

And now that same hot, sexy guy is waiting for me somewhere in his house while I shower. I can't keep the smile off my face.

Suddenly, a warm hand slides around my waist until it rests on my stomach. I gasp as Grisham yanks me back against the hard planes of his wet body, and one of my arms immediately goes up to wrap around the back of his neck.

"You're fucking beautiful," he groans into my ear. I can feel it; he's hard and ready for me, and I turn in his arms to face him.

I'm *so* not prepared for the sight of Grisham fully naked in the shower with me.

My eyes roam greedily from his broad, tattooed shoulders to the muscled wall of his chest. Then they drift down to the rack of abdominal muscles that could and should definitely be in a magazine. A trail of dark hair leads down to the impressive length of his cock, and a whimper escapes me. I pull my eyes away to travel down his thick thighs and cantaloupe-size calf, before my gaze meanders lazily up his body once more. He's wearing his prosthesis, which makes me wonder idly if he always showers with it on.

And when I meet his gaze, I'm instantly wet and ready for him, more so than I've ever been before. Because the sight of a man that looks like Grisham devouring every inch of me in return is beyond hot.

"I'm done waiting," he grinds out, just before his lips collide with mine.

17

Grisham

Stinging nettles of hot water hit my back as I spin Greta around and press her against the shower wall. But the water is ice-cold compared to the raw heat of her kiss. A million thoughts run through my head as my hands blaze a trail down her bare sides, but short of the bathroom falling down around us or her pushing me away, nothing is going to stop me from seeing this through.

Surfing with her today just created too many feelings for me to contain inside me any longer. She's been through so much with me in a short time, I feel like every time I'm with her I'm going to explode. She's pulled me with her over hot coals to the other side of the darkness; she's opened me up from the inside out, and she's quickly becoming an addiction I don't want to quit.

I want her so bad I can't think about anything else.

I tease her lips with my tongue and she opens up for me. Placing my hands under her thighs, I hoist her up and she doesn't waste time wrapping her legs around my waist. She's exactly where I want her and her mouth is warm and wet where our tongues play together.

My hips pinned against hers hold her up against the wall while one of my hands delves into her hair and the other slides up her flat belly to cup her breast. She's a handful, the perfect size, and I squeeze gently while she breaks away from my mouth and cries out.

I watch her face, fascinated, because this is a side of Greta I haven't seen since the night in my kitchen when I stopped things before they went too far.

Tonight, there's no stopping this.

My thumb flicks the hardening tip of her breast, and her eyes close.

I can't wait anymore to have some part of her in my mouth, so I drop my head and lick a circle around her nipple before closing my teeth on the pebbled flesh.

"God, Grisham," she moans. "Yes."

"Yes?" I repeat, glancing up at her. "You're telling me yes tonight?"

"I'm telling you yes every night," she hisses as my mouth closes around her nipple and sucks. "Every single night."

I hum against her skin, and her hands tighten painfully in my hair. But the pain is pure pleasure.

I know I don't have long before the shower water runs cold, so I gently place her back onto her feet and pull away slightly. I allow both hands to cup her full breasts as I stare down into her eyes, playing, teasing.

"You're so fucking sweet," I tell her. "I've wanted to taste you since that night in my kitchen."

She catches one side of her bottom lip between her teeth as I drop to my knees in front of her. I take a few seconds to just take in the sight of her. Water from the shower drips over her stomach, down past a thin line of hair leading to the most beautiful sight I've ever seen. She shifts her weight, and I glance up at her and grin.

Impatient, Grits?

Then I use my hands to part her legs as I plant a kiss to each inner thigh. Still just needing to watch, my finger slides into her folds and finds her hot little clit, drawing a slow circle around her. Her entire body shivers, and I tighten my grip on her thigh to steady her.

"Please, Grisham," she whimpers.

I can barely hear her voice over the trickle of water around us, but I know what she wants. Slowly, I dip my tongue into the very center of her and take a lick.

She moans, her hips thrusting forward to meet my tongue, and oh *fuck*, it's sexy as hell to watch. Hearing her and seeing her receive pleasure, there's nothing in this world like it. It's like when she's just going about her day, she's this sweet and innocent thing. But when she's here with me like this, she's responsive and sexy and I'm the only one who gets to see it.

It's going to become my goddamn drug.

I ease one finger inside her and groan when I realize how wet she is, how free flowing she is, all because of me, my touch. It sends a painful jolt of pleasure through my already throbbing cock, and I tighten my muscles in order to remain on my knees at her feet.

"That's it, angel," I murmur as she shudders. "Let it go."

I swipe at her with my tongue again and again, pumping my finger inside her while she moans and writhes, and I think I'm literally getting high off of everything that is Greta right now. I can't get enough. She's sweeter than my imagination gave her credit for.

She tugs my hair extra hard as she cries out, and I suck her clit into my mouth and give it one last, hard suck. I raise both of my hands to grip her legs hard, holding her in place as she falls apart above me. When my name falls from her lips again I can't take it anymore.

I thrust open the shower door and pull a wobbly Greta out behind me. I wrap her in a towel and sweep her into my arms, carrying her from the steamy bathroom into the much cooler bedroom. As I set her down on the bed, her eyes are half-closed and there's a sated smile on her face. Her wet hair spreads across the pillows, and her skin is flushed pink. Whether it's from what just happened in the bathroom or from the steam, I'm not sure. I only know the effect is absolutely beautiful.

I wonder if she thinks I'm done with her yet.

Because this night is just getting started.

18

Greta

It's difficult for me to think straight right now, but I'm pretty sure Grisham should have an award stowed away somewhere labeled "Orgasm-Giving Champion." The things he did to me in that shower, with his tongue...I'm going to remember it every single time I'm in that room.

With ridiculous pleasure.

When I feel him sliding on top of me, I open my eyes, completely alert again. He hovers above me, supporting himself on his arms in a push-up position as he stares down at me. I'm trying to figure out the expression in his dark green eyes, but I can't quite place it.

Awe? Adoration?

Imagining that he could feel either one of those things for me is insane. But then he reaches and brushes my cheek with the back of his knuckles. The motion is so sweet, so tender, that an instant lump forms in my throat.

"Do you have any idea how fucking beautiful you are?" he whispers.

I can feel his erection prodding me, and I know he's ready to give himself over to me tonight. Physically. But is he ready to give himself to me in all the ways I want him?

I know it doesn't matter. I'm going to make love to Grisham tonight. I'm going to let him have me in any and every way he wants me, because I'm tired of waiting, too. I've wanted him since the second I laid eyes on him, and the fact that he wants me, too, makes risking my heart something I have to do.

I reach down, find his shaft hard and ready, and grip him tightly in my hand. He hisses, air escaping through his clenched teeth.

"Shit." He gasps.

I watch him, his expression holding me captive as I slowly stroke him. His biceps are straining, the muscles bulging. I watch his eyes darken, and another curse falls from his lips when the pad of my thumb strokes the smooth head of his cock.

Biting my lip, I say what I'm thinking and to hell with the consequences. "I want you inside of me, Grisham. Right now."

"Fuck, girl. You're gonna kill me."

I smile to myself as he reaches over me and pulls open his bedside drawer. He pulls out a row of foil packets and tears one away from the rest with his teeth. I grab it from his mouth, ripping it open as we hold each other's stare. Not looking away from him, I reach between us and roll the condom on over him. Then I position him at my entrance.

Grisham hitches one of my legs up behind my knee, pushing my thigh into my chest. I feel the stretch in my body at the same time I feel the stretch of him filling me up as he pushes inside me with one firm thrust.

My eyes flutter closed and I moan, the feeling of having Grisham inside me exquisite and wonderful. He begins to move, and my body is awash in sensations *everywhere.* I feel it where we're connected; I feel it where his hand grips the back of my raised thigh. I feel it when he drops down and his chest pushes me into the bed, his forehead connecting with mine. I feel it where his knee beside mine digs into the bed, supporting his steady movements.

My hips rock with him, meeting him thrust for thrust, and a chorus of whimpers echoes around the room. When I realize that I'm the one making those sounds, I'm not even embarrassed. Being with Grisham like this has completely changed everything for me. I'm open to him, laid bare, and I don't give two shits.

I'm his.

Almost as if he can read my thoughts, he whispers, his lips brushing mine: "You're mine, Grits."

I simply answer with the truth. "I'm yours."

A possessive growl leaves him, and he thrusts harder, faster, which amps my sensations up to a dangerous level. Without any warning at all, I'm climbing high again, and my nails rake down his back. I'm falling over the edge with an intensity that scares me but that I know is right.

Grisham turns his head, whispering in my ear as his hips continue to piston into mine. "Listen to me, Grits. Making you come has just become the single most important goal in my life. I want another one."

He slows down his rhythm, and our eyes both drift to the place where his flesh slides slowly in and out of mine. It's like a fantasy for me, watching a guy this hot watch me. And just like that, my intensity is ratcheting up again. My hands fly to the sheet, gathering up handfuls and squeezing. Grisham sits back, not allowing our bodies to disconnect, and reaches between us. As I feel his finger find my clit, stroking me once, twice, three times, I fly to pieces again right in front of him.

This time, I think a piece of my soul came apart with me.

Then Grisham leans forward again, and he's thrusting into me with reckless abandon. When his breath comes fast and hard, I know he's almost there. I allow my nails to drift up over his perfect ass, up the sides of him, and over his chest, and he trembles above me.

"Oh, my God," he rasps as he comes, his body jerking wildly for a second before he collapses on top of me.

We lie there for minutes or maybe an hour, just breathing each other in. When Grisham rolls over, I miss him immediately, feeling cold and lonely. But he doesn't go far, merely removing the condom and throwing it in the trash can in the bathroom before walking back to the bed and climbing in beside me. He folds his arms around me, bringing my body to rest on top of his.

My hair creates a veil over us as we stare into each other's eyes.

"That was..." I trail off.

"Something we're going to repeat later," he finishes with a slow and sexy grin.

I nod my head, a giggle escaping me. "Yeah."

We lay silently, he on his back, cradling me into his side. I allow my fingers to trail lazy figure eights along his shoulders, chest, abdomen. Marveling at how he's made of steel.

"I really like these," I admit, tracing the lines of his colorful ink.

"Yeah?" he murmurs, glancing down at me. "You don't have any, though."

I shake my head, still eyeing him. "I've always thought about it, but never could decide on a design I wanted on my body forever. Tell me about yours?"

He's quiet for a moment, and my hand stills. I begin to wonder if maybe he doesn't want to discuss his tats.

"This one," he says softly, pointing to the right side of his chest, "is a knight with his steed. It represents all the times I needed to be that for my mom, and that if I ever had the chance I would be."

My heart swells. "You've done that."

He nods slowly, tracing the thick, black, tribal markings in between the large, colorful images. "I hope so."

He points to the opposite side of his chest. "This anchor, obviously, is for the navy. I thought the rope tied around it just made it look even more awesome. I thought I'd be tied to the navy for life. I was wrong."

His voice gets lower, fuller of unshed emotion, and I brush my hand softly over the anchor. His muscles jump under my touch.

"What about this one?" I run my fingers over the reptilian scales covering the tops of both arms. They're green and gold, and blue and red, the colors shifting and blending perfectly together. "They're so awesome."

"These signify me shedding my skin." His voice is wry, one eyebrow quirking upward. "They were the first tattoos I got, when I chose to go my own way. After everything that happened with Berkeley, and my dad...I broke free from him for the first time in my life. I was finally doing what I wanted to do." He chuckles lightly. "I knew it would piss him off. That just made it sweeter."

I kiss the scales, and then I allow my lips to trail across his chest. My tongue darts out to lick first one nipple, and then the other. Grisham sucks in a breath, his hand tightening on my hip where it lay.

I glance up at him. "I think I'm ready for you to make good on that promise."

I close my teeth around his skin and he hisses.

"Fuck."

I kiss the sore spot and trail my tongue over it to soothe the sting.

"What promise?" He grinds out the words, all of his muscles going taut.

"The one you made about promising to make me feel like that again."

His lips tip up in a smirk. "Oh, that promise."

Those are the last words he says before he pushes himself up and hovers above me. His eyes sear me as he lets them travel slowly over my body.

"I'll make good on that one as many times as you want."

19

Grisham

Just before the sun was up this morning, I was awake, just like normal. Something that wasn't normal was the fact that a naked Greta lay next to me, tangled in my charcoal-gray sheets. I couldn't help what happened next, rolling her over onto her back and running my hands and my tongue over every inch of her gorgeous body.

The memory of it causes a smile to cross my face as I walk into work this morning at the base.

Knowing that my team will be deploying without me at the first of next year is still rough, but I'm dealing with it much better, now that Jacob has decided to hire me as part of the team at Night Eagle.

As the end of my naval career draws closer, I'm putting less time in at the base. I usually just go in for the mornings, and then I stop at Night Eagle after lunch to consult on assignments there.

Today goes exactly this way. After I grab a quick sandwich at a deli following four hours working at the base, I pull into the Night Eagle parking lot and lock the Jeep. The first face that greets me when I walk in the door is Greta's, and I'm pulled right back into the previous night spent holding her in my arms. My body reacts to the mere sight of her, and a big, goofy grin spreads across my face.

She looks up from the desk, smiling when she sees me, too. I walk straight to her desk, lean over the front of it, and brush my lips across hers.

When she pulls away, her face is flushed and her eyes shine up at me. "Hey, there."

Her voice is a little breathless, which I like. It means I affect her the same way she affects me, and it's nice not to feel alone in this whole crazy thing that's happening between us. I can no longer deny or refute the fact that it's happening.

And even though the thought of my darkness swallowing up her light scares the shit out of me, I'm beginning to think her sunshine may be the only thing lighting my way.

And after last night, I damn sure want to make certain it's happening with me and only me.

Propping a hip on the side of her desk, I lean toward her.

"I haven't been able to get you outta my head this morning, Grits."

A pretty pink tinge spreads across her cheeks, and she glances up at me through her long, black lashes. "Me, too. Last night...and this morning...were incredible."

I nod. "It was that. So, this"—I gesture between the two of us—"it's happening. And I want it to be happening on repeat. And only between the two of us."

A slow smile curls her lips upward. "Are you saying you want to make this official, Abbot?"

I only have to lean forward another inch to recapture her mouth. I let her know with my kiss that hell yes, I want to make this official.

When I pull away, she nods. "Okay, then. We're doing this."

Elation fills me up like a helium balloon. "Yeah, girl. We're doing this."

A throat clears behind me, and when I turn, Kyle is standing next to the office door. He looks uncomfortable, clearly not having meant to walk in on such an intimate moment.

"Oh, hey, man," I greet him, rising from Greta's desk. "I was just heading in to see if Jacob needs me for anything today."

Kyle nods, continuing his path toward the desk. As we pass each other, he doesn't glance at me. I shrug, throwing a wink back at Greta before closing myself inside Jacob's office.

He's alone in the room, poring over some documents at his desk. But he looks up when I come in, and nods briskly at me. It's rare for Jacob Owen to smile, so a nod is all I expect in greeting.

"Afternoon, son," he says gruffly.

"Good afternoon, sir. Just checking in with you to see if you need me today. Where're the guys?"

Jacob points toward the brown leather couch, indicating that I take a seat. I do so, facing the row of windows overlooking the ocean while he sits opposite me.

"Teague is delivering a threat assessment system we developed for the state police. Should be a one-day job. Conners and Shaw are on a security detail over in Raleigh for the remainder of the week. They'll be back Saturday for the event."

I rack my brain, certain I haven't been told about an event. "What event would that be?"

Jacob's lips twist in what could be a smile, although it could also be a grimace. The dude's face just doesn't give much away. He's super hard to read. "That's what I wanted to talk to you about today, Abbot. Do you own a nice suit?"

I nod solemnly. I own several nice suits. But what...

"Yes, sir."

He nods. "Good. On Saturday, we're having an event for our current and potential clients. All of our local clients are expected, and several of our long-distance clients will likely be flying in. There will be shitloads of possible future clients, and we're putting our best foot forward on this. Greta's a huge part of the details, but Kyle has planned the whole thing from the ground up. We do these a few times a year. I fucking hate them. But I know the ass-kissing has to be done."

I try to rein in my grin. Picturing Jacob Owen kissing anyone's ass is a stretch. But he runs a successful firm here, and I know he knows exactly what he's doing.

"And you want me to attend?"

Now Jacob throws me a rare smirk. "Shouldn't you already be attending? I don't expect Greta plans on going alone."

Okay, so the man's not blind. Shit, was I supposed to ask his permission to date his daughter or something?

Clearing my throat uncomfortably, I look him in the eye. "Sir..."

He waves a hand dismissively. "Don't, Abbot. My daughter's a grown-up. She'd kick my ass from here to kingdom come if she thought I was interfering. But if you ever hurt her..." He lets the sentence die, but I catch his meaning in its entirety.

"I understand, sir. I would never hurt her."

He nods, like that's enough for him. "I know you're not starting full-time at NE until January, but I'd like to introduce you as the newest member of the team, get clients used to seeing your face."

"Wow. Yeah...okay. I'll be there."

"With a suit on," he reminds me.

"With a suit on."

Kyle opens the office door then. Closing it behind him, he heads over to his desk and sits down.

"That's it for today, Abbot. Tomorrow you can work with Teague on drawing up a master security plan for Jettison Labs' corporate offices. They're opening sometime next year, a new branch of their multinational here in Wilmington."

I stand. "I'll be there. Greta and I are going to train this afternoon, though. So I'll be around if you need anything."

He nods, already absorbed again in whatever task he was working on before I arrived. I exit his office, looking for Greta.

I find her in the lounge. Sneaking up behind her, I wrap my arms around her waist and move her long braid to one side, revealing the slender perfection of her neck.

I put my lips there, sucking lightly as she tenses under my hands. Then she immediately relaxes.

"Hey," I murmur. "How'd you know it was me? I could be some stranger, kissing on your neck. You just relaxed right into me."

She sighs, her eyes closing. "I knew it was you."

"How?" Curiosity gets the best of me, and I lift my head to look at her.

Her eyes remain closed. "Your smell. The feel of your hands. The way your lips mold to my skin. All distinctly Grisham."

Pleasure rockets through me, accumulating in my chest. I pull her closer, allowing my hands to slide down the skirt she's wearing and pull up the material of her skirt just a little bit. My palms rest on her thighs. Her perfectly shaped, supple thighs.

"Ah," I whisper. "So you always know when it's me?"

Her head falls back against my chest. "Always."

"Good." I bite her earlobe, and I'm not gentle. She moans, which causes my manhood to stand at attention. Her hips press back into me, and my fingers dig into her thighs.

Remembering where we are, I reluctantly release her, coming around to stand beside her. I grab a bottle of water out of the fridge. "You know your dad knows about us, right?"

She chokes, sputtering on the sip of coffee she'd just downed. I rub her back, smiling. "You okay?"

She nods, looking at me with an alarmed expression on her face. "Did he say something to you?"

I lean casually against the counter and sip my water. "Just that he'll kill me if I hurt you."

"Oh, my God."

Laughing, I kiss her cheek. She's fucking adorable. "It's to be expected."

"You're okay with him knowing?"

I hold her gaze. "I told you earlier, remember? We're doing this. For real."

She breathes an obvious sigh of relief. "Okay, then."

Tapping her lightly on the nose, I frown at her. "Are we doing something important this weekend?"

She gazes at me blankly.

"Isn't there an important client event you forgot to tell me about?"

She jumps. "Oh, yeah! You're coming, right?"

Putting my water down on the counter, I put my hands on her waist and pull her toward me. "Oh, I'm coming. With you as my date."

Her mouth tips up in a smile. "Okay."

I grab my water and smack her ass. She yelps, scowling at me. "Now, go get that cute ass in some sweatpants. We've got training to do."

"That's it. One, two, switch your feet. Knee up!" I grunt as her knee plants sharply into the pad at my midsection. With every training session she takes, she's growing more confident in her movements. She trusts her body more now than she did when we first started, throwing punches with smooth calculation. She never takes her eyes off her target, never leaves her face unprotected.

It's amazing.

She's amazing.

She's strong, and she's confident.

And she's my girl. Which is the most inspiring part of all.

Smirking, she pulls off her gloves and wipes at her forehead. "I did good, right? That hurt, didn't it?"

I shake my head at her, smiling. "Yeah, Grits. You did good. You didn't hurt me, though."

Quick as a flash, she brings her knee back up. But I'm quicker, catching her foot with one hand and letting the other wrap around her hips so she won't fall.

"Damn," she curses through clenched teeth. "I thought I had you."

I drop her leg and pull her in close until I can smell the heady mixture of flowers and sweat radiating from her skin. I nuzzle her neck, and she gasps. "I know you, Greta. So I anticipated what you were going to do. An attacker won't be so lucky. You're capable of kicking some serious ass. I swear."

She winds her arms around my neck. In her tight, hot-pink pants and the black sports bra she's wearing, I can feel every curve in her body molding to every flat plane of mine. Fire races through my veins, and I wish like hell we weren't at Night Eagle where anyone could walk in on us at any moment.

I need her to myself.

"Come over tonight?" I ask, my voice like the rough slide of sandpaper.

"Count on it," she says, just before her mouth sears to mine.

20

Greta

It's not until later that week that I think about the roses and the person who sent them.

I usually leave my apartment in Lone Sands in order to drive into Wilmington around eight. Today, however, is a day off of school for my sisters. My mom still has to go into work, so I used the convenience of working for my dad to ask off. Of course he conceded, telling me to kiss my sisters and my mother for him.

Mea is never up this early, since she doesn't teach her first yoga class until eleven. The apartment is quiet as I toast my bagel, add some goat cheese, and pour my coffee. When there's a soft rap at the front door, I look up in surprise.

"Who the heck..." My bare feet pad across the living room to the front door. Pulling it open, I look out onto the landing. But it's empty.

I poke my head out, looking left and right, before I step out onto our mat. I almost trip over the pristine white box sitting on the ground.

I frown as I bend to pick up the box.

Where did this come from?

Taking one last glance around the landing, noting that the other three apartments on my floor are quiet, I back into my apartment and close the door behind me. I turn the box over and over in my hands, studying it. It's plain and white, and could be a bakery box. It seems like it could hold a small cake. And the contents match the weight of a bakery treat.

Taking the mystery box over to the counter at the breakfast bar, I put it down and lift the lid. There's a note sitting on top of the box's contents. I can't see what else the package contains, because it's wrapped up in brown packing paper.

Picking up the typed note, my lips move as I read it to myself.

GO SURFING WITH ME?

Immediately thinking of Grisham, I smile and tug the thing inside the box out into my hands. Taking off the brown wrapping, I see a beautiful pale-pink surfboard made of a heavy blown glass.

Turning it around in my hands, I see a giant crack in the center of the board. When I turn it back over, the two pieces fall apart in my hands.

"Aww," I murmur mournfully. "It's broken." A punch of sadness hits me.

I wrap both pieces back in the paper and place them in the box. The white cube slides on the bar, knocking the note onto the floor. When I pick it up, I read the words I hadn't previously seen on the back side.

STOP SURFING WITH HIM.

My blood chills. The fingers holding the note stiffen, and the white paper flutters back to the floor. Staring at it, I take a step back and then another. I know the note can't hurt me, but whoever sent this to me is a different story. I hold my hands out in front of me and see that they're shaking.

And then I get pissed.

Why am I letting a stupid box with a broken gift scare me?

The person who sends these gifts is too much of a coward to hurt me, clearly. I could go and make a complaint at the police station, but there's no point. The words in the note aren't written as a threat.

For as long as I can remember, I've been scared of the things I can't see. I was scared of the bad people in faraway places who could hurt my father while he was working, and cause him not to come home to us. I was scared of the disagreements and distance that tore my parents' marriage apart. I was scared when my sister was diagnosed with CF, that the next germ she got could kill her and there would be nothing I could do to stop it. Fear is a living, breathing dragon that breathes fire into your soul and paralyzes you until you curl into a ball and stop fighting.

But now I'm in control of my own situations, and I can make the decisions. It's time to stop being afraid and learn to empower myself. I don't have to be scared of some secret admirer I can't even see.

I toss the note in the box. And then I throw the entire thing into the trash can. Feeling a little bit better, I head to my bedroom to finish getting dressed. I'll eat my bagel and drink my coffee in the car on the way to my mom's house.

And I decide not to talk about this gift with anyone. Talking about it, worrying about it, gives the sender power.

I refuse to empower any more unseen threats in my life.

"This is so good!" Gemma's voice is saturated in ecstasy as she swallows another bite of cheesecake. "Whose idea was this again?"

I finished chewing my bite of chocolate soufflé and grin. "Mine."

Gabi, always more reserved than her outgoing younger sister, smiles at me around her fork. "It was a great idea, Greta. Thanks for bringing us out for dessert tonight."

I squeeze her hand gently before pulling out my phone and checking the time. "I love spending time with you two. You know that. It's easy to think of fun things to do when your sisters are the coolest people on the planet."

Gemma snorts. Both of my sisters are younger, spitting images of my mother and me. My mom's side of the family must have really strong genes, because none of us received the light hair and brown eyes of my father. Nor did we receive his olive complexion. Gemma is currently sporting indigo streaks throughout her long, curly dark locks. Gabi wears her hair shorter, and it's thick and straight, like mine.

"Mom should be home soon. You two want to blow this joint?"

The girls nod, cleaning their dessert dishes with last bites before we all stand. Walking toward my car in the parking lot, I put my arm around Gabi and squeeze her close into my side.

"You're doing okay, right?"

She nods. "I'm okay, Greta. You worry too much. I've been dealing with CF since I was a little kid. I've got this."

Looking down at her, my heart grows a size, and tears sting my eyes. I don't let them fall. She does have this. She shouldn't have to, but she does. She's a tough cookie at sixteen years old, way older than her physical age shows.

I watch Gemma climb in the car, but squeal when Gabi pokes me in the rib.

"Hey. What was that for?"

"Something's different about you." She opens her car door and climbs into the backseat. I sit in the driver's seat and glance at her in the rearview mirror.

"What are you talking about?"

Gabi buckles her seat belt and then folds her arms across her chest. "I mean you're different. Happier. Is it the new job with Dad? Or is it a guy?" Her voice rises on the last word, a teasing lilt full of humor.

I narrow my eyes at her. "How did you...?"

"Oh, please. You're usually wound tighter than a two-dollar watch. But now you're all loosey-goosey and relaxed. What's up with you?" Gemma weighs in, agreeing with Gabi. Her arms flail around as she demonstrates exactly how I've been feeling lately. She resembles a limp spaghetti noodle.

Smiling, I glance at her where she sits in the passenger seat. "Well...there might be a guy."

Both girls squeal and clap their hands. "Tell us the sitch."

I bite my bottom lip to keep from laughing as I ease my car out of the dessert bar parking lot and head toward my mom's home. "The *sitch* is that I became reacquainted with a guy I met awhile back. And he's...complicated. But he's a really good guy. And I like him."

"How much do you like him?" asks Gabi in a hushed tone.

I think about Grisham. About his handsome face, his scarred and beautiful body, his loving and capable hands. Every single part of him flashes through my head, and every single picture is good.

"I like him a lot."

The girls are still giggling and teasing me when we pull back into Mom's driveway.

My dad has taken care of my mom and sisters' needs, even after the divorce. Secretly, I think he knows that the marriage didn't work out because of his messed-up priorities, and he's trying to compensate for it now. I've heard my mom tell him numerous times that she doesn't need anything extravagant. But he makes sure she has everything she could ever want.

I wish he'd just admit what I know to be true: he still loves her and misses the family he left behind.

The house is located in a gated beach community where all of the houses are large and modern. It's not a mansion, but it's a really nice home, and my mom and sisters are more than comfortable here.

"Hello?" I call as we walk in the front door. "Mom?"

She comes around the corner still wearing her blue hospital scrubs. "Hey, girls! Where have you guys been?"

Gemma breezes past my mom on her way to the stairs. She doesn't usually stay and talk to us long, because all of her technological devices are waiting for her in her room. "Dessert. I'm going upstairs."

"Of course you are." My mother sighs as she scoots over to accommodate Gemma's passing.

Gabi walks right up to her and puts her arms around her waist in a hug. "Hey, Mom. How was work today?"

My mother's weary eyes soften as she gazes down at Gabi. "It was fine, sweetheart. You doing okay?"

Gabi nods. "Answered the same question from Greta. I only need one mom, guys. You have to stop tag-teaming me."

Mom glances at me and smiles. "We'll try."

I nod. "Sure."

Gabi gives us a dubious glance. "I'm going to go make sure Gemma doesn't send out sexts pretending she's me."

My mouth drops open and my mom sighs. "You two need to get ready for bed in a few minutes."

Gabi turns back over her shoulder as she places a foot on the stairs. "By the way, Greta has a boyfriend." Then she runs, giggling, up the stairs before I can snatch her up.

My mother's brows lift nearly to her hairline. Her long, dark hair is swept back into a braid, but a few pieces hang around her face. My mother is absolutely beautiful, and I hope to look as good as she does when I reach my late forties.

"Boyfriend?"

We walk down the hallway together toward the family room in the back of the house. My mother settles onto the sectional couch while I perch on the end beside her. She crosses her arms and points to me.

"Tell me about him."

I sigh. Every time I talk about Grisham, I have to try hard to get a grip on the cheesy grin that plasters across my face.

But with my mom, I'm not sure I'll be able to hide it. "Well, I'm not sure how serious it is yet. That's why I haven't said anything."

She scrutinizes my face, and I know she's reading every feeling I harbor for Grisham on my face. Her lips twitch.

"You like him," she surmises. "Where did you meet?"

"We actually met almost two years ago. He's a longtime friend of Berkeley's." I leave out the part about Grisham wanting to be much more than that to Berkeley back then. As sure as I am that he's over it, I don't want someone else shoving any questions in my mind about his loyalty.

"And then," I continue, "I ran into him again a couple of months ago, when he gave me...."

I trail off, feeling guilty. I haven't told my mom about what happened on the beach because I didn't want her to worry. She has one child she constantly worries about. Why give her another thing to keep her up at night?

"When he gave you what?" Curiosity leaks from her tone.

"Mouth-to-mouth resuscitation." My voice is almost nonexistent, but I can tell from the expression on her face that she heard my quiet mumble.

My mother's eyes widen to a dangerous size. "*What*?"

Quickly I explain what happened on the beach, and how it felt to awaken with Grisham's green eyes staring into mine.

"It was...I don't know, Mom. Something about him that day gave me hope. Like everything was going to be okay. It's stupid, I know."

My mother is nodding, fiddling with her empty ring finger the way she does sometimes when she thinks about my father.

"It's understandable. He saved your life. I'm sure that created a strong bond. For you and for him."

I smile gratefully, happy that she understands. "It did. At least for me. And now, we see each other at work, too."

Her eyes cloud with confusion. "At work? At Night Eagle?"

I nod. "Yeah. He's...a navy SEAL."

My mother's jaw slackens. I'm not sure how she's going to feel about this piece of news. Marrying a guy in the military might have seemed glamorous to her when she first met my dad, but she quickly learned how difficult it is to be a military wife. And she's never said it, but I'm not sure if she wants the same thing for me.

"He's retiring at the end of the year," I quickly continue. "He...he was injured overseas a few months ago. He...he lost his foot, Mom."

Her eyes soften, immediately growing wet with unshed tears. "Oh, Greta. I'm sorry to hear that."

I nod. "I know. It just about broke my heart when I found out from Berkeley, and I hadn't even started dating him yet. But now that I am, I see that it hasn't slowed him down one bit. Heck, he dove into the ocean to pull me out, didn't he? But he can't keep doing his job in the navy. So Dad hired him at Night Eagle. He's a great addition to the team."

My mother sighs. "I'm sure he is. How do you feel about that, though, Greta? We've never really discussed it, but I think you might have some trust issues with men. Right? Because of how devoted your dad always was with his job? What if Grisham's just as devoted?"

I sink back against the couch cushions. I don't want to allow my brain to go there. I close my eyes. What I have with Grisham is something I don't want to doubt. The way we are when we're together, the electrifying chemistry and utter safeness I feel when I'm in his arms are things I've never felt with anyone else. And if Grisham ever did choose work over me, it would break me. Completely. I can't go through the same thing with him that I went through repeatedly with my father. The same thing I watched my mom suffer from every time my dad left us alone.

I can't.

My mother reads my expression once again. "You've thought about it. Haven't you?"

The gentle coaxing in her voice has me nodding my head. "Yeah. Maybe I have."

She leans forward and pats my knee. "Let me meet this guy. Maybe I can read in his eyes how 'into you' he is."

My lips quirk upward. "You want to meet him? I would love to introduce you and Gabi and Gemma."

She nods firmly. "Of course I do. Why don't you bring him by for dinner next Saturday night? I know this weekend is the client thingy for the firm."

I tilt my head, looking suspicious. "How do you know that?"

She shrugs, pulling an afghan from the back of the couch to cover her legs. "I just know things. Want to watch a movie?"

I nod. Mom and I have been through a lot together. I'm always going to want to kick back on the couch, cuddle up with her, and watch a movie. It's one of my favorite ways to calm my overactive brain.

And tonight, my brain is in danger of overuse. Between thoughts of Grisham, and thoughts of whoever it was who may have sent me that broken surfboard figurine, I'm completely maxed out on anxieties for one day.

But I have two things to look forward to in the very near future.

1. Accompanying Grisham as his date to an event thrown by my father's company, which I now work for.
2. Introducing Grisham to the most important people in my life: my mother and sisters.

Even rogue thoughts of lurking, menacing individuals can't keep the warm, comforting feeling covering me like a fuzzy blanket.

21

Grisham

W hat a motherfuckin' big shot." Ben's drawl holds a touch of pride as he inspects my suit and tie.

I'd decided to go with a dark charcoal-gray suit, crisp white shirt, and dark red tie. I know from the mouth of a little birdie that Greta's dress is a deep shade of red. I can't wait to see her in it, but I also want us to coordinate. Surprise her a little.

I have a night full of surprises planned for her.

"Just watch and learn, Cowboy." My teasing tone lets Ben know I'm not being a cocky bastard.

He sprawls out on my living room floor while I adjust my tie. He and Lawson came by to drink a beer and help calm my nerves before tonight's client event. I'm nervous as hell.

It's a big night in more ways than one. I'm being introduced to the pool of current and potential Night Eagle clients as a member of an elite team. One that I'm pretty damn honored to be a part of. With the skills Jacob has, combined with the strategic knowledge and general badassness that Dare and the other guys bring to the table, it's a privilege to be considered one of them.

And Jacob's giving me a soft place to land after leaving a job I thought would be my lifelong career.

I still hadn't spoken to my father. The navy was being surprisingly cooperative with my mother's lawyers. My father was considered a flight risk and a danger to my mother, thanks to the police report and bruises on her body that she'd taken the time to report. He's not getting out of prison until he goes on trial and is found not guilty.

And I have a lot riding on the fact that won't happen.

But I'll be there when his trial rolls around, making sure my testimony helps keep him under lock and key.

Working for Night Eagle is helping to pick up the pieces. I now know where my life is headed. And there isn't a single time when I picture the future that Greta isn't by my side.

Tonight, not only do I want to jump feet first into my brand-new job, but I also want to show her that I'm serious about her and this relationship. I'm exclusively hers, and I want her to be mine. I have something waiting for her when we arrive back at my house tonight that will prove just that.

I smooth out my tie and turn to face Ben and Lawson.

"Hey. You two lock up when you leave. And you better be gone by the time I get back here later tonight with Greta. You have your own houses to wreck."

Without looking up, Ben waves me off. "Me and Stealth got this. We'll take care of your pet project, too. You're all set."

I nod. "Thanks. I mean it. You two are there for me when

I need it, no matter what. And I appreciate it."

They both glance over at me, and then grit their teeth.

"Enough of that shit. Get going. We're all good here." Lawson gives me a shooing motion with his hand, silently telling me to quit acting like a girl. So I just grin at them and make my way out to my Jeep.

When I arrive at Greta's apartment, Mea swings the door open with a wide smile. She's a petite little thing, way shorter than Greta. I bend down and hug her after entering their place.

"Hey, Mea. You doing okay?"

She gestures toward the couch. "Greta should be out in a minute. Have a seat, sailor-boy. I have some questions for you."

Oh, boy. I sit down on the couch, spreading my legs wide and placing my forearms on my thighs. Then I clasp my hands and lean forward, giving her all of my attention.

"I don't falter under questioning," I point out. "I'm well trained."

Her eyes narrow. "We'll see."

She begins firing off a round of questions that she clearly expects me to answer without any hesitation. Questions like "what are your intentions toward my friend?" and "what's your favorite Greta quality?" are easy to rattle off answers to. In the couple of months that Greta and I have been seeing each other, I've learned a lot about her. Some of it is too personal to share with our friends, but I think I pass Mea's test with a perfect score. Or damn close to it.

Mea's serene face looks pleased. She leans forward from her cross-legged position on the floor and smiles. "You're golden, sailor-boy. I'm impressed."

I spread my arms wide. "What can I say? Greta's got me wound around her little finger."

Mea gives a firm nod. "It better stay that way."

Just then, Greta floats into the room on three-inch heels. My eyes land on those sexy, strappy sandals first before they slowly make their way up her body.

Insane. Gorgeousness. Just entered the room.

"Damn, Grits," I murmur. "You look stunning."

Stunning doesn't even begin to cover how she looks.

Why isn't there a word better for this than stunning?

Her dark crimson dress swishes around her ankles, exposing the fuck-me heels she's wearing on her pretty feet. The material of the dress is made from something that clings to her willowy curves like a vine on a trellis. There's a split on one side that exposes skin that I feel the need to have my hands on *now*. I pause at the slit, imagining where my tongue will meet the warm skin of her leg later tonight...

I shake my head to clear it, feeling like I'm under some kind of witchy spell. I could give a shit. If this is a spell, I just want more of it.

The dress is free of sparkles and glittery stuff, which make me really, really happy. The feisty color is enough of a statement. And so is the deep, plunging neckline that hints at the curves of her breasts without outright showing all her goods. But wow...she still must have had some work to do to keep the ladies hidden.

The dress has long sleeves that fit her like a second skin. When I finally make it up to her face, she's giving me a soft, sultry smile that snatches the breath right out of my chest.

She's a priceless work of art.

And she's with me.

I move toward her like a puppet on a string.

"You like it?" she asks, turning away from me so I can see the back of her.

And when I see it, my cock jumps against the restraint of my pants. The back of the dress is completely open, exposing the delicate blades of her shoulders and gorgeous expanse of ivory skin on her back.

No longer able to wait to touch her, I clasp my hands in front of her and pull her back against me. She smells heavenly, like something sweet that I can't wait to get my mouth on. I press my lips to the skin on her neck.

"You look beautiful, Greta. Like you should be walking down a runway somewhere, not showing up at an event with me."

She turns in my arms, and her gaze is hot and sweet as it holds mine. "I don't want to be anywhere but at this event with you, Grisham Abbot."

An enormous smile makes the ripping of my face a real and present danger. "I'm happy to hear you say that. Because when you look like that, I'd go crazy if you were anywhere but by my side." I kiss her, just below her ear, and I feel her shiver in my arms.

Maybe we can take just a couple of minutes... My fingers make their way to the fabric at her shoulders as I begin to tug it down.

Mea clears her throat.

I freeze, having completely forgotten I'm not alone in the room with Greta.

"You guys better get going," says Mea pointedly. "Or you're going to be late."

Greta's face is deep crimson, and I kiss her cheek as I entwine our fingers together. I pull her toward the door with me.

Grabbing a clutch purse off the counter, she calls back toward Mea, "I'm probably gonna stay at Grisham's tonight." She glances at me to confirm, and I give her a firm nod. She giggles, and then looks back at Mea. "Okay?"

Mea shoos us away flippantly. "Please. I've got a hot date tonight."

That stops Greta, and she turns completely around. "Again?"

Mea avoids Greta's gaze. "You know my style. I've gotta love 'em and leave 'em."

Greta shakes her head. "One of these days, a guy is gonna make you want him to stay."

Mea laughs, her wild curls flying around her head. "One of these days, they'll learn that they can't tie me down. Ever."

Greta flies back to hug her friend. "Love you, Mea. Be careful."

As we walk out the door, we hear her response. "I always am!"

Greta is quiet on the ride to Wilmington, where the event is being held. I glance over at her a few times, only to find her lost in thought. I don't want to disturb her, so I let her be.

But when we're nearly there, I grasp her hand in mine and bring it to my lips. The feel of her soft, satiny skin against mine calms me. "You okay?"

She gives me a small smile. "Yeah. I worry about Mea."

"Why?"

Sighing, she looks back toward the dark night beyond her window. "Because she pretends a lot. She's been through a lot in her life; that's why we instantly bonded when we met in college. I figured out pretty quick that she had some deep scars on her soul. But she never really lets anyone in. I'm worried that she'll always be that way."

I mull over what she just said. I've known Mea for a while, but only through Berkeley. I don't really know anything about her, only that she and Berkeley went to high school together and then when she went to college she became good friends with Greta. She's a little spitfire, and she's absolutely beautiful, but I've never seen her with a guy.

"She dates a lot?"

Greta snorts. "More like, she uses guys and then tosses them away."

Well, damn.

Greta rushes on. "I mean, I don't fault her for it. She's young and she's single, and guys do it to girls all the time. I think when they meet Mea, she turns the tables, and they're left wondering what the hell happened." She laughs softly.

Thinking about that brings a smile to my face, too. "Don't worry about her. She just hasn't met the guy that makes her want more. She will."

Greta turns to me, her face turning serious. "I did."

My heart stutters once before picking up its regular beat. I pull up to a valet stand at a luxury hotel before bringing her hand to my lips again. This time I plant a trail of light kisses along her hand, her wrist, her forearm. The material of her dress doesn't deter me from kissing her again and again.

"We're going to have a great night."

"The best," she agrees as the valet opens her car door.

The event is set up as a meet and greet, and as we enter the executive gala room on the fifth floor of the hotel, a classically decorated atmosphere greets us. There are black-jacketed servers walking around with trays of champagne and hors d'oeuvres. There are so many people in the room, milling around, laughing and joking, clinking glasses...but all I can see is Greta.

It's obvious she's unaware of her utter beauty. Of her ability to command attention in a room. As I scan the crowd around us, I observe that she's caught the eye of several men around us. But she's completely oblivious. Smiling to myself, I put my arm around her waist and pull her a little bit closer. Her dress swishes around her ankles, and that one exposed leg is bared.

God. How am I going to make it through this night without pulling her into the bathroom or out to my car and showing her exactly how fucking sexy I think she is?

Her azure eyes focus on me, and she tilts her head. "What are you thinking?"

My voice is rough as I lean in, my lips brushing her ear. "You don't want to know."

She pulls back, shocked pleasure written on her face. "I think I know. Guess what?"

"What?"

She lets her eyes make a slow, simmering perusal of me in my fitted suit, from my messed-up hair to my black dress shoes. Then she makes her way back up, sliding a finger along the silk of my tie, moving up until she's gently stroking my bottom lip.

She taps my mouth with her finger. "I'm thinking the exact same thing."

Yeah. That's it.

I grab her by the arm, steering her gently-but-firmly toward the door we just entered a few minutes ago.

"Hey, guys!"

Berkeley's bright voice stops me in my tracks, and we turn slowly to face her and Dare. They're both grinning at us, holding glasses of champagne. Berkeley looks great in a royal blue dress, and Dare's rocking a black suit with no tie.

"Where were you headed?" asks Berkeley with a hint of suspicion in her tone.

Dare laughs outright, spotting the pained look on my face. "We need you here, brother." He slaps me on my back. Then he leans in. "If I can handle it for a few hours, with Berkeley looking the way she does, so can you."

I nod, but I still can't keep my eyes off my date.

"Let me go introduce you to a couple of people. Then Jacob wants to see us before the big intro. Think you can handle leaving Greta with Berkeley for a while?"

I look toward Greta, thinking how badly I don't want to leave her side tonight. But she nods toward Dare, urging me to go on without her.

"You're here to work, too," she reminds me. "I'll be fine."

I take another glance around the room, noting that she still has the attention of a lot of guys. And now that Berkeley is with her, they're like magnets for men.

I look sternly at Berkeley. "Stay with her. You two watch out for each other."

She salutes me. "Yes, sir." She deepens her voice in jest, but she needs to know how serious I am. I don't like leaving Greta alone in a room like this.

"Oh, chill, Grish." Berkeley smiles and gives me a shove. "She'll be fine. Geez."

I follow Dare through the crowd, taking one last look at my gorgeous date standing like a dark angel in her bloodred dress.

"And I'd like you to give a warm welcome to the newest member of our team, Grisham Abbot."

There's a polite round of applause throughout the room, and as I stand on the small platform I listen to Jacob give a list of my accolades and accomplishments from my time in the naval academy, OTS, and being a SEAL. It feels surreal, having someone list all of the important things you've done.

I find Greta's face in the crowd and lock onto her. Letting everything else fall away, I realize that I don't care about how any of my credentials look on paper. All I care about is whether or not I'm a good enough man for her.

She smiles at me from her spot in the crowd and gives me a tiny nod. A pang of something sharp and sweet hits me in my gut like a punch.

She sees me. Through all the stuff that most people think are most important about me, she sees underneath all of that. To the real me.

As soon as Jacob's done introducing me as part of the team, he goes on to outline some of the services Night Eagle can offer for potential clients. I'm already well versed in what the firm can do, and I zone out a little bit. I realize I've lost Greta in the crowd. I see Berkeley standing in the exact same spot she was before, but the place beside her where Greta was is empty. I frown, scanning the crowd.

No Greta.

Jacob's speech drones on. He discusses Night Eagle's growth, and the fact that the company is the most reliable private security firm out there. Just when I think he's finished, he goes on to list, in great detail, every single service N.E. has to offer, and why potential clients should choose our firm over the competition. He skims over special government assignments N.E. has been a part of, or headed, and the sea of faces in front of me is more than impressed.

But right now, I don't care about any of that. Because in the entire time Jacob has been speaking, Greta hasn't reappeared in the crowd.

When Jacob's speech is finally finished, we stand beside the podium to answer questions from potential clients. And then Jacob excuses us to "enjoy the night."

I grab Dare by the arm as we're released. He's heading back to Berkeley.

"Hey. Have you seen Greta?"

He shakes his head, glancing at me. "She's not with Berkeley?"

I shake my head, impatient. When we reach Berkeley, I immediately ask her the same question. I glance around us, but I still don't see Greta.

"She went to powder her nose. Relax. She's not walking out

of here without you, silly." Berkeley smiles at me, but I frown again.

"She's been in the bathroom this entire time?" Doubt plagues me. I had to have been standing up there looking for her in the crowd for the past half hour.

Berkeley's smile falters, and I see her eyes dart toward the exit. The restrooms are outside in the hallway.

"Hmm. It has been awhile..."

I take off, shoving servers out of my way to get to the exit door. Dare is right behind me.

"Talk to me, man. What do you think happened?"

Dare's voice is calm, and I can tell he's trying to pacify me.

He can't pacify me in this situation. For some reason I can't put my finger on, Greta not being visible is making me feel very uneasy. Droplets of sweat bead on my forehead and my pounding heartbeat is taking up residence in my throat.

"I don't know. I just have a feeling..."

We burst into the hallway, and I look left and then right. There's no sign of Greta, but there are a few guests lingering in the hall having conversations or walking to and from the restrooms. The restrooms are to my right, while the elevators and stairwell are to my left and down another hallway.

If this were any other situation, one where I weren't looking for my girlfriend and worrying that something bad might have happened to her, my natural instincts and training would kick in. But right now, I can't think straight.

Do I go left, or right?

I start in the direction of the restrooms when Dare grabs my shoulder and spins me around to face him.

"Stop. Grisham, *why* do you have a feeling? You're freaking out on me, man, and I need to know why."

His gaze is intense, focused, and it causes my brain to snap into place and start to think rationally. I focus on him and take a deep breath.

"She's been getting notes. I mean, she was. Awhile back."

Dare frowns. "Notes?"

"Yeah...like secret admirer shit. Flowers and weird messages. Someone broke into her car to leave them. Someone broke into her desk at work. I don't know, dude. Nothing really seemed that serious. But as soon as I couldn't find her in the crowd..."

Dare's eyes widen. "Shit. Okay. Check the bathrooms. I'm heading for the stairwell. We'll find her, Ghost. It's probably nothing."

I nod, my jaw setting firmly as I head for the restrooms. I knock on the ladies' room door once before poking my head inside. It's empty, save for one woman putting on lipstick at the sink.

She gasps when she sees me.

"Have you seen a dark-haired girl in a red dress?" I ask her quickly.

She shakes her head mutely, eyes wide. The lipstick tube is frozen halfway to her mouth.

I back out of the restroom and perform a thorough check of the men's for good measure.

I stand out in the hallway once again, my brain working furiously to decipher this mystery. *Where is Greta? Could she have gone out for some air?*

That thought immediately drives me forward, and I head in the same direction as Dare had moments before, toward the stairwell. I glance at the elevator and quickly disregard it.

The stairs will be faster.

I push the door open and begin descending them as quickly as I can. My prosthetic doesn't slow me down as I jump from the third stair to the landing, continuing my progression downward. It's when I reach the landing on the third level that I hear something strange, and I stop moving.

Listening, my ears strain for another hint of the sound I heard that doesn't belong.

I hear it again, the sound of a quiet sniffle and then a muffled sob coming from the floor below me. I take the steps two at a time until I reach the second-floor landing.

Greta is huddled on the steps, hugging her knees to her chest. She's crying.

The sound of her anguish sends a shard of pain slicing through my chest, and I almost have to double over with the pain of it. But my eyes are focused on Greta and what she needs, and she sure as hell doesn't need me to fall apart. I need to find out what the hell is making her cry.

"Baby..." I kneel down beside her, taking her into my arms. "What's wrong? What happened?"

I attempt to keep the frantic tone from my voice, but I'm pretty sure I fail because when she raises her tear-streaked face to me, I almost lose my mind.

"Tell me," I instruct, cupping her face in my hand.

Her eyes focus on me, a watery blue abyss that I can't afford to fall into right now. "He...he hurt me."

Anger, furious and white-hot, threatens to overwhelm me. I grapple for control over the emotion, focusing on Greta and only Greta. "Who hurt you?"

"I didn't see his face, Grisham. He was wearing something over his eyes...oh, my God. I didn't even get a chance to remember everything you taught me! God...I'm such an idiot!"

Now I move so that I'm crouching in front of her, cradling her face in both of my hands. "No, angel. If someone attacked you, none of this is your fault. Did he grab you?"

She shakes her head frantically. "No, I was outside, just catching a breath of fresh air. It's kind of stuffy in there, you know?"

I nod, patiently waiting for her to continue. Meanwhile, there's a flurry of activity inside me, urging me to let Greta go and chase down whoever the hell had attacked her.

"So I was heading back inside, taking the stairs instead of the elevator because I didn't want to wait."

I nod again.

"And then this guy was just...*there*. I don't know where he came from, but his mask scared me. He was running straight at me, and he used something in his hand—I don't know, a knife? Something cut my arm."

She indicated her forearm and my eyes locked in. I saw that there was a tear in her dress, and I caught a flash of blood.

"Mother*fucker.*" The curse flies from me before I can control it as fury roils outward from the very heart of me.

"Then Dare came, and the guy kept running down the stairs. Dare checked to make sure I was okay, and then he ran after him."

"Dare's gone after him. That's good." I stroked her cheekbones gently with my thumbs, trying to ease the fear still lingering in her eyes. "I'm not going to let anything happen to you, Greta. I'm sorry he got to you. I should have been here."

Her eyes widen, and her fingers circle my wrists, holding on tight. "Grisham, you had no way of knowing this would happen. I should have been safe, this is a nice hotel. It's not your fault."

I close my eyes briefly. Because no matter how many times she says those words, I will always feel like protecting the people I love is my purpose. So when she's hurt, hell yes it's my fault. I have the ability to keep her safe, and I damn well need to do it.

I couldn't do it for my mother for years, but I will do it for Greta.

I lean my forehead against hers. "Let's go inside and find you some medical attention, okay? I want someone to look at your arm."

She shakes her head. "No, I don't want to go inside. I don't want the circus my father will turn this into."

I give her a small, regretful smile. "We can't hide this from him, Greta. He needs to know that you were attacked by some psycho at his event."

She sighs. "I guess you're right. Damn it."

I pull her to her feet. "How bad does it hurt?"

She glances at her arm and frowns. "I think it's a shallow cut. Hopefully it won't need stitches." Her eyes swim at the thought.

I nod, pulling her into the crook of my arm where I need

her to be. She may be okay, but I need to feel her body beside mine. I'm still struggling to keep my breaths even, to control the rage building a stone wall inside my chest. Now that I know she's safe, all I want to do is make sure her father has her and go after the person who dared to make her bleed.

I want to make him bleed.

An eye for an eye.

The event is winding down, thankfully, and people are leaving as we enter. We receive a few strange looks from parting guests, but I ignore them and hustle Greta to a table in the corner. I sit her down, and turn to look for Jacob.

Berkeley rushes over. "Oh, my God, Greta! What happened?"

She sees the tear in Greta's dress and her eyes widen. "Are you hurt?"

Greta's face is pinched, exhausted. Her skin is paler than usual, her eyes standing out starkly against the pallor of her face. I can't keep my eyes from roving over her body again and again, checking for more injuries I may have missed.

"Some asshole attacked her in the stairwell. Dare went after him."

A flicker of worry shoots through Berkeley's eyes, but she covers it well and comes to Greta's side. She scoots a chair closer and places an arm around her. Carefully pulling up Greta's sleeve, she examines her wound. I lean closer, wanting to see for myself how bad it is.

"Oh." Berkeley catches her breath. "Not too bad. It doesn't look like you need stitches. It's a long gash, but not deep. Do you want to go to the ER?"

"Yes," I answer at the same time Greta gives a resounding "No!"

I stare at her, and she stares back. There's a stubborn lift to her chin that lets me know she's not budging.

"No ER, Grisham. I'm okay. I can check in with my regular doctor tomorrow if it'll make everyone feel better."

"Greta?" Jacob has appeared at my side, concern etched on his face. "What..." He trails off as he sees her wound.

It's stopped bleeding, but it's obvious she's been hurt. "What the hell happened?" His voice is nothing more than a growl, and I understand exactly where he's coming from.

Quickly, I recount what Greta told me about the attack, and Jacob's scowl grows deeper with every word.

"Why would someone attack you?" he asks.

I've asked myself the same question over and over again since I found her huddled—crying and alone and hurt—on those stairs. That was the moment I realized that what I thought was a harmless admirer situation was really something far more sinister that we could no longer just keep an eye on.

My voice is steady and grim as I answer Jacob's question.

"She has a stalker. And he's escalating."

22

Greta

The word *stalker* hits me in the gut like an uppercut.

I don't have a stalker. Celebrities have stalkers. Girls who are important, who have a public platform. Not me. I'm just Greta.

Staring at Grisham, I shake my head. "A stalker? You think I have a stalker?"

He kneels down beside me. "Angel, I know you have a stalker. The signs are there, especially after this attack. It can't be coincidence, or random. The same person who sent you those flowers is the same person who attacked you tonight. I'd bet my life on it."

He stands again, turning away from me and running his hands through his messy locks. "Dammit! Why didn't I see this coming?"

I just sit there, mute, turning this new information over in my mind. I think about the other gift I was sent by an anonymous party, and I sit up straighter.

"And the surfboard," I mutter.

Grisham's head swivels around until he's staring at me. "Come again?"

My father's voice interrupts me. He's speaking quickly into his cell phone. He has a friend on the Wilmington police force, and it's clear that's who he's speaking with. I turn my attention back to Grisham. Berkeley is listening with rapt attention while she rubs comforting circles on my back.

"I got another gift."

Grisham opens his mouth, then closes it again. A look of awed frustration crosses his face, and I know exactly what he's thinking.

"I didn't tell you, because I knew you'd freak out. And it was just another harmless gift, but it had a note that scared me a little. And I didn't want to give the sender power by making a big deal about it. I just wanted to ignore it, pretend it never happened."

Grisham places his hands on his waist, and I can see a muscle tensing in his jaw. "What did the note say, Grits?"

I take a breath. I'll never forget what that note said. I recite it as if I'm reading from it at that moment. "It said *GO SURFING WITH ME?* And then when I flipped it over, it said *STOP SURFING WITH HIM.*"

Grisham mutters a curse, and as my father hangs up the phone, he pulls him aside and begins talking in hushed, urgent tones. I can only imagine what they're saying, and I place my forehead in my hands, wishing this night could just end.

I hear Dare's voice when he returns, but I don't bother to lift my head.

"He disappeared in the alley behind the hotel. Couldn't

find him, even though I combed that damn alley. He's a fucking magician."

Both my father and Grisham were less than thrilled with this news, but all three men are already formulating a plan to keep me safe. I don't even hear what it is, because I'm suddenly being introduced to two police detectives.

I give my statement to the police. It's surreal, experiencing the notes and gifts through their eyes. I'm realizing, as I recount everything that's happened with my stalker thus far, that I'm in much deeper than I thought before. This situation has somehow spiraled out of my tenuous control without my knowing it. The thought is harrowing and disconcerting. I don't understand where I went wrong.

I also don't understand why this is happening to me.

By the time I'm finished giving my statement to the detective asking me repetitive questions, the entire Night Eagle team surrounds me. The guys are being protective and strong, and I'm so grateful I'm a part of this band of brothers. They'll keep me safe.

The determination on Grisham's face takes me aback. It's like he's made a vow to himself to never let something like this happen to me again. I know that he's feeling a sense of déjà vu. He's thinking that he couldn't protect me tonight, the same way he couldn't protect his mother from his own father for all those years. I have to let him know that this is different, that I can handle this and I trust him implicitly to be there for me when I need him.

To me, Grisham is nothing but a hero. But proving that to him is turning out to be a daunting feat.

Before I know it, the questioning is over and my father is leaning down to speak to me.

"Are you all right?" he asks. "Do you want me to call your mom? Do you want to come back to my condo tonight? I don't want you to be alone."

I open my mouth to say no at the same time Grisham speaks up from my side. "She won't be alone, sir."

My dad takes a long, hard look at Grisham. Something seems to pass between them and my father gives a curt nod.

"You'll be okay if I let you go with Grisham, sweetheart?" he asks me seriously.

I don't hesitate before I give my own nod. "Absolutely."

Grisham takes my hand, pulling me to my feet and immediately cradling me to his side. I feel his lips brush the top of my head, and all of the stress and anxiety and fear the night caused me leave me in a whoosh of air. Being in Grisham's arms again makes everything seem like it'll be okay. I can survive a stalker if I have him by my side.

My dad places his hands on my shoulders and kisses my cheek. "I'll give your mother a call, so you can just go home and settle in, okay? I'll make sure she knows what happened, and that you're fine. You give her a call in the morning."

I nod and disentangle myself from Grisham so I can throw my arms around my dad. We've been through a lot together. And it hasn't all been good. But when it comes down to it, if I'm ever in trouble, he's someone I can depend on, and that counts for something. I squeeze him tight.

"Thank you, Daddy," I whisper in his ear.

When he pulls back, his eyes are moist and he quickly

turns away. "See you Monday morning, pumpkin."

The childhood nickname he gave me almost does me in, and Grisham seems to sense my impending emotional collapse. Without another word, he sweeps me out of the room. He appears to sense the urgency of my need to get out of there. With just a few short words and the slide of a bill into the valet's palm, his Jeep is brought around much more quickly than I could have hoped for.

He gently places me in the passenger seat and takes the time to buckle me in. His face is tender and concerned as he looks into my eyes. Without saying a word, he brushes my lips gently with his. Then he's gone. He rounds the hood of the Jeep, slides into the driver's seat, and we're on our way back to Lone Sands.

When we arrive at his beach house, Grisham is around to my side of the car quick as a flash, helping me down from the SUV.

He keeps an arm slung around my shoulder, walking me up to his front door, opening it, and closing it behind us. Grisham's big body shielding mine calms the thudding of my pulse. I watch with focused attention as he locks the dead bolt, and he glances over at me. His eyes soften as he takes my face into large hands.

"You're safe, Grits," he whispers, searching my eyes. "You're safe with me. I won't let anything happen to you." His thumbs rub feather-light circles on my pallid skin.

I nod wordlessly, letting my head fall against his shoulder. His arms wind around me, and I'm lifted into the air and carried to the couch.

Grisham sits on the edge of the cushion and looks down at me. Reaching out to tuck a piece of my hair, fallen from my elegant updo into what I can only imagine to be a bedraggled mess, he bends to claim my lips.

His lips are warm and welcome on mine, and I instantly open my mouth to accommodate him. The kiss turns urgent and feverish, him leaning into me and me capturing the hair at his nape with my fingers. When I whimper with a sudden fiery desire I can feel throughout my entire body, he pulls back and stares down at me.

"You're hurt," he whispers, his eyes dark with warring emotions. I stare up at him, wondering which one will win out. "I should..."

"You should make love to me." My voice is impatient as I interrupt his good-guy spiel. "Until I feel safe again."

He doesn't hesitate. He yanks off his suit jacket, throwing it to the floor. I use greedy fingers to unbutton each button on his shirt, yanking it open and feasting my eyes on his sculpted chest. I'm so suddenly overcome with a need to have Grisham on top of me, surrounding me, *inside me,* that I can't contain the desire overflowing from my veins.

I use my fingers to rake a path up his chest, and the answering rumble of a growl in his chest spurs me onward. Making a path back down, I find the belt on his pants and unfasten it with sure and steady fingers. Grisham watches me, but his hands aren't idle as he strokes my face, my hair, my neck. He finds the edge of fabric on my collarbone and pulls my dress down my arms. I pause in my feverish work to let him pull the garment free from my torso and I'm bared to him.

Then I'm sliding his gray pants down his hips, and he kicks off his shoe and steps out of the pants. He kneels between my legs, pushing my shoulders down to the couch and pulling my dress down over my thighs. All that's left between us is a pair of barely there G-string panties I wore underneath my dress.

Grisham hovers above me, using his knee to spread my legs farther apart. His eyes search mine, holding me steady with his touch and his gaze. "Tell me what you need right now, Grits. I want to give it to you...whatever you want."

A rattling breath leaves me, because it's the simplest question I've ever been asked. All I want is him. I don't want to relive what happened to me tonight. I don't want to discuss who might have been behind the attack. All I want is to feel Grisham moving inside of me, taking all the bad feelings away and replacing them with good ones. Amazing ones.

"I want you inside me," I whisper. I don't shift my gaze from his for a second, letting him know that I mean what I'm saying. "That's what I need. I need you."

"Fuck."

The black boxer-briefs come off like quicksilver, and my panties follow suit, landing somewhere on the floor beside us. I can feel Grisham between my thighs, and when I glance down I can see the hard, long length of him pressing gently against my folds. I reach around him to grab his ass; it's taut and perfect and I squeeze, giving him a not-so-gentle push to continue.

"Now, Grisham." My voice is strained, and I can hear the note of pleading as I pull him closer.

His eyes, the darkest green and glowing with embers of fiery need, burn into mine as he slowly pushes inside me. I moan, closing my eyes and allowing my head to loll against the couch cushion.

With a guttural groan, Grisham pushes forward to the hilt, and then slowly pulls back out, dropping his eyes to watch the place where our bodies meet. I watch, too; it's the mesmerizing dance between us that I needed. Watching Grisham stake claim on me steals away every second of terror my stalker put me through. I pull on his hips, urging him to move faster.

Realizing what I want, he thrusts inside me again and again, moving faster and harder until I can no longer watch our bodies move. I'm just lost to the sensation of him stroking against the pulsating point inside me that makes me relinquish control. I close my eyes, willfully losing myself in Grisham.

And when he reaches between us to rub his thumb against my slick, swollen clit, I come apart harder than I ever have before. His name bursts from my lips in a scream, but he doesn't stop. He continues pounding, driving onward until I'm dizzy with pleasure. Overwhelmed by his touch, his smell, the rhythm our bodies make when they slam together. My hands leave him to scrape a jagged line up his back.

My nails on his skin is the last straw for Grisham. He falls forward, burying his face in my neck as he begins to tremble. I can feel his release streaming inside me, and the sensation makes me smile. I want to be marked by Grisham tonight in every way possible.

I lose track of the minutes we lay there afterward, Grisham still inside me and my arms draped lazily over his back. Our breathing returns to normal, and then his satisfied hum of approval vibrates against my throat.

"You. Are. Incredible." He punctuates each word with a kiss to my neck. My skin is still sensitive, tingling with each kiss, and my inner walls squeeze around him where he's still inside.

"Shit, baby...you can't do that. I have to get up. We can't go again just yet."

My lips push outward in a pout. "Why the hell not?"

He pulls back, eyes me, and bursts out laughing. "Well, damn. I really like this side of you, Grits."

"I really like all sides of you."

Chuckling, he rises, pulling out of me. Then he freezes. "Greta..."

My eyes have drifted closed, and I'm sure nothing can erase the smile on my lips. "Hmmm?"

His voice is laced with worry. "I...damn. I was caught up in you. I didn't use a condom."

I shake my head, keeping my smile. "It's okay. I'm on the pill."

I can hear his answering smile as he climbs off the couch. "Okay, then. Hey, Grits...I know it's been a long night and you're probably ready to pass out. But can you stay right here for a second? I have a surprise for you. It's not the exact moment I thought I'd bring it out, but..."

My eyes snap open and I sit up. Dragging a blanket from the back of the couch to drape over my bare body, I look at him questioningly. My brows pull together. "You got me something?"

He hesitates, running a hand through his hair and shooting

me an almost shy grin as he steps into his underwear. "More like I got us something."

He kneels down beside me and takes my hands in his. Raising them to his lips, his face holds a serious expression. "I wanted to do something to show you that I'm ready to be all in. It's me and you, and that's how I want it. I want this, Grits. I didn't think I would. I thought that I needed to be alone, make saving people's lives and keeping them safe my only mission in life. But then you showed up that day on the beach, and everything changed. As much as I tried to fight it, I couldn't stay away from you. I don't want to."

His words are stealing my heart away, one tiny piece at a time. It's everything I ever wanted to hear him say, and he's speaking these words with all the feeling and meaning I could ask for. I brush away a tear, and he raises a hand to my face, caressing it softly with the back of his hand. "You and me?"

I nod, leaning into his palm. "You and me."

He breaks out into one of his beautiful grins, the skin around his mouth creasing like parentheses. He sweeps his lips across mine once, twice, three times before he rises to his feet and turns for the kitchen. "Close your eyes. I'll be right back."

Totally mystified, I settle back on the couch and close my eyes. I can hear Grisham walking through the kitchen to the little mudroom that leads to his carport, and I can hear the scraping of metal and lots of rustling. Then I hear him padding back toward me, and I'm itching to open my eyes and see what he's doing.

"Okay, Grits," he announces. "Open."

My lids fly open and then I raise both hands to my lips

too late to cover my gasp. "Oh, my God, Grisham! You got a puppy?"

He comes closer and dumps the warm and wiggling little bundle of fur on my lap. It's a fawn-colored boxer puppy with an adorably sad-looking face and huge brown eyes. The top of his head is dappled with white spots, and his feet are white, too. He's staring up at me while his little body fights furiously to get closer to my face. I cuddle him to my chest, nuzzling his fur, and then he's licking me everywhere he can reach.

Giggling, I glance over at Grisham. He's sitting beside us, smiling like he just won an enormous prize.

Like *I'm* his enormous prize.

"No," he corrects me. "*We* got a puppy. And please tell me I made the right decision, and that you are a big dog person. Because this little guy is gonna grow up to be about seventy pounds."

The puppy takes this opportunity to squirm out of my arms and leap onto Grisham's lap, jumping up to lick his face before racing around the couch like an Energizer doggie.

I climb onto Grisham's lap, straddling him. His eyes immediately go dark as he stares at me. "This is the most perfect gift. Thank you."

A smile tugs at one corner of his mouth. "You take care of everyone around you, Grits. Your friends, your mom, and your sisters. I thought we could add this little guy to the list."

The puppy gives a short, sharp bark, as if he agrees with this sentiment completely.

"What are we going to name him?" I look lovingly at the puppy as he turns in a circle and flops down against my thigh.

Grisham takes my face in his hands, bringing it to within an inch of his, and I immediately forget what question I just asked him. My breasts push against his bare chest and my nipples instantly peak. His hands drift up my back, and he whispers just before his lips meet mine.

"We'll have to figure that out later. Right now, you're too much of a temptation."

Greta

The following morning is Sunday, and when I wake up I find Grisham sitting on the floor in the kitchen with a tumbler of coffee beside him. He's pulling on one end of a frayed multi-colored rope, and our new addition is savagely tugging on the other end. Frantic little growls are emitting from his tiny furry body, and I burst into ecstatic giggles at the picture they create.

Grisham looks up, and the smile he gives me is like the reward for something good I did but can't remember.

"You laughing at us?" He points at me and throws the rope at my feet. "Get her, boy."

Our puppy rocket-launches himself in my direction, his little paws skidding on the hardwood kitchen floor. I bend down to scratch him on the head, and he rolls over onto his back to beg for my attention on his belly instead.

"Aw, come on, man! You are such a sucker," Grisham playfully chides the puppy.

I raise a brow. "You're not a sucker for a good rubdown?"

The teasing grin freezes in place on his face and his eyes narrow dangerously. "I am a complete sucker for you rubbing anything on my body." He stalks toward me, and my insides turn to molten lava. When he's close enough to reach out and grab me, the puppy darts between our legs and begins jumping up, nipping at Grisham's and my bare toes.

"Cock-block," mutters Grisham.

I gasp and slug him in the arm.

"We have to name him," I remind Grisham as I begin pulling out pots and pans to make breakfast.

He watches me for a moment as I begin preparing his now-favorite breakfast item: cheese grits. "Hey, what goes perfectly with grits?"

I play along. "Um, eggs?"

He nods, a knowing gleam lighting up his eyes. "So, haven't we just named our puppy?" He slowly points between me and the dog. "Grits...and Eggs."

I turn the name around in my mind. Then I grin. "Eggs is perfect."

He climbs onto a barstool to watch me cook. "Hey...I've been thinking."

My hand falters in my stirring before I pick up the pace again. You never want to hear your boyfriend say "I've been thinking." It's terrifying.

"About?" My tone is cautious, and I keep my eyes on the mixture of grits, milk, and cheese in my bowl.

"You can look at me, angel." His tone is gentle. "It isn't anything bad."

I glance up at him. I was able to fall asleep in his arms before the thoughts of last night's attack reared their ugly heads. I was able to find shelter in his strong arms, from everything and anyone who wanted to hurt me. This morning, the lurking fear is back. I have to face the facts. I have a stalker. This person is unknown. I now have an open case file with the police department, and I've been labeled a "victim." The thought turns my stomach.

"I want to skip your regular training this morning."

I start to protest. "My arm is fine, Grisham, really. Training with you is going to help me—"

He interrupts, holding up his hand. "We're going to do a different kind of training. I mentioned it to your dad last night, and he thinks it's a good idea. So...we're going to buy you a handgun."

I drop the spoon, staring at him.

I grew up in a house with a gun. My father even made sure my mother knew how to use it when he was gone. So guns are nothing shocking or alarming to me.

But what was stopping me cold was the reason behind my needing a gun. Grisham must think that I could be in serious danger.

"You really think I need one?" My voice comes out as barely a whisper.

His eyes go soft, and he pushes off the barstool, coming around the counter to pull me into his arms. "It's a precaution. I need to know that if I'm not there...you're protected."

I nod, absorbing the tenderness I feel emanating from his embrace. "I already know how to use a gun. My father taught me years ago."

I feel his nod. "That's what he said last night. But you don't own one. So we'll go to the shop today and pick one up, and then we'll take it to the range for some practice. How does that sound?"

I look up at him. Staring into his eyes, I see confidence and empowerment as he gazes down at me. He believes that I can handle this.

So I will.

"It sounds like I'm getting a gun today."

After a lengthy morning at the local sheriff's office, applying for a handgun, and having my background check and finger-prints scanned, Grisham escorts me gun shopping.

He takes my hand as we walk inside POW Shooting Sports. I raise my eyebrow at him, and he grins. His smile parentheses make me feel giddy, because he's obviously enthusiastic about this adventure.

"Don't knock the name," he suggests. "It's awesome in here."

The place is enormous, boasting a retail gun store in addition to a full shooting range and gun classes. Grisham pulls me up to the gleaming sales counter where there are firearms hanging on the wall behind the clerk and also locked in glass cases before us.

Telling the burly man behind the counter why we're here, he begins pulling out handguns at Grisham's instruction. Soon, there are three guns sitting on the counter. Grisham points them out by name: a steely gray 9 mm Glock, a shiny silver .38 Special, and a flat black Sig Sauer.

I stare at the firearms, trying to decide which one I'm supposed to like best. Grisham gives me a gentle nudge with his arm. "Pick each one up, Grits. Test it out, hold it in your hands. Feel the weight of it to see what's comfortable."

At his encouragement, I nod and begin picking up each weapon one at a time and doing exactly as he said. I find all three have a very different feeling in my hands.

Grisham leans into me, his voice tickling my ear as he looks at the selection through my eyes. "Which one of them feels like something you'd feel comfortable using to defend yourself?"

I toss him a quick, startled glance. His expression is somber, like what he's saying is a matter of life and death.

It may be.

"You aren't just purchasing a firearm to practice with, Greta. If you own a gun, you need to be prepared for the day you'll have to use it. It's a serious thing. I want you to think really hard about it."

I nod and then look at the three weapons again. All I can do is go with the one that I felt an immediate connection with when I held it. The Sig Sauer had felt hefty in my hands, but comfortable. Like I could wield it as an extension of my own body.

"I want that one," I say softly, pointing to the black pistol.

Grisham gives me a smile full of pride, and then he nods to the clerk. Pulling out a credit card, Grisham starts to slide it across the counter.

My eyes widen, and I grasp Grisham's arm, halting his progress. "That pistol costs nine hundred dollars," I hiss. "You're not buying it for me!"

The corner of his lips quirk as he gives me an amused expression. "Your safety is at risk, Greta, and I'd damn well buy you ten guns if it were going to help keep you safe. But this one"—he indicates the credit card—"is on Night Eagle. Work expense."

Breathing a sigh of relief, I release him.

After I fill out the required paperwork and the clerk tells me that I can pick up my gun in a few days pending approval, Grisham leads me to the shooting range.

POW has an indoor practice range, a massive space where target practice commences. Armed with a pistol similar to the one I just purchased, I stare at the man-shaped target standing thirty feet in front of me. As I peer at the targets, a shiver rockets through me from head to foot. Grisham, noticing, moves to stand behind me. With his arms around my waist, he leans in to speak calmly in my ear.

"It's okay. No one is going to hurt you. You're just here to practice. To get better at using your firearm. You can do this, Grits. You're the strongest woman I know."

I allow his words to wash over me like a salve, soothing all the scared bits and pieces in order to make me feel like the brave person he believes I am. I close my eyes, and then when I open them again the tremors are gone.

"I'm ready," I say clearly.

Grisham places a set of protective gear over my head for my ears. Then he steps back and stands by my side. When I glance at him, his eyes are on the target. Waiting.

It's like riding a bike. There's no safety mechanism on this gun, only a hammer and a trigger, and both must be engaged in order to fire the weapon. The training sessions I had with my father years ago roll through my mind like a slide show, and I aim for the chest. I steady the gun and keep my eyes wide open.

Focus, Greta. Focus on the target, eyes wide open, squeeze...

The shot resounds off the walls and rafters and a hole opens up in the chest of my target. A satisfied smile settles onto my lips. When I look at Grisham, he's grinning at me. He gestures toward the headpiece, and I pull it down around my neck.

"You were holding out on me," he says. "You're a good shot. What aren't you good at?"

I shrug. "It's been awhile. I wasn't sure I'd remember what to do. But I did."

He shakes his head, staring at me with wonder in his eyes. That expression will never, ever get old. I want to put it there every single day. For Grisham to look at me like I'm something special, like I'm important, makes me feel like the luckiest girl on the planet.

And he just gave me yet another gift: confidence. I know that if I ever have to use a firearm to defend myself, I'll be able to do it. But I don't want it to have to come to that.

"I want the police to catch this bastard so I'll never have to use this gun." My tone is flat and hard.

Grisham places his hands on my shoulders, forcing me to look into his eyes. I set the revolver down carefully on a metal rail beside me and then place a hand on Grisham's chest. "Me, too. In the meantime, you're going to have to be extra careful, Greta. I don't want you going anywhere by yourself. If I have to, I'll be your shadow."

I smile. "You can't be my shadow. You're still working at the base until December."

He frowns. "Halloween is next week. We don't have much longer until the end of the year. And then I'm all yours. Until then, make sure you let Mea know that you two need a buddy system going. And the guys will walk you to and from your car at work every day. I want you to stay with me at night."

My ears perk up. Grisham wants me to stay with him at night? As in...

"Grisham, I really don't want to hear this wrong. You want me to stay at your house every single night? Wouldn't that mean I'd need to keep my stuff there?"

His lips curl upward. "Would that be a problem? I kind of like your stuff. And Eggs needs a mom *and* a dad."

I just gawk at him, mouth agape.

He sighs, then patiently spells out his request. "Greta...I want you to move in with me."

The first emotion I feel is shock. It threatens to knock me off my feet. Then elation buoys my spirit, lifting me so high I feel like I could become airborne at any moment.

Holy hell. He just asked me to live with him. Grisham Abbot wants me in his home...all the time.

Then I think of Mea. She's my best friend, not just my roommate, and I don't want to leave her hanging.

"I want to live with you and Eggs. I really do. But I can't just leave Mea hanging without any notice or without knowing what she'll do next about a roommate. I'll talk to her about it and maybe we can figure it out. But I'm not saying no."

God, I'm definitely not saying no.

He nods resolutely. "Okay. Talk to Mea and then get back to me. Because I want you all up in my space, Grits. Not just because I want to protect you. But because you're mine."

I'm yours.

My eyes are moist as I gaze up at him. I've never lived with a boyfriend before, and I realize with a jolt of surprise that I want nothing more than to share a home with Grisham. Share a life with him.

It could have happened when I woke up to see him staring down at me on the beach that day. Or maybe it happened when he stayed with me the night I had a concussion. Hell, it could have even been when he made love to me for the first time.

It doesn't matter. At some point in this roller-coaster ride with Grisham Abbot, I'd gone and fallen in love with him. There is no question about it; it's just a true and simple fact. And now he'd bought us a puppy and he wants me to move in with him. But the *L* word hasn't yet come into play.

Am I alone in my amorous feelings for this sexy Navy SEAL who saved my life? Or is he falling for me, too?

23

Grisham

By Wednesday of the following week, I'm pretty sure I've annoyed Greta with the amount of time I'm spending with her. I don't want her to feel trapped by my presence, but I'd rather that than something happen to her on my watch. She's received no more "gifts" from her stalker, and I'm grateful for that. But I'm sure he's lying low after the attack. Maybe he knows that Greta filed a police report, and that his unwanted attention is now on file.

Either way, spending time with her just feels...right. It gives my life a different kind of purpose. I want to protect her, but I also have an unyielding urge to make her happy. To make her smile. To make her feel the kind of pleasure that makes a woman want to stay.

I want her to stay with me.

It's a foreign concept to me, wanting a woman to stay. Relationships for me have been purposely short and to the point. Mutual casual affairs have been all I've allowed in my life for a long time. But with Greta, I want so much more than that.

I want *life*. I want the whole package. Sitting on the couch with Greta's legs draped across my lap in the evening is more enthralling than a wild night with some faceless woman from a raucous bar. But I'm not sure how to convey my feelings.

I don't want to scare her away, and I don't want to jump the gun. I want to make sure she's ready for all I have to give.

Or, if I'm being honest, I want to make sure that *I'm* really ready.

I've never committed to anyone in my life. Maybe I don't have the first clue how to be good at it.

But, as I walk into Night Eagle that day, I have a firm grip on exactly what I *am* good at.

"Hey, you." Greta greets me from her desk, pausing in whatever work she's doing on her computer to stand, coming around her desk to walk right into my arms. I hug her tight, resting my chin on top of her head and sighing with absolute contentment.

"I always feel better when I'm holding you," I say honestly. "That way, I know you're safe."

She tips her head back to look up at me, smiling indulgently. "I'm fine, silly. I've just been here working. And I have a literal army of guys to watch my back."

"True. But physical contact is always better."

She pulls back completely and gestures toward the office. "Dad wants you in there ASAP. I think they've got something they're working on that's short notice. So they've been trying to sort things out and come up with a working plan. I think it might be a rescue of some sort."

I nod, my mind immediately transitioning from boyfriend-mode to work-mode. I kiss her lips quickly and walk into the office, closing the door quietly behind me.

Jacob is situated on the couch, looking thoughtfully at something on his laptop screen. Kyle glances at the screen over his shoulder, seemingly reading what his boss is looking at. Dare, Teague, and Shaw are poring over a map of some kind, blown up to large scale.

"What's going on?" I ask as I enter the room and sit down at Jacob's side.

Everyone glances up, surprised to see me. They were all so absorbed in their tasks that they hadn't heard me open the office door.

"It looks pretty serious," I offer cautiously.

Jacob looks back down at the computer. "It always is when there's a child involved."

My stomach sinks. "What's up, boss?"

Dare sits up and rubs his hand over his head several times. In weeks of working with him, I've learned that it's his telltale sign of stress and worry.

"It's not good, dude," he says grimly.

The foreboding feeling I'm experiencing increases. I can feel a bead or two of sweat break out on my brow as the fist of anxiety in my stomach grows and clenches.

"A little boy has been taken."

The sentence drops on the room like a bomb, carrying me to a dark and deadly place where there are no survivors. Anybody who takes a child from his family has a sick, twisted soul and that means we're dealing with a monster.

"FBI's on it?" I ask.

"Yes. They've located the place where the child is being kept. We're all just hoping he's still alive. They've asked us to go in to help extract him. Just south of the state line there's an underground network of tunnels that have been around since the Civil War."

Frowning, I look at the map spread out on the table. "Like from the Underground Railroad?"

Jacob nods. "Sick fucker took the kid and escaped into the tunnels. No ransom note. So he's not after money. He just wanted a kid to play with."

My stomach rolls. "Oh, fuck."

Kyle speaks up. "We're communicating regularly with the feds, but this team doesn't have much time to strategize. Every moment counts. We don't want to go in and fuck it up, but we don't want the kid to have to stay there any longer than necessary."

Dare nods. His face looks strained. I can see it on all the guys' expressions. This case is wearing them down. "We need you on this, Grisham. Your stealth training is going to be essential. We plan to be down there Friday, ready to go in the middle of the night Friday night or early Saturday morning."

I nod, already all in on this mission. "You've got me. Let's get this shit figured out. I want to bring that kid back alive."

Jacob nods, and we all get back to studying documents and begin planning out the details.

It's Friday afternoon, and I've decided to take Greta out for lunch. We're leaving in a couple of hours for our kidnapping rescue assignment, and I want to spend a moment with her before I leave.

She sits across the table from me, her long dark hair pulled into a high ponytail that shows off the elegant lines of her neck. She's casual today in a pair of jeans and boots, with a thin, long-sleeved sweater that accommodates the continually dropping fall temperatures.

Whatever look Greta decides works best for her on any given day is a look that grabs and holds my attention. She's so much more beautiful than she even knows, and it's a quality that draws me toward her like iron filings to a magnet.

The server at the casual eatery we've chosen brings us platters of sandwiches and chips, and we dig in. I watch Greta take a dainty bite of her pastrami and Swiss, and then close her eyes in pleasure while she savors it. Swallowing hard, I turn my attention to my own sandwich. The girl is pretty damn distracting when she's eating. I didn't even know a girl could be sexy while she ate.

"So you guys are all set for this mission?" she asks cautiously. "Everything has been practiced and you know what you're doing like the back of your hand?" Her voice carries a hint of anxiety, lilting upward ever so slightly at the end of her question.

"Yes, angel," I answer patiently. "We've got this. There's no way we're letting this monster hurt that kid. We go in and grab him, bring the guy down, and get out. He won't even know we're coming. We don't have to follow the same procedures the FBI does; that's why they called us in on the case."

She nods. "I know that. But I worry. I want my father and my boyfriend to come back in one piece."

"We will."

"If you don't think you'll be back by tomorrow night, just tell me now. I can change the plans with my mom and sisters and you can meet them another time."

I shake my head, forcefully rejecting that idea. "No. You planned this, and I know it's important to you. It's important to me, too. I'll be there. We'll be back in plenty of time."

She nods, stark relief apparent in her eyes. She asked me to have dinner with her at her mom's house earlier this week, before I found out I'd be leaving on assignment this weekend. But since we were planning to grab the kid in the middle of the night tonight, I know I'll be back in time to make good on my plans with Greta. I don't have any worries that I'll miss it.

"Sounds good," she replies. "I'll be counting down the hours until you're back safely."

As we finish lunch, we talk about what our friends have been doing lately. We've been wondering what's taking Dare and Berkeley so long to get engaged. As right as they are together, I'd have thought it would have happened a year ago. But they seem content just as they are. And Greta hasn't brought up a potential new living situation to Mea.

"She's just been kind of stressed-out lately," she admits. "Mea's usually just so zen about everything. She lives life in the moment, never worrying about what comes next. But opening a business goes against all of that. For the first time in her life she can't just throw caution to the wind. I think she's adjusting. Plus, there's something else going on with her that she's not telling me about. I just don't think it's the right time to up and leave her, you know?"

I nod, trying to hide the disappointment that rips through me. "Okay. In the meantime, though, Eggs is starting to like me better than you." I shrug, feigning indifference.

Greta gasps, pointing a finger at me. "Low blow, Abbot!"

I shrug again, and then stand. Holding out my hand to her, I say, "Ready to go?"

She takes my hand and I lace our fingers together as we begin the short walk back to Night Eagle. "Hey, maybe you two can bond some tonight when you take him to your place. Hey, Mea's going to be home tonight, right? I don't want you alone."

She nods. "I think so. It's Friday night, though, so she could be out. If she decides to stay somewhere else, I'll go to my mom's. I don't want you worrying about me while you're working. Okay?"

"Okay." I pull her into my side.

When we pass the parking lot adjacent to Night Eagle, I immediately sense that something's off. I stop walking, surveying our surroundings and trying to put my finger on what exactly is different. My eyes gloss over Greta's car, and then they snap back to the blue paint of her RAV4.

Scratched. Someone keyed her fucking car.

I release Greta's hand as I head over to her car in a brisk jog. She's calling out behind me, but I don't stop until I reach the car. I stoop, fury igniting a fire in my chest as I read the words etched in the side.

SLUT

The letters are large, flowing in jagged succession from one end of the doorframe to the other.

"Goddamn," I mutter angrily. "He did this to your car."

By this time, Greta has pulled up short beside me, and when I glance over at her face her bottom lip is caught between her teeth and her eyes are aimed at the disgusting word scrawled out in the language of hate on her vehicle.

"Come here." I drag her into my arms and turn her away from her car. "Don't look at it. It's hate and it's a lie. We're going inside, and we're going to call the detective assigned to your stalking case. This guy won't get away with it, Grits."

She nods, allowing me to tow her around the corner and into the building. I take one last look at her car before it disappears from view, and all I can think of is how badly I want to meet this guy in a dark alley one night rather than allowing the guy who's been terrorizing her to be brought to justice through the law.

Guys like that don't deserve a trial by jury.

And now, a new thought crosses my mind: *I have to leave her tonight for a mission hours away. How the hell am I going to be able to do that?*

24

Greta

Thanks for coming over tonight, B." I smile gratefully at Berkeley as I pull my legs up beneath me on the couch.

"I don't think Grisham was going to go on his assignment with the team if I didn't agree to this," teases Berkeley.

But she's right. Grisham was adamant that he wanted all three of us to stay together tonight. He claimed there was safety in numbers.

"And this whole situation with your stalker is freaking Dare out, too. He's relieved I won't be alone at our place tonight. I won't complain, though," she continues, as a tendril of her blond curly hair falls into her face, "this spread equals pure happiness to me."

She gestures toward the three fondue pots spread out on the coffee table. Mea dips a fluffy marshmallow into the steaming turtle fondue. When she lifts it, a drizzle of chocolate drips from the powdery treat back into the pot.

"I might want your boyfriend to freak out and overreact

more often if it calls for a fondue sleepover party." Mea pops the dessert into her mouth and moans in delight.

Berkeley frowns. "I don't think he's overreacting. I can't believe someone keyed your car. And after the incident last weekend..."

The subject of my stalker feels like a black cloud following me around, drizzling ice-cold drops of rain over every aspect of my life. I reach for a strawberry and dip it into the white chocolate fondue. Taking a bite, I eye Berkeley.

"They'll find him. And then this will all be over." I sound much more confident than I feel.

"In other news," I continue, "Grisham is going to meet my mom tomorrow night."

Mea and Berkeley both pause with bites of dessert halfway to their mouths.

"Really?" asks Mea. "You two are getting serious. You never introduce guys to your mom."

I nod.

"Well, he's already met your dad. That was the hard part. Your mom's a sweetheart. She's going to love Grisham." Berkeley smiles sweetly.

I've had the same thought many times since I arranged this dinner. Neither of my parents ever get to meet the guys that I date, because I've never seen the point of introducing any of them. But Grisham is different. His presence in my life feels weighty, as if it has significant meaning I want my family to share in and be a part of.

"The only hard part will be convincing Gemma she doesn't have a chance with him!" I giggle, thinking of my outgoing, flirty younger sister. She's going to fall hard for Grisham. With his tattoos, sexy, messed-up hair, and the fact that he practically had the word *HERO* written across his chest, she's going to be totally in love.

Too bad. He's all mine.

The thought sends me spiraling off into a happy land where Grisham and I end up together.

Well, he's meeting my mom tomorrow. He asked you to move in with him. I now share a puppy with him. Is the happily-ever-after part really that far off?

Mea scrutinizes my facial expression. "You're totally gone over this man, Greta. I've never seen you like this before."

Her uncharacteristically somber tone makes me sit up straighter, paying closer attention. "Yeah, Mea. I really am."

Her expression darkens. "Make sure he feels the same way before you let yourself fall. I mean it. Sometimes guys change up the plan at the last minute, leaving you reeling and confused. Don't give him your whole heart, yet."

Berkeley and I both turn to gawk at her. "Are we still talking about Grisham?"

Mea meets my gaze levelly. "Absolutely."

Berkeley and I exchange a glance. We both know Mea well enough to realize we aren't going to be able to delve any deeper into her statement, but she was clearly hinting at something. I just wish I knew what.

"Noted," I finally answer.

Her comment rockets Grisham's job back to the forefront of my mind. Dating him will not be like dating a regular guy. When he travels for work, he won't be able to text me and call me at any given moment. He'll need to stay focused on his mission, watching his team's back, and getting the end result accomplished while keeping everyone's safety uncompromised.

How will I deal with that?

My mother's face flashes in front of my eyes like an apparition. My father's work had come before her and my family, time and time again. Am I just setting myself up for the same fate? I'm not willing to come second to a man's career. I know that. There are too many scars left from seeing how sad and unhappy my mother was all the time. I don't have it in me to suffer silently, even if the man in my life is a hero like Grisham.

Berkeley reaches out, touching my shoulder softly. "Hey, Greta. It'll be okay. Grisham is a great guy, and when he commits to something, he does it with his whole being. You'll see."

Her comment, meant to buoy my spirits, only deflates me further. *When he commits to something...* That's my biggest fear, in a nutshell. That Grisham will commit...to Night Eagle. To the missions.

But not to me.

We move on from that topic, and our night continues pleasantly. But my mind is always on Grisham and what I can expect from him moving forward. As I drift off to sleep, Mea and Berkeley slumbering beside me, I find myself wondering if I can really give myself over to Grisham.

Can I allow myself to love a man who may not fully love me back?

I arrive at my mom's house the following afternoon well before dinnertime. I promised my sisters some quality time alone with them before Grisham joined us. We've been gathered around in the kitchen, baking together. I couldn't decide what to make for tonight's dessert, so I took requests from the girls. I'm currently popping a peach cobbler into the oven, while Gabi stirs up a marshmallow crème frosting for red velvet cupcakes.

We're laughing and joking and teasing, and I'm grateful that the little bit of distance having my own place provides keeps our relationship strong. There's not enough time for them to get sick of me or vice versa.

My mother walks into the kitchen, a sunny smile on her face. "So nice to see all three of my girls having fun together."

I return her smile. Gemma shrugs and tries to pretend like she wasn't just having a blast a moment ago. My mother cocks her head toward Gemma and rolls her eyes at me. Pressing my lips together, I hide my smile.

"So what time does the man of the hour arrive?" asks Mom.

I check the clock on the oven. Five o'clock. I told Grisham we'd have dinner around six. I'm expecting him to text me any minute to let me know he's back in town and on his way.

My phone dings just as that thought flits through my head, and I run for it. My mother laughs as I trip over my feet lunging for my purse.

My face lights up when I see the text from Berkeley.

Dare just got home! I'm guessing Grish is on his way to you?

My lips curving into a smile, I glance at my mom. "Time to put the Cornish hens in the oven!"

She helps me spread apricot glaze on all five birds, and then we place them in my mother's stainless steel double ovens. Her kitchen is top-of-the-line. Cooking at her house is a much different experience from trying to throw a meal together at my apartment.

I make sure my side dishes, baby new potatoes with rosemary and garlic and zucchini casserole, are ready. I prepared them earlier, so all I'd have to do when Grisham arrived was heat them up while he got a chance to chat with my family.

Everything is perfect.

Smoothing the one-piece shorts romper I'm wearing, I pace the kitchen nervously while I wait for him to arrive. Until I notice my mom watching me.

"What's wrong?" My alarm is palpable, spreading through me like a virus. "Did I forget something?"

"No, honey," she says gently. "Everything is going to be fine. Why don't you grab a glass of wine and go relax?"

Without waiting for my response, she uncorks a bottle of Riesling and pours me a glass. I take it gratefully, sipping and letting the cool liquid slide down my throat.

"Thanks."

"Don't worry." Mom pours her own glass of wine. "I can't wait to meet the man who has you so tied up in knots."

I take a seat at her distressed antique kitchen table. "He doesn't usually. I mean, we're great together. We really are. It's just that tonight means so much to me. You and the girls are the most important people in my life. You're meeting the man I'm in love with. Pair that with the fact that I'm cooking an enormous meal and I'm definitely coming apart at the seams. Just a little."

Mom studies me intently. Her eyes, with just the finest of lines spreading out from their corners, are shrewd. "You love him?"

I study my wine. "I do."

We sit in silence, sipping our wine. Before I realize it, I've finished my entire glass. When the oven dings I walk over to take out the hens.

"What's keeping him?" I wonder aloud. "He should be here by now."

As if on cue, Gemma strolls into the kitchen. "I'm hungry. Where's your man, Greta?"

Panicked, I look to my mother.

"You should just text him if you're worried," she suggests.

Great idea. I can text him. Or better yet, I can call him. He's not on the mission anymore.

I wander down the hallway as I push the little phone icon beside Grisham's name in my Favorite Contacts list, and I hold the device up to my ear.

"Hey, Grits."

The relief that just the sound of his voice brings me is like a salve. My body instantly relaxes, the previous tension ebbing away. I smile as the tranquilizer known as calm assurance works through me.

"Hi." My voice is breathless. "I miss you."

His voice drops. "I'm in a meeting with your dad."

The steady flow of repose halts. "In Wilmington? But...Grisham! I just pulled dinner out of the oven. You're still forty minutes away?"

My voice rises, and I struggle for control, taking a deep breath and releasing it slowly.

Breathe. Hold yourself steady and just breathe. He's going to explain this.

Grisham's voice sounds pained when he answers. "Oh...shit. Baby, I forgot. Your dad asked if we could meet to debrief and to discuss my future at Night Eagle. I'm still high on adrenaline from the mission...damn. Can I come over later?"

I pull the phone away from my ear and just stare at it. *I can't believe this is happening right now.* The soothing effects from my glass of wine are instantly vanquished by the dirty feeling of second place. To my father's firm.

This is what you've been afraid of though, isn't it? The tiny, spiteful little voice inside my head mocks me. *You aren't enough for him. His job is always going to be more important. It doesn't matter how important this night is to you. He isn't here. He doesn't care.*

My hand trembling, I place the phone back at my ear. Grisham is calling my name, seemingly since I stopped listening a few seconds ago.

"Greta? I'm sorry. I promise I'll make this up to you, okay? Stay at your mom's tonight. I don't want you going home alone."

I almost laugh. This is just getting better and better. He doesn't want me to be alone, but until a moment ago, he'd forgotten all about me.

"It's fine, Grisham. I'll talk to you tomorrow."

I'm proud of how calm my voice is. Inside, turmoil is raging, but on the outside I sound distant and polite. Detached.

"Oh, man. You're mad. Right? Grits?"

"Have a good meeting with my dad, Grisham. Good night."

I end the call.

Clutching the phone in my hand, I turn and walk back down the hallway to the kitchen. Both girls are sitting at the table now, teasing each other while my mother watches with her glass of wine. She looks up when I enter, an expectant smile on her face.

The smile fades away when she gets a good look at my expression. She immediately asks my sisters to go wait for dinner in the living room. They start to groan, but when she gives them her sternest "Don't Mess with Me Right Now" look, they make themselves scarce.

And when she stands up and faces me, my stoic steps finally falter. I stop, grabbing hold of the countertop with both hands and leaning into the granite with every ounce of strength I can muster. That countertop is the only thing holding me together right now.

"What happened?"

My voice breaks. "He's not coming."

"Oh, Greta..."

That's all it takes. Just those two sympathetic words, crawling under my skin and into my bloodstream, embedding themselves into all the fibers of my being. And I crack.

The sobs burn my chest. I'm not sure what emotion is more prominent: my seething anger, or my profound sadness?

I fell for a man because I felt safe enough with him to believe he'd put me first. *Could I have been wrong about him?* I know how important the opportunity to work with Night Eagle was for him. But was it more important than me?

Deep down, I think I always expected him to choose work over me, because that's what men like Grisham do.

Turning my face into my mother's shoulder, the tears continue to roll. I'm just not sure Grisham is the man for me anymore.

25

Grisham

I know.

As soon as she hangs up the phone, an acute sense of aware-ness slams into me.

I fucked up.

As soon as I leave my meeting with Jacob, I turn down Teague and Shaw for drinks at the bar down the road from Night Eagle. Instead, I get in my car and call Greta's number.

"You made her cry, you asswipe. I know some guys...big guys. I'm going to have them pay you a visit. I'm gonna specify where they should hurt you first, and the first place is to kick you right in your b—"

I interrupt the sassy voice on the line. "This must be Gemma."

"I don't care that you know who I am. You made my sister *cry*. She never cries."

I sigh. "Yeah, I know she doesn't. But I made a mistake. You understand mistakes right, Gemma?"

Silence on the other end of the phone.

"So, will you put her on the phone?"

Gemma laughs. *Damn, this kid is tough.*

"She's in bed. She went upstairs right after she talked to you and hasn't been back down since. You're out of luck. I suggest you take a hint and find yourself a new girl to screw over."

And for the second time tonight, an Owen woman hangs up on me.

I don't sleep that night. Sitting on my back patio, I stare out into the blackness where I know the ocean is answering to the pull of the moon. There's no way I'm letting Greta go. I can't. She's become a gravitational force in my life. I'm helpless against it.

I don't bother going inside; I know the emptiness in my bed will haunt me. Greta belongs there. Eggs sits in my lap in the lounger. His occasional whine tells me that he misses her, too.

Rubbing the top of his head, I try to soothe him. "Shh. It's okay, boy. Daddy messed up, but I'll get her back for us. Promise."

When the sun breaks over the horizon, my eyes are grainy and dry. But I'm alert with a purpose: finding Greta. She spent the entire night thinking she isn't important to me, that I won't put her first. And I showed her exactly that.

Giving Eggs a quick rub under his chin before sticking him in the mudroom with his bowls and his toys, I head out. I climb in the Jeep and drive away from my house.

But I'm not going far. If Greta is upset, I have an idea of exactly where she'd go as soon as the sun came up. Or just before.

When I arrive at the surf spot, I park and walk down the steep wooden staircase.

Ah. I do know her. Better than she thinks I do.

She's sitting in the sand, facing the crashing waves. Not many surfers this morning. The early November air is chilly in North Carolina, though not biting. All of the tourists are gone. There are a few true blues, though, catching the waves and riding them to shore on their boards. Greta is watching them.

"This is where I thought you'd be," I say as I approach. My voice is quiet, deeper and rougher than I expect. "I'm glad I found you. You shouldn't be alone."

She doesn't turn as she replies, "Is that why you're here, Grisham? It's always about duty with you, right? I'm not a damsel in distress. If that's all you see me as, our relationship wasn't going anywhere, anyway. Because as soon as I didn't need saving anymore, you'd move on to the next woman."

More than anything, I want to touch her. My hands curl into fists with the strength it takes not to. But I can see that right now, she doesn't need my touch. She needs my affirmations, and my explanation.

"You're not a damsel to me. I think you're strong...and capable. I'm so sorry about last night."

She doesn't reply. Her eyes are still focused on the salty sea, but a single tear drives a wet trail down her cheek. My heart cracks when I see it.

"Greta? I want this. I want *us*. I'm sorry I didn't show up last night. I never want to be that guy. The guy who disappoints you. The guy who isn't there for you. I know—"

Her head whips toward me as she interrupts, and there's a fire in her eyes. "You know I went through years of watching my father do that to my mother? Of watching him do that to *me?* My dad's a good man, Grisham. He's a hero. He wants to save the world. And I see so much of you in him. I have a feeling that's what drew me to you in the first place. But I can't be with you...it's not the life I want. I know you're a good guy, and this is killing me to say. I just need some time."

Disbelief forces me to remain exactly where I am. My words aren't going to fix this situation, not when my actions are the thing that destroyed it.

It feels like déjà vu, but as I lean over and place a soft kiss on her cheek, and then stand up, I'm struck with one thought.

In order to show her what kind of man I can be for her, I have to do something it might kill me to do.

I have to give her the space she's asking for. I have to walk away from her.

I'm able to wrap up my discharge with the military earlier than I expected, and the second week of November is my first one working full-time at Night Eagle.

And it happens to also be my first week without the extreme comfort and simmering satisfaction of knowing Greta is mine.

I walk into work at 8:30 a.m., and she's not at her desk. Simultaneously sighing in relief and acute pain, I walk back to the break room to grab a cup of coffee.

Greta is there, watching her large white mug fill under the single-cup dispenser. She turns her head, a greeting hovering on her lips, but when our eyes meet she falls silent. Time is frozen for a moment while she holds me in her startled blue stare.

Her eyes dart downward, a quick once-over of my body, and when they draw back up to my face there's desire in her eyes.

That's a fierceness I remember very well, and my body answers her perusal with stiff recognition.

There's nothing I need more right now than to cross the cavernous divide she's placed between us and pull her into my arms.

"What are you doing here?" she blurts.

"It's my first day as a full-time member of the team. You're looking at a proud *ex*-Navy SEAL."

Her expression shutters. "Congratulations."

"Greta—"

The door swings open and Kyle enters. He looks back and forth between us before walking to the counter and grabbing a mug. "Everything okay in here, Greta?"

He ignores me completely and addresses her, which sends a bolt of anger searing through me. *I always knew he had a thing for her.*

Kyle's interest never fazed me, because I knew without a doubt that Greta's heart belonged to me. But now...

"It's fine. Good morning, Kyle."

Her voice is pleasant, and you wouldn't know anything had passed between us just a moment ago.

Kyle gives me a funny look. "Morning, Greta."

They begin talking together and I can't stay in there any longer. Coffee can wait. I leave the kitchen and head for the office.

This is going to be a rough fucking day.

Word travels fast. Greta told Berkeley about our break, who in turn shared it with Dare. Dare must have let the rest of the guys know, because I receive more than one sympathetic eye as I enter the office for our morning meeting.

"Fuck," I mutter. "Everyone knows?"

"You're just lucky it's my fault she ended it," offers Jacob. "Otherwise, you'd be dead."

Dare claps my shoulder. "That's rough. Have some hope, though. Berk and I split for a while before we ended up together. Remember?"

Grunting, I give him a sideways glance. "Yeah. I remember. I almost killed you for hurting her."

His smile is regretful. "You did. And I would have deserved it. But it all worked out in the end."

He's wearing a lightweight jacket, and he reaches down to pull something out of the pocket. A small, black velvet box. When he opens it, a diamond ring gleams from its pristine perch inside.

"Whoa!" Shaw's exclamation is full of surprise. "You're finally doing it?"

Dare's grin is full. "I might as well, right? I knew I wanted to spend the rest of my life with the girl a long time ago."

"Why'd you wait so long?" I ask, curiosity pushing aside my own pain.

Dare shrugs. A determined gleam lights across his features. "I wanted to win over her father."

I throw my head back and laugh. "Shit, man. I could have told you that was impossible."

There's only one man in the world who's a tougher son of a bitch than my old man, and that's Berkeley's father. He views the world in a very one-dimensional way, and he had his sights set on his daughter creating a life with me. When Berkeley and I didn't fall in line, he was pissed. He placed much of the blame on Dare, and I thought he'd forever hold him responsible for Berkeley's kidnapping.

"Ah, ye of little faith." Dare elbows me in the ribs. "He gave me his blessing last night."

"You slick son of a bitch!" Now it's my turn to pat him on the back. "That's pure magic. Congratulations!"

Everyone takes their turn congratulating Dare. He and Berkeley are the perfect couple; everyone knows it. They can survive anything.

I'd hoped Greta and I were that strong. But maybe I was wrong.

I'm getting lost in that dark thought as Jacob sits down beside me.

"My daughter knows what she wants," he says. "She's a smart girl."

"Yeah." I nod. "She is. She's realized that I'm not it."

Jacob sighs. "She's scared. She doesn't want a man who loves his work as much as I did. I made the biggest mistake of my life, giving up when her mother decided she'd had enough. I should have told my job to go to hell, and fought for my family. I want you here, and I want you to give it your all. But if you're going to be with my daughter, you have to put her first. And I understand that, Grisham. I'd never fault you for it."

I stare at him. "Are you telling me not to give up on Greta?"

"I'm not telling you anything. Just hate to see my mistakes made twice."

He rises and calls our meeting to order. I lean in and try to concentrate, but my thoughts all keep drifting back to one person.

Greta.

26

Greta

The week flies by, and by Friday I can almost ignore the slicing pain that brings me to a sudden halt every time I see Grisham.

Hearing his voice is almost worse. The rich roughness of his voice is nearly enough to make me run into his arms. All I want is to be able to turn back the clock. What I can't decide is whether or not I want to go back and undo the relationship, or whether I want the night that he didn't show up to never have happened.

Either way, every single time I hear that sexy, all-male voice that just makes me want to wrap my entire body around his, my heart shatters a little more completely.

Every day this week, Dare came to me after lunch and insisted I train with him. At first, I resisted. If I couldn't train with Grisham, then I didn't really want to train with anyone. But Dare was so persistent that I started to suspect him asking me to train was Grisham's idea.

So, weak as I am for what Grisham wants, even after everything, I agreed.

I've also succeeded to turning our office into a fall wonderland. Every available surface is covered in colorful leaf garlands or pumpkins. I've added pumpkin spice coffee cups for our coffee machine. And there's a "Welcome Fall" candle burning on my desk. It's just another tactic I've been using to distract me from thoughts of the man I loved and lost.

But Berkeley's face says it all as she bursts in through the front door. She stops short, staring around her in shocked, horrified awe.

"Oh my *Gah*." She catches her breath. "What the hell have you done to this place? And why didn't you call me first?" She turns in a slow circle, taking in every last gaudy decoration. "This is..."

"Festive? Heartwarming?" I offer hopefully.

She glances at me, her expression turning from stupefied wonder to sympathetic concern. "Um, it's definitely festive." She swallows audibly. I can see her forced focus as she struggles to keep her eyes on me, and I use my hand to cover a giggle.

"What's up, Berk?"

"I'm here to see you."

My brows arch. "Me?"

She nods firmly. "Yep. Dare wants to have a get-together tonight. And since we don't have a house yet, Drake offered up his. You're coming."

My mouth is already open to protest. "I don't feel like it."

Berkeley's eyes take on the determined gleam she gets when

she is setting her mind to something. All I can do is groan, because clearly that something is me.

"I said, *you're coming.*" She narrows her eyes. "I'm not going to let you stay home by yourself on a Friday night moping. You didn't let me do that when Dare and I broke up."

"Um, I tried." I pointed out the information she's clearly forgotten. "But if Berkeley wants to mope, Berkeley mopes. There were plenty of nights when Mea and I couldn't get you out of your sweats or off the couch."

She waves a hand, dismissing my argument. "I need you to help me make appetizers. You know I can't do it!"

Her voice takes on a pleading note that she's hoping I can't refuse.

"Mea's not going to want to come either, if it's at Drake's. She doesn't like that guy."

Berkeley huffs. "She has absolutely no reason to hate Drake. So if I have to, I'll make Dare pick you two up and toss you into his truck."

I scowl. "I just...don't think I can do it, Berk."

My voice is quieter, more serious. Her mouth turns down at the corners when she realizes that there's no convincing me to come to this party. She rubs my shoulder. "I want you there, but I understand."

"I can't be around him any more than I already have to."

Just then, the Night Eagle security team exits the office and heads off into separate directions. As Shaw and Teague head toward the stairs to train, they greet Berkeley and shoot me sweet smiles. Grisham's eyes burn into mine as he heads down the hallway, and Dare stops to put his arms around Berkeley from behind.

"So, we'll see you tonight, Greta?" asks Dare.

I shake my head, a regretful smile on my lips. "Sorry. I can't make it."

Dare's eyebrows lift in surprise. "Really? I know one person in particular who will miss you."

Berkeley twists out of his arms and kisses his cheek. "I'm gonna run and speak with Grish for a sec. Be back in a minute."

He nods, watching her go the way a wolf keeps a close eye on its mate. There's a pang in my chest, and I place my hand over my heart absently.

As soon as Berkeley is out of sight, Dare leans closer to me. "I'm proposing to Berkeley tonight. I want to make sure all the people we love are there. Please don't stay away. It's just one night."

He leans back and holds my gaze as my mouth drops open. "Ohmygod, Dare! Of course I won't miss it!"

His answering grin is genuine and lights up his entire face. "Good. I know she's going to want to remember this night with us having all our friends around us."

This changes everything. There's no way I'm going to miss Berkeley's engagement because of my fear of sharing a room for an evening with Grisham. I want to be there for her.

Kyle comes out of the office door with a file. He walks toward my desk and places the manila folder on top. "Your dad wants this info plugged into a spreadsheet."

I nod, taking the file and placing it beside the laptop. "Got it. Hey, Kyle? What are you doing tonight?"

Dare does a double take, looking from me to Kyle and back again.

Kyle shrugs. "I don't have any firm plans yet. Why?"

Dare glances at me quickly. "Greta..."

I move on, in a hurry to finish my statement before I can think too deeply about it, or change my mind. "Well, now you do. You can come with me to Dare and Berkeley's party tonight."

Kyle glances at Dare.

"Uh, yeah, man. You're welcome to attend. It's just a small get-together at my buddy Drake's place. But we'd be happy to have you there."

I turn a sunny smile on Kyle. "What do you say?"

Kyle's eyes light up behind his glasses and he runs a hand through his sandy hair. "Sounds good. What time should I pick you up?"

"Eight o'clock. You're right on time." I give Kyle a quick peck on the cheek as I close the apartment door behind me. After I lock it, we walk to his car where he opens my door.

Kyle is dressed casually in crisp, dark jeans and a white button-down shirt. He looks handsome; he always does. But I'll never be able to look at him as anything other than a nice guy. A friend.

Not after Grisham.

I'm quiet on the ride over, and I notice Kyle glancing at me a few times as he drives. "You okay?"

I nod absently, staring out the window.

"Look, Greta...I know about you and Grisham. If you want to talk about it, I'm here to listen."

I turn in my seat so that I'm facing him and prop my elbow

up on the console between us. "Why do you men live and die by what you do for a living?"

He shoots me a quick, confused glance. "Uh, what?"

Shaking my head, I direct my gaze back out the front window. "Nothing, Kyle. I'm fine. People break up, and then they move on. It's just what happens."

He nods slowly as we pull onto Drake's street. "And are you? Going to move on, I mean?"

His question is almost shy. I close my eyes for a moment, breathing in and out. The thought of moving through my life without Grisham fills me with emptiness.

But no matter how hard I try, I can't forget him.

When Kyle pulls into the drive, I open my door and exit the car without answering his question.

He puts an arm around me as we walk toward the front door. "You will. It doesn't seem like it right now, Greta, but you'll move on. You're too amazing to spend your life pining away for a guy who didn't deserve you."

I want to protest. I want to argue with him, because I know better than anyone what an incredible guy Grisham is.

He's just no longer *my guy*.

But I keep my mouth shut, and I allow Kyle to lead me into the house.

We walk into Drake's foyer, and to the left is his large living room. An enormous stone fireplace sits as the focal point of the room. Currently, there are several people gathered on a large sectional sofa.

Mea has already arrived, flying solo as usual, and she's sitting right beside Ronin Shaw with her feet tucked up beneath her. She's giggling prettily, and I almost roll my eyes because I've seen Mea's flirtatious act before. It's fluid and flawless, and she's broken many a heart with it. Drake stands at the fireplace, working on building a fire. But as he stokes the logs, he continues shooting glances over at Ronin and Mea.

Hmmm. I see you eyeing them, Drake. Why do you pretend? Just ask her out.

Before I can speak, Mea spots us and jumps up. She comes rushing over and gives me a big hug, like I hadn't just seen her getting ready for the party a couple of hours ago.

She glances at Kyle in surprise. I didn't tell her I was bringing him. I'd already made the decision and I didn't want to deal with any adverse reactions.

"Mea, you remember Kyle, right?"

She nods, eyeing him curiously. "Of course. Hey, Kyle."

He greets her warmly. "Hey."

"You'll excuse us, right?" She aims the request-that-isn't at him and then grabs my elbow. Dragging me toward the dining room where a table is laden with food, she stops and pulls me closer to her.

"What the hell are you thinking?" Her voice is a hiss.

I pull my arm away. "I needed to get through the night. Kyle is good company."

Her eyes are slits. "Kyle is into you."

"He knows we're just friends."

A tense silence pulsates between us. Mea's tiny size is no match for the energy that threatens to overtake any room she's in. But I can be stubborn, and I've decided that I can't listen to what anyone else says right now. I'm just trying to get through each day one at a time.

Finally, Kyle clears his throat at the opening between the living room and the dining room. "Greta? Why don't we go grab a drink?"

Tossing Mea a pleading glance, I walk away from her and follow Kyle. "That's a great idea, Kyle."

He leads me through the dining room's opening to the kitchen. Drake has the granite island set up as a drink station. There's bottles of liquor and mixers, bottles of wine, and beer in tubs of ice. Set up on his kitchen table are glasses for every type of drink.

Kyle whistles. "He didn't spare any expense on the drinks."

I smile, actually relieved to see the array of alcohol covering the table. My heartbeat is pumping much more quickly than it should be, and my hand tightens so harshly in Kyle's I'm sure I'm hurting him.

Grisham is standing at the bar, talking to Drake.

They both turn and look at us as we enter, and Grisham's eyes immediately drop down to Kyle and my clasped hands.

They fly back up to my face, and all I want to do is turn around and walk right back out the front door. Grisham's Adam's apple bobs as he swallows, and his jaw clenches.

This was such a mistake.

But Kyle pulls me forward, asking me what I'd like to drink.

"Oh, hey, Greta." Drake's voice is smooth, covering whatever I'm sure he's really feeling inside. He holds out a hand to Kyle. "Kyle, right?"

Kyle drops my hand in order to shake Drake's, and I take the opportunity to slide away toward the kitchen table. I pick up a wineglass.

Walking over to the table, I grab a bottle of something red. I uncork it, and then I pour the garnet liquid into my glass.

"Grits."

His voice stops me cold. The bottle clinks back down onto the table. I don't glance up, keeping my eyes glued to the trembling hand holding my glass.

"I can't do this, Grisham. Not now. I just want to be here for Berkeley."

"We need to talk."

"I don't think she wants to talk right now, Abbot. At least, that's what I heard."

Shock permeates me from the inside out as my head snaps up. Kyle is standing behind me, aiming a steely gaze at Grisham.

Oh, crap.

Grisham's voice is low and even, but I can hear the danger lurking just under his words. "I wasn't asking you, Wessler."

Kyle places his hand at the small of my back. Grisham's hands ball into fists at his sides. Drake steps up beside Grisham, his eyes on Kyle.

I quickly turn, causing Kyle to spin with me. "Let's go, Kyle. I want to sit on the couch."

I don't look behind me as I tow Kyle to the living room. I don't have a chance to grab my glass of wine before I go, which is a shame.

Because tonight, I'm going to need it.

27

Grisham

You know what, Drake? I'm going to jail tonight. Because I'm going to kill that son of a bitch."

I start in the direction of the living room, but Drake's iron grip stops me in my tracks. I look down at my arm, where his hand is fastened tight, and then up at his face. Drake's teeth are clenched together and his eyes are narrow slits. He's just as pissed as I am.

"Everybody knows she's your girl, Abbot." He hisses, low enough for my ears only. "But you can't start something here. Did you see her face and how fast she was pouring that glass of wine? She's miserable."

"Exactly!" My urgency to get to Greta, to make her understand how much I care about her, makes me lunge in the direction of the living room again. "She needs me. Not him."

Drake growls, a low sound deep in his throat as he now uses both arms to restrain me, wrapping me up in an unbreakable hold. My chest heaves as I suck air in and out of my lungs. "She also looked like she just needs to get through a night in the same house as the guy she loves."

My body stills upon hearing this. Drake releases me when he sees I've stopped fighting. I stare after Greta, even though I can't see her anymore. There's a pounding in my ears that has nothing to do with anger, and something in my chest squeezes painfully tight. I recognize the feeling, but I'm too much of a coward to put a name on it. "You think she loves me?"

Drake shakes his head and goes to grab a beer from the bucket of ice on the island. "I thought you were supposed to be smart."

He peers at me over the top of his bottle. "You good? Do I need to get your boys in here to take you out?"

I shake my head. No way I'm leaving Greta alone with Kyle. He's obviously a goddamn predator, moving in on her when she's been single for exactly five minutes.

A niggling, out-of-reach thought tugs at a far corner of my mind, prompting me to reach for it. But I can't quite pull it into focus, and it floats away before I can figure out exactly what bothered me.

"I'm good."

He nods. "You'll get her back. But tonight is Dare's night."

I nod. Circling my shoulders as if I'm about to go into a ring and fight, I shake my head a few times. I'm not just angry. I'm pissed and I'm helpless and that combination is unacceptable for me. I can feel it taking hold in my chest and clasping something tighter and tighter until I can hardly breathe. I don't just want Greta back. I need her.

Drake slaps my back, and then we head into the living

room. I make sure to grab a beer before we leave the kitchen.

Gathered around various seating choices in the room are all of our closest friends. My SEAL buddies are missing because this is Dare and Berkeley's party, but I know every attendee well. Everyone is chatting and drinking, with plates of food in their laps or on tables. The atmosphere is jovial and happy, except for the gray cloud that hangs between Greta and me.

I can't keep my gaze from straying to her as the night drags on. She's the most gorgeous girl in the room, in my opinion. She's *my* gorgeous girl. Her tight leggings hug her legs, and the long button-down shirt she's wearing is cinched at her small waist.

I remember exactly how it feels to have my hands wrapped around that waist, while she hovers over me in my bed.

I shake my head and sip my beer. I close my eyes tightly, but I can't keep the memories of having Greta in my arms, in my bed, at bay. They just keep coming, a flood that I can't dam.

Dare claps his hands together. "Hey, everyone! Can I get you all to take a quick field trip with me for a minute? Feel free to bring your drinks."

Everyone rises, bewildered looks on their faces. Some of us know what's coming, but I'm not sure why we have to leave in order for that to happen. Dare takes Berkeley's hand and leads her through the kitchen and out the back door, and we all follow.

We walk through Drake's awesome backyard setup toward the back gate that leads to the shore. Dare walks right through it, then removes his shoes. He helps Berkeley do the same, and we all follow suit. We walk along the sand, the lights from the beach cottages illuminating part of our path, the crescent moon high in the sky exposing the rest.

When we've passed maybe five houses, Dare opens the back gate to one with every light inside aglow. We walk through the backyard with a stone patio and fire pit, a small grassy area, and a hot tub.

"Dare! Whose house is this?" Berkeley glances around, clearly concerned about being arrested for trespassing.

Dare just smiles down at her, no answer crossing his lips. Then he reaches for the handle on the back door and pushes it open. He holds out his hand and gestures for Berkeley to enter. She hesitates for a moment, then steps inside.

As we all file in, Dare leads Berkeley through a gleaming kitchen. The cabinets are white, the countertops a polished marble. Stainless steel appliances shine brightly from their places. Everyone murmurs about the beauty and functionality of the room, as we pass through it to a stately dining room.

There's a painted detail lining every wall, and the paint color is a dreamy blue. But the room is empty of furniture, and we pass through on our way to the living room. The house is decked out with wide-planked dark wood floors that shine in the light from each room. When we reach the living room, Dare turns to face us.

"What do you guys think?"

I glance around; everyone's expression is completely lost. I note how close Kyle is standing to Greta, and then quickly avert my eyes. This is clearly an important moment, and I can't get lost in rage right now.

"Berkeley, I want you to go check out the view from that

window." Dare points. "It's dark, but you should still be able to see it."

"But the ocean is in the back of the house," protests Berkeley.

Dare pulls her close, bending down close to her ear. His voice lowers, but we all hear clearly his reply. "You'll like this one better. I promise."

Berkeley shrugs and heads for the window. She peers out, and while she does, Dare drops down to his knee behind her. Mea gasps, placing both her hands over her mouth. Berkeley, glancing at Mea in concern, turns around. When she catches sight of Dare on his knee, her eyes immediately fill with tears and her mouth falls open.

Holy shit. That look...that's true, pure happiness. She's going to remember this moment forever.

I've known Berkeley for my entire life, and I've always wanted her to be happy. When she found her perfect match in Dare, I resisted it. But in the end, even I could see how happy he made her. And I could see that she'd changed his life from the moment he met her.

"Berkeley Holtz." Dare's voice is clear and strong, if a little thick with emotion. "You're the only woman I will *ever* love. I've known that since the first time I laid eyes on you waiting tables at See Food. We've been through so much together since then, but you stayed by my side every step of the way. No one believes in me the way you do, and I can't imagine my life without you. Spend it with me here, in *our* house." Berkeley's eyes widen considerably, and she glances around the room. Dare continues. "Will you do me the honor of becoming my wife?"

Even though tears glisten at the corners of her eyes, Berkeley doesn't let them fall. She lowers herself to her knees in front of Dare and wraps her arms around him. I'm sure he doesn't need any more answer than that, but she gives him one anyway.

"This is our house?" Her voice is a wonder-filled whisper.

"It's ours, baby."

"Yes...yes, I'll marry you, soldier."

The room erupts. Dare stands up with Berkeley still wrapped in his arms, lifting her off her feet and twirling her around. When he puts her down, he slides the ring onto her finger. She gazes down at it, awe and utter happiness written all over her face.

The girls swarm her, pushing Dare out of the way as they hug her and ask to see the ring. I can't keep the smile off my face while I watch the blissful beam of light radiating from the newly engaged woman.

Dare sidles over to me and murmurs, with his gaze still glued to Berkeley, "How did I do?"

I turn and we clasp hands, giving each other a one-armed, backslapping hug. "You did good. She's happy."

He grins, still watching his fiancée. "Yeah, she is."

Then he finally tears his eyes away and turns to me. "I didn't miss who Greta came in with tonight. You good?"

I shake my head and glance over at Kyle. He's watching Greta, his eyes following her every move. "No. I'm not good. But it's your night. I'll deal with it later."

Dare nods slowly. "Yeah. I like Kyle. He's a nice guy. But Greta's yours. We all know that. It was a dick move to come here with her tonight."

"Definitely a dick move. And it's the last time he's going to take her out."

As if he can sense me talking about him, Kyle turns to look at me. Our eyes meet, and an unspoken challenge crosses the divide between us.

Okay, Kyle. You win tonight. But only tonight.

"I'm going to go hug Berk, and then I'm gonna get out of here."

Dare's forehead wrinkles. "You going home?"

"Nah. I'm gonna head to Night Eagle. I won't be able to sleep tonight, might as well catch up on some of what's coming up for our clients."

He nods. "I'll keep an eye on her."

I slap him on the back. "Thanks. Congrats, man."

I use my key card to swipe into Night Eagle, then let the door close and lock behind me. The front room is dark, and I glance over at Greta's empty desk before opening the office door. I leave it standing open as I plop down on the couch and close my eyes. I just sit for a few minutes, letting the night sink in.

Watching Greta walk into the kitchen with Kyle's hand in hers.

Greta refusing to speak to me, because speaking to me hurts her.

Berkeley and Dare getting engaged.

Kyle, challenging me through his stare.

It's been a long fucking night. With a sigh, I make my way over to Jacob's desk to pull a couple of client files. I find one of the clients I'm looking for, an executive of a multinational who uses our firm to install security systems when he opens a new branch. The other file, that of a client who uses us as personal security when he travels, is missing. I look up, frowning, and glance around the office. Locating Kyle's desk in my line of sight, I cross the room to get to it.

I've never been in Kyle's desk, never having a need, but since Jacob's desk is available to us if we need it, I assume Kyle's is as well. I sit in the leather chair and open his top drawer.

"Bingo."

There's a manila folder sitting on top. Opening it, I leaf through. There's a stack of receipts inside, and I sigh with disappointment. *Not the file I'm looking for.* I'm just about to close the folder when a receipt catches my attention, sliding out from behind the one on top.

Surveying it more closely, I see that it's from a local florist. The order was for a dozen red roses, dated when Greta received her mysterious bouquet.

What the fuck?

Instinct tells me to search through his desk to see what else he's hiding. A black, oily fear is forming in my gut, but I push it back, needing to see if I'm right. Before I flip the fuck out.

I place the framed photo of Greta on top of the desk and dive back into the drawer. I don't see any more photos, but after searching a bit, I come up with a note written in Greta's handwriting. Then I find several more, written on small pieces of notepaper or Post-its.

Kyle, made two copies of these documents for you.

Kyle, you have a phone conference with Davidson Chemical at 2:30 p.m. today.

Kyle, I outlined the main principles of this company's bio for Dad's meeting. Check it out.

Kyle, Daniel Waller from Lexeme Industries called at ten o'clock.

There are several of these, all held together with a paper clip. I stare at them, feeling like they're burning my hands but I can't put them down. I just keep reading them, over and over again.

Has Kyle saved every secretarial note that Greta has written him? What the hell? No...that would be crazy. That would make him...

Her stalker.

The errant thought that drifted through my mind back at Drake's house pops back into my brain, clear as a sunny day this time.

Predator.

Kyle struck me as behaving in a predatory manner.

What if he always had?

Memories come back to me as quick flashbacks. I think about the fact that the flower that pricked Greta was left in her desk at work. Who had access? Kyle did. He also could have grabbed her keys at any time to get into her car without her knowledge. He knows her home address, so he could have left the gift on her doorstep.

And now...he's with her.

Fuck.

"Piece of shit!" My fist slams down into the unforgiving wood of the desk.

I sprint out of the office, not bothering to close the door behind me. I exit the Night Eagle building quickly, knowing the door will automatically lock as it closes, and run for the Jeep like my life depends on it.

Because *hers* might.

I pound the steering wheel as I drive, cursing myself for not seeing it sooner. But everyone thought Kyle was such a *nice guy*. It was impossible to see the kind of sick creep he is underneath.

As I'm driving back toward Lone Sands, I put in a call to Jacob, explaining. My words tumble over each other and several times he asks me to slow down and repeat myself.

"Are you sure?" he asks urgently. He sounds like he's already on the move.

"Pretty damn sure."

"We need to be completely sure. Call your friends and make sure Greta stays at that party. Meet me at Kyle's apartment."

When we hang up, he texts me the address, and I head for Kyle's apartment.

"Ronin." I bark into the phone when Ronin answers his phone.

He listens as I ask him to keep Greta in his sight.

"You sound off. What's up?"

In my haste, I don't explain the situation. "Just do this for me. I'll fill you in when I know what's going on."

"You got it." In the background, a loud cheer goes up from the party. I disconnect the call.

Kyle's place is located just outside of Wilmington, in one of the beach communities between the larger city and Lone Sands. When I pull up to the duplex, it's dark.

I don't bother to sneak, knowing Kyle is still at the party. I reach both hands into my pockets, patting, searching.

"Dammit!"

Realizing my lock pick is in the glove compartment of the Jeep, I hustle to get it and arrive back at Kyle's doorstep. Kneeling, I stick the small metal pick into the lock and snake it around inside, searching for the small groove. When I hit pay dirt, the lock turns easily in my hands. I turn the knob and let myself into the darkened house.

I enter into a dark, narrow hall. Flipping the lights, I follow a tiled floor past a living room, a dining and kitchen combo, and a bathroom. When I arrive at a bedroom, I flick the light, and all of the air escapes my lungs on a strangled cry.

I freeze, horror descending on me like a swarm of locusts invading an unsuspecting town. The words I want to shout are stuck in my throat, and I can't speak.

Greta's face is plastered all over the wall behind Kyle's bed. Her face, animated in some, still in others. He's caught her from a distance, and from closer up. Greta on a surfboard, riding a wave. Greta, smiling and laughing with Berkeley and Mea in a girly boutique. Greta, getting out of her car. Greta sitting in her car. Greta, walking up the sidewalk to her apartment.

It's just Greta, over and over and over again.

In his *bedroom*.

"Abbot!" Jacob calls my name from the front of the duplex.

"In here." My voice doesn't sound like my own. The dull ache of fear combined with the laser-hot streak of anger make it scratchy and raw.

On his dresser, there's dozens of surfboard figurines, much like the one he anonymously sent her. An array of women's jewelry in assorted boxes on his nightstand.

"Sick son of a bitch!" My voice is hoarse. My stomach is

rolling, tumbling over and over again until I have to run to the bathroom to empty its contents. When I finish, I stand up and wipe my mouth. On shaky legs, I return to the bedroom. Jacob is on the phone with the detective he's friendly with in the WPD, the same one who is assigned to Greta's stalking case.

"Get here, now," Jacob says loudly. "We've got him."

I have no doubt that when they begin combing through Kyle's things, they'll find more receipts for the flowers and gifts he bought her. He's definitely going to go down for this.

As long as I don't get my hands on him first.

My phone vibrates in my pocket. When I see Ronin Shaw's name on the screen, I pick up immediately.

"Dude. I'm not sure why you didn't want Greta to leave, but she said she wasn't feeling well."

Panic rises inside of me, threatening to boil over and consume me completely. Never, in all the times I've been sent on a dangerous mission, have I felt fear like this.

"She's gone? Dammit, Shaw! I told you to keep her there! Kyle is her stalker."

I hear the sharp intake of breath on the other end. "You sure?"

"Yes, dammit!" I look at Jacob, who has finished his call and is watching me intently.

"Fucking shit. Kyle took her. They left ten minutes ago."

With an ever-tightening fist of terror in my stomach, I relay the information to Jacob.

"Go," he orders. "I have to stay and wait for the detectives. Go *now!*"

I don't need to be told twice. I break into a run and don't stop until I reach the Jeep.

28

Greta

My head is pounding, and I blame the headache for making me hear the sentence that just came out of Kyle's mouth incorrectly.

"Kyle...*what* did you just say?"

We're sitting in front of my apartment, in Kyle's car. I turn to face him, my mouth hanging wide open in utter disbelief.

Kyle blinks rapidly, looking everywhere but directly at me. When his gaze finally settles on mine, his face is almost pained. "I said *I love you, Greta.* I always have. Since high school. I just think that now is the perfect time for me to say it. This can be our time."

His tone is soft, and there's an expectant expression of pleasure on his face. Whatever he's expecting me to say, however he's expecting me to react to his proclamation, it's drastically different from the reality.

"Oh, Kyle," I say softly. "That is so sweet. I had no idea...that you felt this way."

He nods eagerly, reaching across the console to take my hand. "It never seemed like the right time, you know? I mean, I was kind of shy in high school. And then we were at different colleges. But then you started working at Night Eagle with me. And I thought..." His voice trails off, and a dark expression crosses his face. "And then you started dating Abbot."

I nod sympathetically, my mind spinning in a million different directions. It's not every day that someone professes their love for you. Looking into Kyle's eyes, I only wish I could feel the same way.

But I don't.

I squeeze his hand gently. "Listen, Kyle. I'm flattered, I really am. I wish I was the right girl for you. You're a great guy. But...things are super complicated right now. I'm still tangled up in my feelings for Grisham."

Kyle's expression is blank. "But you broke up with him."

I nod. "Yes, but that was only a week ago. And I *love* him, Kyle. That doesn't just go away overnight. Maybe in a year or two..."

I watch as Kyle's eyes shutter. His expression is completely bland. I can't read anything from it. "Yeah, okay. You're letting me down easy, but you're basically saying it's never going to happen."

All I can do is look down at my lap. "I'm so sorry, Kyle."

Kyle says nothing; he just stares out the windshield.

I wish I could read his expression. I wish he'd say something.

After a few tense moments of silence, I grab my bag and unlock my car door. "After you think about this, Kyle, you'll see that I'm right. We're not right for each other. I'll see you at work on Monday, okay?"

He doesn't answer, just continues staring out his front window.

I sigh as I exit the car.

Wow, Greta. You're bowling a strike tonight. No pins left standing.

The tiny hairs on the back of my neck begin to strain outward as I walk up the sidewalk. They're literally standing on end. It's a sensation I can honestly say I've only felt once before. And I don't like it. I'm almost at the stairs when I turn back to face the parking lot.

Kyle is still sitting there in his car. His eyes are burning into me. A shiver slithers up my spine. Quickly turning back around, I force myself to take the stairs one at a time until I reach the second floor, and then I unlock my apartment door with trembling hands.

Mea isn't home yet. She's either still at Drake's, or she's found a hot date for the night. Sometimes, she stays at her cousin's in Wilmington. Either way, my stomach tightens at the prospect of spending the entire night alone. As soon as I place my purse on the bar top, there's a knock on the door.

With a sigh, I walk back toward the door. I reach for the knob, and then hesitate. "Who is it?"

"It's Kyle. Greta...I just didn't want to leave things that way. Let me apologize."

"Oh, Kyle, you don't have to—"

I pull the door open, and my sentence is cut off as Kyle violently shoves his way into the apartment. He slams the door behind him with his foot, and the anger on his face transforms him from the sweet guy I know into a stranger wearing a mask of rage. I stumble backward so fast my feet begin to twist. A barstool catches me before I fall. It tumbles to the ground.

"Seriously, Greta."

Kyle stands before me, his hands fisted, his chest rising and falling with his heavy breaths. "How can you be such a fucking *idiot*? Everything you could ever need is standing right in front of you."

I blink. My mind hasn't caught up to the action in the room. Did Kyle really just *force his way* into my apartment? And now he's yelling at me? What the hell?

"Kyle! What are you *doing*?"

He ignores my question. Spittle is forming in the corners of his mouth as he speaks quickly. His brown eyes light up with fury. "When's the last time *Abbot* sent you flowers? And your favorite...roses?"

"How do you know that my favorite..." My voice trails off as I stare at Kyle. Something clicks in my brain, and suddenly, my limbs are paralyzed with fear.

"He's all you can think about. What is it, the sex? I never had you pegged for a *fucking cunt*, but I guess I could have been wrong. Maybe that's what you need from me."

It was Kyle.

He sent the flowers, the box at the door. He keyed my car...

He's my stalker.

When I realize the truth, it sends a reaction through my body that I don't expect. Instead of becoming more frozen in fear, my limbs immediately loosen. My head clears, because

I'm in a bit of a situation here. I've thought a million times about what I would do if I came face-to-face with my stalker, but I never, ever, thought it could be someone I know. Someone I *like*.

"You're not going to hurt me, Kyle." I sound calmer than I feel. I concentrate on taking slow, deep breaths as I edge sideways toward the end of the bar. All I can think about is making it down the hallway and to my bedroom before he can get to me.

His lips twist into an ugly sneer. It's an expression I've never seen on him before, and I pause to stare at his face.

"No, it's not going to hurt, Greta. You're going to *like* it."

I don't have time to react as he lunges for me. I turn, attempting to run, but he's on me before I can take a single step. I only succeed in knocking my bag and everything else off the top of the bar. He grabs me from behind, squeezing me painfully tight. I immediately begin to struggle. As his grip continues to tighten, Grisham's voice comes to me from somewhere deep in my mind. *"Struggling to free your arms first will just expend your energy, giving him the advantage."*

I stop struggling. Remembering everything Grisham taught me in the training room, I take a step to the side. It's small, but it's enough. Then I squat down suddenly. Kyle stumbles forward a bit, his arms loosening their hold on me considerably. Then, closing my eyes, I jerk backward with my head. The back of my head slams into his chin, and as I stumble forward with stars in my vision, Kyle's arms release me completely as he lets loose a string of curses.

I'm free. I'm free. I'm free.

I twist to the side, throwing my elbow up high. I connect with hard tissue; his stomach. He grunts, taking a few stumbling steps backward.

It only takes me a split second to realize that I have an opportunity. I turn and begin to run. I can hear Kyle; I can *feel* him as he comes after me.

Make it to the gun. Make it to the gun.

But I don't make it. Kyle tackles me from behind. I sprawl out on the floor, the wind leaving me as I hit the ground. Flipping me over so that I'm trapped beneath him, Kyle looms above me. Panic saturates every part of me, keeping me still and lifeless on the floor. My body is beginning to ache in the places where I've hit the floor, but I ignore the pain.

Kyle's lips curl in a cruel grin. I can't see any light in his eyes; he's gone completely dark. The friend I've known for years is gone, replaced by the stalker I never wanted.

"You like it rough." He says it like it's an observation, a fact.

Then he hits me, his open palm striking the side of my face with a resounding slap. The sharp stinging is enough to bring tears to my eyes, and my vision swims for a moment before my eyes widen in shock. I have no time to react before Kyle grips both sides of my shirt and gives it a violent jerk, scattering buttons all over the hall.

Shaking my head feverishly, I try to reason with him. "No, Kyle, stop. I don't want this."

Somewhere in the distance, probably still in my purse, I hear my phone ringing. The ringtone is the one I set for Grisham, "Halo" by Beyoncé. I try and focus on Kyle while simultaneously wishing with all my heart that Grisham would choose now to be extra persistent. Maybe when I don't pick up my phone, he'll come to my apartment. Hope blossoms in my chest, a beautiful flower I firmly grasp in my desperation.

"That's Grisham," I warn Kyle. "He'll show up"

Kyle sneers. "Then I guess we better make this fast. He'll make a quick exit if he finds us together."

My stomach lurches. "Don't, Kyle."

He just shakes his head at me. "Stop acting like you don't want it, Greta. The hard-to-get game is over."

Desperate, I draw my knees up beneath me. "Then let me be on top. That's the way I like it."

He freezes, clearly not expecting me to say such a thing. "You're fucking with me."

Yes, asshole, I'm definitely fucking with you. Fall for it. You sick bastard.

"No. You were right, Kyle. I do want you. So let me have you...just the way I like it."

I can see the shocked indecision in his eyes, and in the second that he hesitates, I use my knee to thrust upward as hard as I can. He howls as I connect with his testicles.

Kyle falls forward, but I scoot out from beneath him and half-crawl, half-lurch for my room. I slam the door behind me and lunge for my nightstand. I fumble, then pull the drawer open and pull out my loaded handgun. Its solid weight settles in my hands as I hold it steady and aim for my bedroom door.

It takes a few beats, and he's clearly moving slower than before, but I hear Kyle on the other side of the door.

Go away, Kyle. Go away, Kyle.

He opens the door. Surprise registers on his face as he sees my gun, but only for a second. Then he composes himself and his righteous anger is back in place, a permanent mask.

"Now I don't even want you anymore, bitch. Now I just want to end you."

I cry out. "Don't, Kyle! I'll use this, I swear to God I will."

He laughs. "No, you won't, Greta. You're not brave enough. That's probably not even loaded."

He comes for me, and I squeeze the trigger.

Twice.

29

Grisham

The ride to Greta's apartment is torturous. I don't stop for a single red light, and I drive like a madman as I swerve around any vehicle stupid enough to be in my way. When I finally pull up, I practically leap from the Jeep. Stumbling slightly before I catch myself, I spring for the apartment. Jacob texted me on my harried drive that the police were on their way to Greta's as well. I don't waste time, thrusting her front door open, glad it's been left unlocked.

Until I discover the state of her apartment.

A barstool is lying on its side. Her purse and the rest of the contents of her bar top lay strewn on the floor. I've only just had time to take in the state of the room before I hear her scream. My head jerks to the back of the apartment in the direction of her bedroom. I've only taken half a step in that direction before the first gunshot rents the air.

Then the second.

In a blur, I'm down the hallway. My heart slamming against

the walls of my chest, my lips moving in a silent prayer. I haul ass until I get to the doorway of Greta's room. She's standing there, eyes wide open, gun held in her hands. She stares at the unmoving form of Kyle on her bedroom floor.

Oh, my God.

I can't stop the relief that flows through me at seeing her standing there, safe, but the state of her indicates that she's been in a fight. She's disheveled, and her hair hangs loosely from its previously neat ponytail. There's also a prominent bruise beginning to form on her left cheekbone.

"Greta, baby." I step over Kyle and walk toward her slowly. "You did good. Give me the gun now, okay?"

Her eyes lift from Kyle's limp body and focus on me for the first time. I can see sheer terror there, and it breaks me in half.

Kyle is so damn lucky Greta already shot him.

Her arms shake as she swallows. "Grisham?"

"It's me, angel. You're safe."

That's when her face crumples and she lowers her arms. I grab the gun and gently take it from her hands. Placing it beside us on the nightstand, I pull her into my arms.

She begins to sob, deep, heaving cries that shake me to the very core. Every single one of them drives me further and further out of my mind, but I struggle to keep it together. For her.

"I got you, Grits. I got you." I hold her, feeling like I need to do it. Like having her in my arms is necessary for me to continue functioning.

"Don't let go, Grisham. Please."

I just grip her tighter, clutch her closer.

"Is he...is he...?"

I know what she's trying to ask, and I gently pick her up in my arms. There are sirens outside the apartment now, and I know that any minute this place will be crawling with uniforms. I carry her to the living room, sit her gently on the couch, and kneel in front of her.

"You stay here. I'm going to go check."

She nods, her expression miserable as she stares down the dim hallway.

I move quickly down the hall to her bedroom. Kyle is still lying on the floor. I kneel down beside his form.

One half of me wants him to be dead.

You deserve it, you bastard.

The way he hurt Greta will stay with me forever, a grudge I'll never be able to forgive. But the other half of me knows that if he's dead, his ghost will haunt Greta forever. She's not a killer; she'll grieve him whether he deserves it or not. And she'll carry the guilt on her shoulders until it finally drags her down.

He's lying on his back, eyes closed. But I see his chest rising and falling. I place my fingers on his pulse point and feel it, though weak, still pumping blood through his veins.

He's alive.

Walking back down the hallway, the police enter the living room. Three officers take a stance, their weapons aimed at me. One of them glances at Greta huddled on the couch, while another yells, "Police! Don't move."

I raise my hands in the air.

Greta looks up in shock. "No...not him." Her voice is shaking. "The man who attacked me is lying on my bedroom floor."

"He's alive," I offer as the officers move farther into the apartment. "But unconscious."

The officers reholster their weapons. One of them addresses Greta. "Miss, are you hurt? There's an ambulance en route."

She shakes her head. "I'm fine."

The officer stays, asking Greta to tell him what happened. He pulls out a pad to take notes. The other two move down the hallway past me to check on the situation with Kyle. I continue into the living room, taking a seat on the couch next to Greta. I don't expect her to, but she immediately scoots closer to me. I instinctively put my arm around her shoulders and she leans in.

She answers the officer's questions clearly and without hesitation, and pride swells inside me. She's been through an ordeal no woman should ever have to experience, but she knows what happened and she's not afraid to tell the truth. I rub my hand up and down her arm soothingly.

From time to time, as she explains something disgusting that Kyle said to her, or when she tells the officer how he tackled her down and hit her in the face, I flinch. She then turns to me and gives me a reassuring nod, like she's trying to make sure I realize she's okay.

As she's talking, the paramedics rush in with a stretcher, and the officer points them toward the bedroom. They emerge a few seconds later with Kyle lying on the stretcher. Greta stiffens, and I pull her head into my chest so I can softly stroke her hair. It's only been a week, but I've missed having her with me.

Finally, the officer is finished questioning her. Her eyelids appear heavy, and her head keeps drifting back to my chest.

When the police officer instructs her to be available the following day for more questioning, I shoot him a scowl.

"Why? She shot him in self-defense. You see her face. He attacked her. He was going to sexually assault her or worse right before she pulled the trigger. He's been stalking her for months. There's evidence inside of the Night Eagle Securities office."

Greta sits up again. "Am I in trouble?"

Jacob and Detective Henderson, his acquaintance from the WPD, step through the open front door, followed by Dare and a panicked-looking Berkeley.

"No, you aren't." Detective Henderson sends the uniformed officer a stern look. "And we'll wrap this case up as quickly as possible. You were the victim here, Greta."

Greta stands and faces her father. He cups her cheeks, stooping so he can look into her eyes. Holding her face to the light, he curses. "Is he dead? If he isn't, I'm going to be the one to do it."

I shake my head regretfully. "Get in line, sir."

"Are you okay?" he asks Greta, his voice breaking. "I was so scared, pumpkin."

She nods, grabbing his wrists with both hands. A fresh tear rolls down her cheek. "I'm okay, Dad."

He nods, and then pulls her to his chest in a hug. I'm watching her face, and I see her wince as he squeezes her.

She's hurt. She's exhausted. I want to take care of her, to make sure she gets some ice, some painkillers, and a good night's sleep.

But will she let me?

When Jacob releases Greta, Berkeley is next to grab her.

"Careful, Berk," I warn. "She's sore."

Dare comes to stand beside me. "Did she give him hell?"

I nod, feeling pride rise inside me again. "Yeah, she did. And then she shot him when it wasn't enough."

Dare whistles low. "Tough girl."

You got that right.

I think about what Greta's been through tonight. What she's been through over the last few months that she's been in my life. She's tough, sure. But she's also warm, tender, and loving. She stands up for what she believes in, and she won't accept less than what she deserves. She's incredible, and I'd be a fool to let her get away again.

"Is she free to go?" asks Jacob, speaking to Detective Henderson.

The detective glances at us from where he's speaking to a uniform officer. "Yes. And don't worry about Mr. Wessler. He'll be charged with stalking, aggravated assault, and attempted rape."

Berkeley gasps, putting her hand to her mouth. Tears fill her eyes, but she gulps, tamping down the emotion.

"Greta?" she coaxes. "Let's go in your room and pack a bag. You can get changed into something comfortable." Her eyes stray to Greta's ripped shirt. A lacy camisole flashes beneath it.

Greta nods.

We all just stand around, quietly waiting for their return. When they do, Greta is carrying a black leather duffle.

"Ready to go?" asks Jacob. "You can come home with me tonight."

My stomach plummets. My skin immediately becomes clammy as I imagine the thought of spending one more night away from her. Especially after what just happened.

I need her with me.

I open my mouth just as Greta speaks.

"Actually," she says quietly. "I'd like to go home with Grisham. I just...need to be with him. We have things to discuss."

Jacob's eyebrows lift and his forehead creases, but he doesn't protest. He looks at me, giving me a serious perusal. Then, making a silent decision, he nods. "All right. Call me in the morning."

She nods, moving to hug him once again. "I will."

Relief sweeps through me. Then hope soars like a hot air balloon, filling me and lifting me higher and higher.

She wants to be with me tonight. Does this mean she's going to take me back?

After all that's happened tonight, this is an opportunity. I want to make sure she's okay, and when she's ready, I want to let her know how I truly feel about her.

I want to make her mine again.

30

Greta

As Grisham drives me back to his beach cottage, I drop my head against the car window, letting the cool glass soothe my aching face.

So this is how it feels to have been in a fight, I surmise. I wonder if my aches and pains are worse, knowing that I was fighting for my life.

Grisham is quiet. He must sense that I need the reticence. Either that, or his head is full of his own complicated thoughts. When we pull up to the house, Grisham turns to me. His eyes are full of shadows, and I can't read them. After everything that happened tonight, I nearly forgot the fact that I haven't been close to him in nearly a week. His eyes still have the power to hold me prisoner.

"Don't move." His voice covers me like a blanket.

I obey, watching as he exits the car and crosses, his slightly uneven gait so beautifully Grisham, to my side of the car.

He opens my door, unbuckles my seat belt, and places his

right hand under my knees. Putting his other arm around my shoulders, he tells me to watch my head as he lifts me from the car. I'm too exhausted to protest. Or maybe I'm just too comfortable in his arms. I rest my head against his large chest as he carries me into the house.

Grisham bypasses the living room, taking me straight to the master bathroom. He puts me down gently, then turns toward the shower. Soon, white steam floats around the bathroom and Grisham turns back to face me.

He gestures toward the glassed-in shower. "First thing to do is get the feeling of the fight off of you. You need to wash yourself clean of it."

I bob my head, grateful that he's doing the thinking for me right now.

"Do you..." He hesitates.

I try to read his expression. Is it uncertainty there in his sage-green eyes? I take in his appearance for the first time tonight. At Drake's I was too busy trying to avoid him. And then, at my apartment...

He's casually sexy in worn, stylishly tattered jeans and a cotton Henley that stretches across his broad shoulders and sculpted chest. I know exactly what his tight, packed abdominals look like underneath, all the easier to picture in my head. His one shoed foot is covered in a navy Nike with a white check. My eyes slide back up, lingering on the way his jeans hug his muscular thighs. My mouth waters slightly, and I force my gaze back up to his.

"Do you want me to help you?" His voice drops to a low, husky tone that only ignites a raw ache deep within me.

Slowly, I nod. He approaches carefully, eyeing me like a wild animal he's cornered in the forest.

I guess I deserve his wariness, but it stings. More than it should.

I stand perfectly still as he reaches for my hoodie's zipper. I threw it on over my camisole while Berkeley helped me pack. He tugs it down slowly until the two sides pop open to reveal the lacy fabric of my tank. His sharp intake of breath is the only indication that he's taking in air, and his hands softly skim my shoulders as he slides the garment down my arms. Placing it on the countertop, he appraises me. It's like he's trying hard not to look at me but can't help it. I raise my arms, and he pulls my cami up over my bare breasts and off of my head. As he stares down at my midsection, a muscle ticks in his jaw and I glance down to see what he's angry about. My rib cage is spotted with bruises, likely from where I scuffled with Kyle on the floor. A shudder goes through me as I think about it, and I turn to check out my other side. Grisham looks on in the mirror as I discover that my back is black and blue.

Holding himself together, but now with trembling hands, he reaches for the elastic waistband of my sweatpants. He's upset, and I cover his hands with my own to still them. He raises his eyes to mine.

"Together," I whisper.

Our eyes locked, we work to slide my pants down my legs. When they're halfway down my thighs I stop, wincing from the soreness in my stomach. I'm not even sure where it stems from. I have a feeling I'm going to have sore spots for days I never expected.

Grisham reads my pained expression and takes over; I step out of my pants once they reach the floor, and he folds them neatly, placing them on top of the counter. I shimmy out of my panties and kick them to the side. Grisham's fists ball up at his sides as he takes in my entire body bared to him.

I step toward him, into his space, and his automatic response is to put his arms around me. His warm hands move up my back, and I sigh. Instead of making me stiff and skittish, his touch is warming me from the inside out, spreading comfort to all the places that need it.

I reach up on my toes to whisper in his ear. "Thank you. For knowing I was in trouble. For coming."

He lets out a shuddering breath. "The bruises...you don't know how badly I want to track down his hospital room and make him pay."

"Shhh," I hush. "I need you here with me."

His arms circle around me, and I rest my cheek against his chest. His heartbeat, thudding steadily beneath my cheek, brings me blissful peace.

"I didn't know if you'd want that," he admits. "I fucked up before, Grits. I know that. After tonight, I know now even more completely than I did before...I can't lose you. You're the most important thing in my life."

I nod, knowing in my heart that he's telling the truth. "I want to know about how you figured it out."

He pulls back and nudges me toward the shower. "I'll tell you everything. Just get into that steam first. It'll be good for the soreness. And I'm going to go get an ice pack ready for your cheek."

"Don't go far, Grisham." It feels silly, needing him this much. But right now, I need his presence just as much as I need to breathe.

His lips brush my forehead. "I won't. I'll be right back."

He opens the shower door for me, and I step inside. I lose sight of Grisham as he closes the door behind me, and I gladly let the healing steam envelop my body.

Twenty-five minutes later finds me wrapped in a new pair of sweats, while Grisham is clothed in a pair of gray fleece pants. His beautifully scarred torso is on display, and my eyes dance between it and his adorable expression of concentration as he holds an ice pack to my cheek.

My stomach turns as he tells me about the pictures of me on the wall in Kyle's bedroom. When I gulp, Grisham's gaze flits to mine. "It made me sick, too. But he can't hurt you anymore."

"I know. I just can't believe he's been watching me, taking photos. It feels slimy, like I've been violated."

Grisham lowers the ice pack and uses the back of his hand to gently stroke the sore area. "You have been. And it's disgusting. I'm so sorry this happened to you."

"You came for me," I whisper, dropping my eyes. "When you found out what he was. You came...even after everything I said and the way I pushed you away."

"Hey." He dips his head down so he can find my gaze, and lifts it to meet his. "I will always come for you when you need me. If the woman I love is in danger, I will stop at nothing to make sure you're safe. It doesn't matter—"

"What did you just say?" The question leaves on a whisper.

His lips are still moving, but I stopped hearing everything he said after those life-changing words.

He stops. A beat passes between us, and then:

"I love you. I tried not to, and then when I realized I did, I tried denying it to myself. But now, you need to know. You, Greta Owen, have all of me. I love you."

I cover my mouth with trembling hands as I stare at him. I'm waiting for the dream to be over. Or maybe I'm waiting for him to realize he's emotionally wrecked and spouting gibberish because of it. I'm waiting for *something*.

But he merely stares right back at me, and the only emotion I see shining out of his stunning green eyes is...love. Pure, unguarded love.

"I fell in love with you when you breathed life back into me on the beach." The words float off my tongue, because I've been holding them back for so long it's a relief to let them go free.

He takes my face in his hands so gently that a hundred emotions shake lose in my chest. And then he kisses me.

And *my God*, it's a kiss I will never forget.

He's gentle at first, and as his lips move against mine I can feel the love inside of him, like he's passing it from his lips to my soul. I open my mouth to him, and he groans as his tongue tastes me. He nips at my bottom lip, and I can't hold back anymore.

I ignore the needling pain in my body as I move to straddle his lap; he leans back to accommodate me, and I let my fingers roam the short, bristly hair at the nape of his neck. I grow hungrier as his hands gently draw a path down my back and around my waist, teasing at the skin on my stomach. Desire unfurls its leathery wings in my gut, and I wriggle against his growing erection.

"Hell." He moans, releasing my lips only to trail kisses along my jaw and down the sensitive skin of my neck. "I want you so damn bad. But, Grits, if you don't want this tonight...I understand. We can wait. I'm not going anywhere."

"I can't wait." The reply is breathless as I'm busy pulling my T-shirt off and tossing it aside. Glad I didn't take the time to don undergarments after my shower, I scoot off his lip so I can remove my pants.

"You're fucking hot when you're horny." His tone is teasing, but his eyes are dark and hooded, with fire brimming in their depths.

He stands in front of me, dropping his sweatpants to the floor. His cock bounces free, and its heavy length only excites me further, makes me want him more.

I push on his shoulders, and he sits back down hard on the couch. He opens his arms for me, but instead of crawling back onto his lap I kneel in front of him.

I've never done this for him before, and his eyes widen with his surprise. But he remains silent as he watches me wrap my lips around his swollen head.

This is something that I need to do. All of the ways I was violated tonight are still with me, and I need to purge myself of those feelings. By being with Grisham in this way, by giving him this piece of myself, I'm setting myself free from Kyle's intimidation.

Grisham's eyes flutter shut, and a string of curses leaves his lips. I pull back so I can lick the line formed by the vein that travels the length of him. I trail my tongue back up to the top. Then I take him fully in my mouth again and suck him as deeply as I can. When he doesn't fit, I use my hands to squeeze the base of him while my head bobs up and down at a steady rhythm.

"Fuck. Fuck!" His hands find my head and he wraps them in my hair, gently pushing my head in time to each stroke of my mouth. I continue to swallow him whole, moving faster until he abruptly jerks free.

"Stop." He pants. "Let me inside you."

He pulls me up, and I climb onto his lap. Without meaning to, I wince with the sharp pain in my thighs. Concern etched in his features, he pulls me into his arms and stands.

Confused, I wrap my legs around his waist. "No, Grisham. I don't care if it hurts. I want to."

"I will never hurt you," he says firmly. "Never."

He carries me to bed, placing me on top of his sheets, and then climbs in beside me. We face each other, and his hand seductively traces lines over my shoulder, down my side, and across my hip.

"We can do this if you want to," he says softly. His eyes penetrate every hidden corner of me. "But let me take care of you."

I nod, ready to give myself over to him completely.

Guiding me onto my back, he supports himself above me. Then he bends his head, taking my mouth and marking me as his. He reaches between us and strokes me with strong, sure fingers. I moan, pushing against his hand with my hips and throwing my head back against the pillows.

"This," he whispers at my throat, "is always, *always* supposed to feel good. I will worship this body, Greta, and the woman who owns it, for as long as you'll let me."

He brings me to the brink of the beautiful pleasure, and then smiles as he pulls his hand away. Before I can protest, he thrusts inside of me, and the fullness is even better than I remember.

Being this close to him, feeling every part of him connect with every part of me makes me feel like my body was created to love his.

He hisses as he pulls out of me, then thrusts back in. He lowers himself to his forearms, and I smile because I know he needs to be close to me as badly as I need him to be.

Then I bite my lip when the angle of his thrusts changes, and he begins repeatedly stroking my clit with an increasing intensity. It doesn't take long until I'm right at the edge of that wonderful precipice, ready to fall.

"I love you, Greta." His whisper is strained, but beautiful. It's the only thing I need to be able to jump.

I ride my orgasm longer than I ever have before, and it's not until I'm coming down that Grisham lets go of his own self-control. He plunges into me, deeper, faster. And then he's trembling and my name leaves him on a shout as his release empties inside me.

This is my SEAL, saving me all over again.

This is love.

Epilogue

Grisham

On Christmas morning, Greta's up early. It's unusual for her to be dragging me out of bed, but when a man stays up most of the night worshipping at the altar of Greta, it can happen.

She's giddy as she leaps onto the bed, straddling my lap and placing the palms of her hands against my chest. "Merry Christmas! Merry Christmas!"

I groan, peeling one eye open and then the other. "Damn, woman! I thought only kids were this excited about Christmas morning!"

She leans over me, her cerulean eyes vibrant and glowing. "I freakin' love Christmas! I thought we established that when I decorated."

"Yeah. You mean the day after Thanksgiving? When you drenched this entire house *and* the firm with green and red? Yeah, angel, I got it. I'm up."

I grip her hips and sit up, moving her with me as I go. "Let's go. If I'm going to be up this early, I want to see my girl in the kitchen cooking.'"

She slaps my chest. "Neanderthal."

Grinning, I attach my prosthetic and stand. I cradle her close to my chest, squeezing her perfect ass and nipping at her plump bottom lip. She moans, throwing her head back to give me access to her neck and pressing her body flush against mine.

"Give me fifteen minutes with you first." My voice comes out in a growl, because that's what she does to me. Still. She takes away rational thought, relocating my center of gravity so that my world revolves completely around her. I can't foresee it ever changing.

She giggles and ducks her head, pulling away from me and allowing her body to slowly slide downward, stimulating every part of mine in the process. "No! It's time for presents. Just me and you, remember? Then we're heading over to my mom's for Christmas morning breakfast and presents with the girls."

"Ah," I say. "Yeah, okay. Let me hit the bathroom and I'll meet you in the living room."

She swats my ass as I walk away from her, and I turn and give her a dark stare. "Don't start nothin', won't be nothin', Grits."

She smiles coyly and then disappears out of the bedroom doorway.

Minutes later, I'm walking out into the living room. Greta sits in front of our Christmas tree, laden with ornaments and colorful lights. Berkeley tried hard to divert Greta from using the brightly colored bulbs, insisting that white lights look better. But Greta refused, and I backed up my girl.

I haven't felt like this about the holidays in a long time. Christmas with my parents always felt like an excuse to show off what a perfect family we were, when I knew the truth. We weren't.

But today, I have Greta, and everything about this holiday feels completely different.

She pats a spot on the floor next to her, and I take a seat. My flannel pajama bottoms, which match hers, fit right in with the plaid Christmas tree skirt she picked up when we cut down our tree. I'm in awe of the way she's turned my world upside down in the best possible way.

Greta leans her head on my shoulder as we gaze at the twinkling lights. "I'm glad we're going to get to see your mom tonight. What's Christmas dinner like at your aunt's?"

I shrug. "I've never been. My dad always had us doing something showy on Christmas for the base we were stationed at. My mom and I never got to spend holidays with her family. I realize now that he isolated her from them a long time ago. I'm happy she's making up for lost time."

"His trial begins at the start of January. I hope it gives you the closure you need to gain freedom from him."

I sigh, kissing the top of her head. "Me, too, Grits. Me, too."

Perking up, she reaches under the tree. "None of that talk today, though. We'll have enough justice and trials in the new year to worry about. Today is about me and you and our first Christmas together."

I smile at her, knowing full well her most important gift isn't sitting under our tree. "What you got for me?"

She slides an envelope toward me. Quirking a brow, I lift the flap and pull out a white piece of paper.

Unfolding it, I see a drawing. It's a surfboard, blue and pink.

The colors swirl together, and there's a G_2 symbol drawn in gorgeous script in the middle.

"This is pretty," I saw quietly. "What is it?"

She bites the corner of her bottom lip as she assesses my reaction. "It's the design for the tattoo I'm getting." She points to her shoulder. "Here. Mea's brother, Mikah, designed it for me."

I'm speechless for a beat. "You're getting a tattoo?"

She nods shyly. "I love all your ink. You got it after you left for SEAL training, right? When we first met, you didn't have it. It represents change for you, when you came into your own after declaring your independence from your father. For me, it's going to celebrate the start of my new life. With you."

I just stare at her, disbelief filling me up. She's incredible.

"Plus"—she shrugs with a playful smile—"I think my skin could use a bit of color."

Laughing, I grab her into my arms and plant a kiss on her sweet neck. "I love it. I can't wait to see it on you."

She grins eagerly, pulling back from me. "So where's my present?"

I tap her nose with my finger. "You'll get it at your mom's. Let's get ready and head over there."

She frowns but allows me to lead her back to our bedroom and we do just that.

Greta opens the front door at her mom's.

"Hello?" she calls as we enter the foyer. "Merry Christmas, family!"

"We're back here, Greta!" Her mom's voice floats from the family room at the back of the house.

Greta takes my hand as we walk down the hallway. When we enter the family room, I'm filled with shock. Greta's two younger sisters are sitting in front of the Christmas tree, still in their pajamas. Gabi smiles sweetly at us, and Gemma's eyes dance with delight. That's my first clue. Gemma's eyes never dance with delight.

My second clue is Jacob's voice. "Merry Christmas, you two."

Greta's head swivels. Jacob and her mom are cuddled together on the couch under an afghan. They look cozy and comfortable, like they sit together like this all the time.

"What the—" Greta's voice drops. "Dad? What are you doing here?"

Jacob and Greta's mother glance at each other. The expression in their eyes is love rekindled.

"How long has this been going on?" Greta's voice is incredulous.

Her mom stands and comes toward her. "A few weeks. After Thanksgiving, Jacob and I had a long talk."

"Sweetheart," says Jacob, also rising, "I realized a long time ago that nothing will ever make me as happy as my family does. I had to figure out how to get your mom back. She's decided to give me another shot."

Gabi giggles from the floor. "Surprise! It's the best Christmas present ever!"

Greta turns to me, her eyes shining. "It is."

My heart fills for them. Their family is back together again. Now healing can begin in Greta's heart. Her trust issues stemming from the breakup of her parents' marriage would no longer scar her.

We spend the morning laughing together, opening gifts and eating a delicious spread. They accept me into their home and their family, and I'm filled with a warmth I've never experienced.

"Are you ready to go?" asks Greta sometime later. "We should get on the road if we're going to make it to Jacksonville by dinner."

We're sitting on the couch in the family room, having just finished watching a classic holiday film. I stand, taking her hand and pulling her up with me.

When I drop to my knee in front of her, her mother gasps. Jacob nods proudly, and the girls squeal.

"Greta Owen, you're the love I never thought I'd find. You've brought sunshine into my life where before there was only darkness. In the new year, I want nothing more than to be the man who makes you happy for the rest of your life. Please, angel, tell me you'll be my wife. I want your last name to be Abbot."

Tears are streaming down her face, and the gorgeous smile I've grown to love crosses her lips. She doesn't need to answer aloud for me to know she's mine.

Forever.

Please turn the page for an excerpt from the first
book in Diana Gardin's Battle Scars series

Last True Hero

Available now

Dare

Welcome to Lone Sands, North Carolina. Where lonely hearts find a home in the sun and the sand.

Seriously? This postage-stamp-size town off the coast thinks that their best feature is that it's full of lonely people?

This is probably the point when I should turn around, drive pell-mell in the opposite direction of Lone Sands. But I don't. I keep plugging. The love of my life, my Ford F-250, has made it this far from Fort Benning. I'm tired of driving, tired of pulling through fast-food drive-throughs. I just want to stop.

I just want to live.

That sounds so simple, just live. But how am I supposed to do that, now? I have no idea what the hell I'm supposed to do with my life from this point forward.

But according to my buddy Drake, this quiet little town is the place to be if you're looking for some peace and quiet after the army sends you packing.

I observe as I drive. That's something I've always been good at. Observing. Reading people. Taking mental notes.

Each new road I turn on is picturesque, dusted with sand. Charming shops and restaurants in bright colors adorn the quaint little streets. The ocean is visible sometimes when I glance down a side street, shining and winking with the afternoon sunlight. Cottages are scattered in clusters, tall sea grass intermixed with small dunes for yards.

I'm going to be living in a town that doubles as the cover of some damn girly book.

When I pull up to the address I'd put in my GPS back in Georgia, Drake strides out of the unpretentious bungalow. The front garden beds are alive with the leafy fronds of palm bushes, waving at me as if in welcome.

"Man, you made it!" Drake is pulling open my truck door and dragging me onto my feet. He proceeds to squeeze me in a bear hug so tight I think a few of my ribs are left cracked in his wake.

"Yeah." I rub my sides as he releases me, wincing. "I made it."

He's already standing beside the extended truck bed, reaching to grab my suitcase, pulling it up and out. "This all you brought?"

"That's all I've got."

Drake nods his blocky, shaved head. It sits atop his neck like a boulder perched on a stump. Every inch of him is like that: big and steady. The dude is as solid as a mountain.

He disappears through the heavy oak front door, and then pokes his head back outside to peer at me. "Get in here!"

When I enter, I look around, my eyes drinking in the living

room. Whistling, I nod my head in appreciation. "This is nice, Drake. Real nice."

The floors are some sort of dark hardwood, and although the living area we've just entered is a little tight, the ceilings are high and decorated with exposed beams. The fireplace takes up the entire far wall, made of some kind of natural stone that makes me stupid with envy. I walk over and reach out a hand, feeling the rough texture beneath my fingers.

"This is amazing."

"Yeah." Drake shrugs. "I knew that would speak to you. I worked on all of this myself. Place was a wreck when I bought it. But I can see the water from here, and I wanted the beach in walking distance. It was worth it to fix this old dump up."

I can tell from the loving way he talks about his house that he doesn't really think it's a dump. Whatever the opposite of a dump is, that's how my friend feels about this house.

"You did good, man. It's beautiful."

He grins his trademark, full-on cheesefest of a grin. "Thanks. Let me show you your room."

The house has two bedrooms; Drake leads the way to the smaller of the two and sets my bag down on a queen-size bed. The room is sparse: a bed, a dresser, and an en suite bathroom off to one side. But the ceilings are high here, too, and there's a sliding glass door that leads out to the sand beyond.

"Drake," I begin. "I don't know how to thank you for this."

He shakes his head and lifts a hand, cutting me off. "Don't. We're brothers. Maybe we don't have the same blood running through our veins, but you'll always be my family, Dare. I look out for my own. And I know what it's like when you first get out. You'll come work with me at the garage tomorrow, and we'll take it from there. You hungry?"

I nod, gratitude filling my chest. The feeling steals my words away; all I can do is nod. "Starving."

"Let's go to a little place I know. Crab legs and shrimp. We can eat till we're stuffed, drink a few, and then come home and crash. Sound like a night?"

"Sounds like the best damn night I've had in a while."

He grins ear to ear and slaps me on the back so hard I'm forced to take a lurching step forward.

A few minutes later, we are rocketing down the town's main drag and my long legs feel like they're wrapped in a burrito.

"I'm used to more legroom than this," I groan. "How do you drive this thing? Your ass is like five hundred pounds bigger than I am."

Drake cuts his eyes at me. "Don't. Talk. Shit. About. The. Challenger."

I roll my eyes so hard my forehead aches. Drake's always had a thing for fast cars, especially if they're packing extra heat under the hood. "Next time, we take the truck." My gorgeous, black, four-door, extended-cab, extended-bed demon.

We pull up in front of the restaurant, and I just sit in the car and study it a moment while Drake lugs himself out of the driver's seat. It's tiny, like everything else seems to be in Lone Sands. It's definitely a hole in the wall, with its gravel parking lot and creaky old sign hanging on rusty chains above the door. Written on it is the name of the place, SEE FOOD.

"Clever," I mutter as I exit the Challenger. Drake's breath hitches as my belt buckle scratches against the side of the car. I wince, checking the dark gray paint to make sure it's intact.

"My bad." I shoot him a chagrined smile. "All good."

When we're seated at a tiny booth inside the restaurant, I've already changed my mind about the sketchy vibes I was getting on the outside. In here, it smells like coastal heaven. My mouth is watering as I gaze hungrily at the menu, and I'm ignoring Drake completely, which is okay because he's ignoring me, too.

"What can I get for you boys today?"

I keep staring at the menu while Drake begins rattling off his food order for the waitress. I can imagine her eyes growing rounder and larger as he keeps going, because Drake normally eats enough for three men. Finally, I zero in on what I want and glance up at her to relay my wishes.

Now is a good time to point this out: I've been in the army for seven years. I've lived all over the United States. I've traveled plenty outside of it, too. I'm not a saint; I've met women all over the place that made my time in their native lands worthwhile. I'm only a man, and I've always enjoyed a woman's company.

But I've never in my twenty-five years seen a woman like *this*.

At first, as I stare, I'm not sure what exactly it is that sets her worlds apart. Her face is gorgeous, yeah. It's the kind of face that keeps men alive in a desert far, far away. The warm, whiskey-colored eyes that pierce me straight through my heart are Disney-princess big, and when she blinks something in my chest explodes. Or maybe it's her hair. All those light-colored curls piled high on top of her head, one wavy tendril hanging into her eyes.

Damn. I physically have to restrain my hand from reaching up to brush it away.

But it can't be any of those things, can it? I'm no stranger to meeting beautiful women in all shapes and sizes.

Maybe it's her body. Which, even covered up in a tight restaurant T-shirt and short-enough-to-peek denim cutoffs, is luring me dangerously closer to those legs that seem to go on for days.

Fucking. Days.

But, as I continue to embarrass myself because I can't pull my eyes away and force my mouth to work, I realize it's her total aloofness that has me salivating at the mouth. She could give two shits about who I am or what I've done. She's barely even looking at me. Wait, she really *isn't* looking at me. She's looking at a spot just above my left ear.

So, I'll make her look at me. I clear my throat and ask, "What's good here?"

Finally, *finally*, her gaze slides to mine, and whatever exploded in my chest earlier detonates once again, only about a million times harder.

"Everything's good here," she replies. Her tone is cool and cautious, as if she thinks I'm hitting on her. Huh. That must happen a lot.

"Okay." I shoot her what I hope is a winning smile. "Then get me one of everything."

Her mouth drops open slightly, and I enjoy watching her tongue play across her top teeth. "What?"

My grin grows as wide as one of Drake's kooky ones. "Just give me whatever you usually eat. I'm sure I'll love it."

She frowns, and a tiny crease forms in the center of her forehead that draws something inside of me up, out, and into the open. Looking at her is causing me to feel too exposed, too out in the open and unprotected. I glance back down at my menu, but the smile doesn't fade from my face.

"All right," she finally says. "I'll bring you a few of my favorites. But don't blame me if you hate them."

Her voice is a little haughty, and so soft and feminine that an extra surge of testosterone races through me. All those hormones centered in one particular place in my body, and I shift in my seat as I feel my jeans shrinking.

When I look up again, she's gone. But Drake is now staring openly in my direction, his grin as wide as I've ever seen it.

"You just fell in love a little bit, didn't you?"

"Shut the hell up."

He laughs. "I don't blame you. She's definitely hot."

"I don't want to talk about it."

"Okay, Romeo, we won't. I just want to watch you make an idiot of yourself for the rest of the night."

I'm halfway through my second bottle of Killian's when she returns, laden down with two trays of food. She sets them down on the table opposite us, and I watch closely as she first lays three platters in front of Drake.

"Thanks, sweetheart." His whole face lights up with his trademark smile, and it appears it's contagious, because she smiles right back at him.

When I see it, I suck in a breath and bite down hard on my tongue.

She has *dimples*.

"You're so welcome," she answers.

I like the slight twang in her tone. I like it a whole damn lot.

"And for *you*," she continues, aiming that gaze, the one that stabbed me earlier, in my direction. "I have a little selection."

She rattles off the name of each item as she sets it down: crab cakes, calamari, mushrooms stuffed with succulent lobster meat, and a metal bucket of buttered corn on the cob.

I'm still starving, and somehow the fact that this food is brought to me by someone who looks like her is making me so much hungrier.

"Thank you. You have amazing taste. Everything looks delicious."

Including you.

"It will be," she assures me, leveling her gaze at mine for another second. When she turns away, she leaves the sweet scent of roses in her wake. I inhale deeply, receiving the blend of seafood and flowers and mentally adding the mixture to the list of things I can't resist.

"Y'all let me know if you need anything else." She flounces away.

"So." Drake begins tentatively, and I know I'm not going to like the turn our conversation is about to take.

I stuff my mouth full of lobster-infused mushrooms and have to close my eyes because they taste fucking incredible.

"Your physical therapy is done, right?"

Drake doesn't waste time; he gets directly to the point. It's one of the reasons he's one of few friends I have in civilian life. I hate bullshit.

"Yeah. It's done, Drake. I'm clear."

"But you weren't cleared for duty. So how much are you going to be able to handle in the shop? I'm serious, dude. I don't want you getting hurt on my watch."

"I'm a grown-ass man, Drake, and an ex-Army Ranger. I can handle getting under some cars and getting shit done. You don't have to worry about me."

Drake continues to chew a mouthful of food while he studies me, and then washes it down with a gulp from his own bottle of beer.

"I know you're tough. But you've gone through a lot, Dare. I wouldn't blame you if you just wanted to take it easy for a while."

"I live at the beach now, right? I *am* taking it easy. But I'm going to earn my keep. Conversation over?"

He nods, not taking his eyes off of me. "Roger that."

I nod, allowing my eyes to wander around the restaurant. I spot Legs over by the computer on the back wall, checking her cell phone. I keep track of her as she busies herself with bringing food and refills to her tables. Other than ours, she has only two others. I've arrived in Lone Sands in April, a good month before the tourists will surge in, searching for summer fun.

Finally, she returns to us, holding our check.

"How was it?" she asks me. The wariness in her voice bothers me. She doesn't seem as cautious with Drake, and I want to know why.

"Drake," I say suddenly. "It's on me tonight. Want to head out to the Challenger while I finish up?"

Chucking, he salutes and heaves himself out of the booth. "Yes, Sergeant."

The waitress—how do I not yet know her name?—glances sharply at him as he speaks, and then aims her steadfast gaze at me while I take the check gently from her fingers.

"Berkeley," I read aloud. Damn, even her name strikes an image of perfect beauty.

"That's me. Did you like everything?" She's asking me as if she doesn't *want* to ask, but she *needs* to know.

"Best meal I've had in a long time," I answer honestly. "Thank you for that."

"I didn't cook it." She finally reaches up to pull that curly tendril off her face. My fingers curl on the table in response.

"I know that. But you chose it. I appreciate that."

She nods. "Anything else?"

"Yes." She waits, and I toy with my empty beer bottle as I talk myself into what I'm about to do. "I'm new in town, and—"

"No."

"What?" I haven't even asked her yet, so I'm more than a little confused about her refusal.

"No. I'm not going out with you."

"I haven't even asked you yet!" I know my mouth is agape, but I'm unable to force it closed. This is new territory for me. I'm drowning in uncertainty.

"Doesn't matter. I get a lot of guys like you in here. Can you understand that? I don't date customers."

I begin to nod. She takes the crisp bill hanging out of my outstretched hand. "Especially not *military* customers."

She walks away quickly before I can tell her to keep the change, disappearing behind a door leading to the kitchen and the back of the restaurant.

I let my head fall back against the booth, muttering a curse and closing my eyes. Somehow, that had gone so much more smoothly in my mind. Not that I'd thought it through well enough.

"Idiot," I whisper as I slide out of the booth and head for the door with my proverbial tail between my legs.

Lone Sands, 1. Dare Conners, 0.

Berkeley

The last two weeks of my college career fly by in a whirlwind of final exams, tearful exchanges with friends, and extra-special pressure from my parents to "get serious" with Grisham.

That would be Grisham Abbot, the man, according to my parents, I'm going to marry.

Grisham, quite honestly, is a great guy. He's the son of a navy admiral, a man who serves just under my father at the base he commands. Grisham's father and mine go way back to their days at the Naval Academy, where they both emerged as officers. Both men met their wives shortly thereafter, and the four of them have been an unstoppable team ever since. It's only natural, at least in their minds, that Grisham and I live happily ever after as a product of their lifelong friendship.

But Grisham's just not *my* guy. He just graduated from the Naval Academy, exactly like our fathers. I don't want to marry a younger version of my dad. I don't want to become the new and improved carbon copy of my mom. That's so not the life I've planned for myself.

What kind of life do I have planned for myself?

Ain't that the question of the century?

I have no clue. Trained chimps have a better grasp on their future than I do. I graduated with a major in interior design. My mother thinks that's perfect, because I'm going to be planning and designing navy events for the rest of my life. Sigh.

My welcome home begins with a bang.

My parents have thrown me a graduation extravaganza. Because my mother can't just call it a party. That would be ludicrous.

It's also, in a sense, my "coming out" party with Grisham. My reflection in the full-length mirror in my bedroom at my parents' house mocks me. The girl staring back at me looks as though she was made for this life. She was made to belong to affluent parents, her father one of the most powerful men in the United States military. Her mother is a flawless version of herself, always on top of her game, always the picture of class and authority. The girl staring back at me looks like she belongs on the arm of a handsome, clean-cut man of privilege who will work his way quickly through the ranks of the navy.

But inside that girl, another is fighting to claw her way to the surface. The real me, just waiting for a chance to spread her wings. The me who loves to run around in funny T-shirts and cutoffs. The me who spends hours in her room drawing beautiful spaces and painting canvases to hang on the walls inside of them. The me who is most at home in a seafood restaurant with old wooden floors and down-to-earth people who love me for me. Not for the future me who will make them proud, just the me I already am.

I leave the room, shutting the door a little too loudly behind me, and crash directly into my mother.

"Honey," she coos. "You look beautiful. Here, let me fix your hair. This piece is falling down again. I wish you'd grow out these layers. And flatiron it. It really would become you so much better."

I puff my lips out and blow, allowing the strand of hair in question to flutter flippantly around my face. "Better?"

She frowns, an expression her face doesn't handle very well due to the monthly Botox injections.

"Don't be smart. Get downstairs. Grisham's been waiting on you for thirty minutes, at least."

"Grish knows me well enough to know he could be waiting all night."

My mother's eyes roll skyward and I can almost hear her counting to ten.

I hold up my hands in surrender. "All right, Momma. I'm going."

The pins holding my hair up are already giving me a headache as I reach the bottom of our grand dual staircase, but I plaster a giant, fake smile on my face and begin to greet guests as they hover near me. Just dying to offer me their sincere congratulations on my completion of four years in college.

The University of North Carolina at Wilmington wasn't at all where my parents envisioned me earning my four-year degree. Since I was born a daughter and not a son, a military academy was out of the question. At least for my father. But they just knew I'd be headed to an Ivy League school after I graduated high school in Brunswick County, North Carolina. The last place my father was stationed when he earned admiral quickly became my home. Even though I've lived in many places before this town, I feel like I belong here. The Carolina coast is in my blood, and leaving it, even for four years, would have completely shattered my heart. So I fought hard, and won.

The faces around me are a blur as I head for the dining room table, which was nearly sagging under the weight of all the food littering the top of it.

"I swear to God, Berk, if you hadn't shown up in the next five minutes I was going to either shoot myself, or just straight-up leave this party and hit the bars."

I whirl around, and the sight of the caramel-brown skin, long, spiraled hair, and chocolate eyes of my friend Mea is so healing that instant tears spring to my eyes. Wiping them away, I slam myself into her arms.

"Mea! Ohmygod, they invited you? There *is* a God!"

"Of course they didn't," she scoffs, cheerful as ever. "I crashed. Just got back into town. I missed you, Berk!"

I just sigh and squeeze her tighter. After high school, Mea and I went to separate colleges, and a friendship with her didn't really fit into my parents' plan, anyway. She comes from blue-collar parents, and our families never ran in the same circles. But we were inseparable as teenagers for a reason. Mea just gets me, and I get her. We know who the other is, and she knows who everyone in my life expects me to be. She doesn't judge, she just loves me unconditionally. The same way I do for her.

"Please tell me you're here to stay." My words are lost in her bare shoulder, and she laughs and pushes me back so that she can look into my eyes.

"You look like you need rescuing. Here, you take this and chug, and I'll keep watch. Do it!"

I grab the silver flask from her hand like a lifeline and let the liquid inside burn my throat. If Mea is going to be in Lone Sands this summer, I can make it.

I will make it.

"Berkeley."

I freeze, but only for a second. Grisham's voice is full of disapproval. But we've known each other for so long, I just don't care. And he knows it. I down about a third of the liquid in the flask before turning around to face him. The grin on Mea's face is so wide, I'm scared that her face is going to crack from the extra pressure.

A not-so-delicate snort escapes me, and I wipe my mouth. Good thing I didn't apply the sensible pink lipstick my mother left on my dresser.

"Grish? You want a sip?"

His thick, blond brow furrows, and I can see the internal battle going on behind his gorgeous, perfectly sculpted features.

Grisham's dirty blond hair is so thick shampoo models everywhere are screaming with jealousy, and it's expertly styled into an array of spikes. His skin is tan and smooth, and his eyes are a green so deep a girl could see the rain forest if she stared into them long enough. There's no denying that his tall, muscular body, the one that helped him earn Navy its first football win over Army in twenty-three years, is every woman's fantasy.

He just isn't *my* fantasy.

But he's my friend, and I love him because he doesn't hold me to the high standard our parents do. I know he wishes things could be different. But he's very aware that they aren't.

"Give me the flask." He sighs after a minute's hesitation.

I grin and hand it over. "Atta boy, Grish."

Grinning at him as he swallows, I chuckle. "Remember the first time we got drunk? We went to Manny Reyes's party sophomore year of high school, and I forced you to play that stupid drinking game with me? We both ended up throwing up in the bushes."

"Uh-huh," he replies with a wry grin. "You were always getting me into trouble." He leans closer and whispers in my ear. "Still are."

"Can we get out of here?" Mea's impatient. She hates being in my parents' house, she always has. I can't blame her. I feel the exact same way.

"Can't." My tone is mournful. "I haven't seen the Admiral yet."

So we stay, and we eat. The three of us stick close together, but each time my mother sends me a death glare fit for the Queen of the Damned, I make a round of my guests. I shake hands and smile, tilt my head and laugh. It's all so empty I'm afraid if I huff out a breath too hard, everything will just blow away. Somehow, hidden in her tank top and short skirt, Mea has managed to sneak *two* tiny flasks of vodka into a party that's only serving champagne.

When the Admiral finally makes his entrance, I'm more

than a little tipsy. Mea is flat-out drunk, and Grisham has his large, strong hands full, trying to contain the two of us. His parents are here, and he doesn't want to disappoint them any more than I do mine. Only my back is so hunched from the load of expectations that I'm sinking, and I'm tired of trying to hold it all up.

"Berkeley." The Admiral states my name with a punctuation point at the end. The sound of his voice sends three different emotions coursing through my body all at once: anxiety, exhaustion, and affection.

Affection because I love my father. He's a good dad. He's been my dad in the only way he knew how. He was forceful at times, and gruff at others. He's firm and immovable in his opinions, and the sky-high standards for his only child are probably just as difficult for him to uphold as they are for me.

Anxiety because every time I see my father, I know that something is going to happen that will inevitably take me farther away from where I actually want to be. Like when I came home at Christmas of my sophomore year, I was excitedly bringing brochures for a spring break trip that all of my friends had been planning since the dawn of time. Only my father preempted me, and informed me that I'd be taking a tour of navy bases overseas with him and my mother for the week of spring break instead. It was like he could feel it when I was finally going to do something for myself, and was compelled to drive me off my course and back onto his.

Exhaustion because the person I am around my father is not the person I really am inside. I've been putting on an act with him for as long as I can remember, and the sand in that giant invisible timer is just about out. I can't pretend anymore. And when the real me finally emerges, it's going to either break his heart or flat out kill him.

I don't want to marry the man he's chosen for me. I don't want a life as a navy wife like he always wanted. I want to be free and independent. And I've never had the courage to tell him, or my mother, how I really feel.

As a twenty-two-year-old college graduate, I'm aware that this makes me a giant wuss.

"Admiral," I say just before pulling myself carefully into his embrace. He's in dress whites, of course, and all of his decorations are badged on his uniform proudly for all to see. He should be proud of everything he's accomplished; I understand that. But to a normal person, all that metal glinting on his shoulders is like a warning. Bright flashing lights that say STAY THE FUCK AWAY FROM ME AND ALL THAT I LOVE.

"Welcome home, sweetheart. Tomorrow we begin planning your future, yes?"

I nod numbly. "Sure."

His eyes zero in on Grisham and he smiles warmly, and then they slide to Mea, and that smile falters slightly. "Grisham, my boy. I've been hearing great things about everything you've accomplished during your time at the academy. You're prepared for your move to San Diego?"

My eyes travel back and forth between the two of them. "San Diego? Grish...you didn't tell me you've been stationed! Congratulations!"

"Got my orders yesterday," he whispered into my ear. "I hadn't had time to talk to you about it yet. Apparently, we've been summoned to brunch with our parents in the morning."

Sunday brunch has always been my mother's *thing*. Even while I was away at college, I was still expected to attend at least once a month. Grisham's family is always there, and our mothers love to *ooo* and *ahh* about how cute we look sitting next to each other at their tables. It irritates the heck out of me.

My father leans closer, eyeing first me, and then Grisham. "No more vodka this evening, understood? You're not in college anymore, Berkeley."

Don't I know it.

My father forgets to greet Mea before my mother pulls him in another direction. I watch him go, my eyes narrowed and the vodka swimming in my veins contributing to the feeling of nausea in my belly.

"Now? Now can we leave?" Mea tugs on my hand.

"Yeah," I mutter. "Now they won't notice I'm gone. Grish, you coming?"

He shakes his head. His mouth turns down on one side in a frown. "If I go, who's going to cover for you?"

I reach up on my tiptoes and wrap my arms around his neck. "You're the best."

He leans into the kiss I plant on his cheek, and the look in his eyes is full of understanding and melancholy. "Be safe. Call me if you want me to come get you."

I don't have time to think about how Mea and I are going to get our drunken asses out to a bar as she pulls me outside into the salty night air. My parents' house is located in the most affluent portion of Lone Sands. They consider this residence their beach house, because my father also occupies admiral's quarters on the base. He stays there most of the time.

The slightly broken look in my mother's eyes when he leaves to go "home" is another reason I have no desire to become a military wife.

There's a car idling at the end of our long driveway, far enough away from the house to be inconspicuous. When Mea opens the door to the backseat, I'm greeted by her brother, Mikah, who is a couple of years younger than us, and one of his friends.

"Hell, yes." Mikah grins over the driver's seat at me as I climb in. "Welcome home, Berk baby."

Mea slams the door behind me and sends me a smug smile as we buckle up.

"Have they been waiting out here the whole time?" I'm already feeling bad for Mikah and his bleary-eyed friend.

"Mikah has been on text alert all night," she answers. "I sent him a message when the Admiral came in."

I nod. "Get me the hell out of here, Mikah."

Chuckling, he takes off, and the large muffler on the little beater he's driving revs loudly. "I'm glad you're home, Berk."

I smile at him. But the jury is still out on whether or not I'm happy about being back in Lone Sands. If it's up to my parents, I won't be staying long.

Author's Note

I have the utmost respect for the men and women who serve our country in the military. I am so thankful for the fact that you risk your life at work every day so that we can enjoy the freedoms we've grown accustomed to. I'm in awe of your courage and dedication to serve.

I grew up in the Hampton Roads region of Virginia, which is home to all branches of the military. The Norfolk Naval Air Base, the Little Creek Amphibious Base, Langley Air Force Base, Fort Eustis, Fort Story, and Fort Monroe. The area is also home to the U.S. Marine Corps Forces Atlantic and the U.S. Coast Guard 5th Atlantic Fleet. My father is retired navy, so I guess you could say I'm a military kid through and through.

I know what families go through when they send a piece of their hearts to a different part of the world and hope and pray each night that piece will return intact. I know the courage that military spouses and families have in their hearts to go months without the person they love. It's a true testament to the strong stuff we're made of as Americans, and I couldn't be prouder to have come from a place where the military blood and tradition is so strong.

Although Grisham Abbot is a character that comes completely from my imagination and is in no way modeled after a real individual Navy SEAL, I hope that his character embodies many of the amazing qualities that the men and women in the U.S. Armed Forces possess. He's truthful, he's brave, and he loves with all his heart. He's encouraging, he protects those he loves, and he's on a journey to see where his life will lead after the navy. Grisham's struggle with a prosthetic leg is in no way meant to be trivialized, but I've never read about a romance hero with one and wanted to bring this incredible sacrifice to light in the most creative way possible.

So Grisham is a tribute to the men and women who give up so much to fight for us, serve us, and protect us. I hope you fall in love with him during his journey the same way I did.

Love,
Diana

About the Author

Diana Gardin was born and raised combing the coasts of southeastern Virginia. She is now a happy resident of South Carolina, as she married into an enormous Carolina-rooted family. She loves the beach; and even more than that, she loves to read while sitting on the beach.

Though writing was always one of Diana's passions, she enrolled in college to become an elementary-school teacher. After eight years of teaching in both Virginia and South Carolina, she decided to stay at home with her first child. This decision opened her eyes to the fact that she still very much loved to write, and her first novel was born. Diana is the author of several works of New Adult romance, including the Ashes series, the Nelson Island series, and the Battle Scars series.

Learn more at:
DianaGardin.com
Twitter: @DianalynnGardin
Facebook: facebook.com/diana.gardin

F Gardin Diana
Gardin, Diana,
Saved by the SEAL /
22960001215317

7/14

WAFI

CPSIA information can be obtained at www.ICGtesting.com
Printed in the USA
LVOW07s0801170316

479551LV00001B/20/P

9 781455 594740